"Leanne Panjer offers a unique and critical insight into the life of angels. Enveloped in a heart-wrenching and powerful story of the love of a mother and a daughter, the reader is taken on a journey from the point of view of the supernatural. She masterfully creates a story that speaks to the intricacies and mysteries of the connections of the natural and the supernatural, the ordinary and the extraordinary, the seen and the unseen. This book will spur many to consider the power, love, and wonder of God's plan for each of us, while the atmosphere of hope and providence amidst provocative themes will teach and inspire many."

Brian Westra, B.A.E., B.Th.
Teacher
Living Waters Academy

"*Tov* is a compelling, page-turning novel you won't be able to put down as you experience a profound connection with this angel, hovering close, fulfilling his role to protect, guide, and stay near Ellen and her wayward daughter Kelly. The understanding Leanne Panjer has of the role and efforts along with the limitations, frustrations, and passion of our angels helps us realize that despite our failings, negativity, struggles, and poor choices, our angels are always near—never forcing, yet ministering to us through their longing to help us make wise decisions, to facilitate healing moments, and to ultimately help us find freedom and peace in God's unconditional love, acceptance, and forgiveness."

Annette Stanwick
International Speaker
Freedom Facilitator and Coach
Author of the bestselling & award-winning book
Forgiveness: The Mystery & Miracle

"*Tov* calls you into the unseen world of angels and demons, challenging you to venture there more often. This book will beckon you to pray more diligently and to engage in the spiritual battle that rages around us. Creative and imaginative, *Tov* draws you into lives both human and divine. Leanne Panjer has been gifted with words and called by God to write beautiful songs and now a beautiful book. Enjoy an adventure in the unseen world."

Kathleen Gilhooly, B.Th., M.Th.
Pastor

Tov

Peace and blessing
to you
who read this.

Leanne Panjer

Leanne Panjer

TOV

Scriptures and additional materials quoted are from the Good News Bible © 1994 published by the Bible Societies/HarperCollins Publishers Ltd UK, Good News Bible© American Bible Society 1966, 1971, 1976, 1992. Used with permission.

Printed in Canada

ISBN: 978-1-4866-0982-6

Word Alive Press
131 Cordite Road, Winnipeg, MB R3W 1S1
www.wordalivepress.ca

Library and Archives Canada Cataloguing in Publication

Panjer, Leanne, 1959-, author
        Tov / Leanne Panjer.

Issued in print and electronic formats.
ISBN 978-1-4866-0982-6 (paperback).--ISBN 978-1-4866-0983-3 (pdf).--ISBN 978-1-4866-0984-0 (html).--ISBN 978-1-4866-0985-7 (epub)

        I. Title.

PS8631.A544T69 2015   C813'.6   C2015-904204-6
                                                               C2015-904205-4

To Joyce, Kath, Laurie, and Sharon,
whose encouragement and friendship
will outlast this lifetime.

God's secret plan is to be put into effect.
God, who is the Creator of all things, kept his
secret hidden through all the past ages,
in order that at the present time,
by means of the church, the angelic
rulers and powers in the heavenly world
might learn of his wisdom in all its different forms.
God did this according to his eternal purpose...

—Ephesians 3:9–11
(Good News Bible)

God revealed to these prophets that their work
was not for their own benefit, but for yours,
as they spoke about those things which you have now heard
from the messengers who announced the Good News
by the power of the Holy Spirit sent from heaven.
These are things which even the angels
would like to understand.

—1 Peter 1:12
(Good News Bible)

The prayer of a good person
has a powerful effect.

—James 5:16
(Good News Bible)

Chapter One

Tov was waiting, alert. He was ready. Leaving heaven for adventure usually thrilled him, but something in the air whispered. Warned. The angels at this send-off were different. His friends were present, but others were here, circling up front. Quieter, more experienced angels had come to this departure.

Ignoring premonition, Tov closed his eyes and let the tranquil music wash over him. The send-off was always amazing. He had been to earth many times, but it was not a fondness of the place that left him wanting to return. His master had a consuming devotion for human life, a boundless depth of interest in their feeble survival. Tov observed this more than he understood it, and he accepted his Creator's unfailing exhilaration that they existed. Nothing could keep him from fulfilling his Lord's purposes and desires. He would go again.

Tov stretched his wings and rose above the choir, scanning the scene below. He was taller than most, his hair longer, wavier, and slightly darker. His features were sharp, lacking the softness of some of his kind. Amid the gallery of faces and shapes, dazzling robes made them all the same from the neck down. Different jobs, varying personalities. All needed. All important. Yet they sang as they were. One voice. One purpose. One. He listened, and drank the encouragement. Few were granted the opportunity to go to other dimensions, but everyone felt the excitement and learned of what lay beyond from the stories that came back. They shared. They lived and existed together. It was how they were made. Tov concentrated, digesting deeply all that was offered to him. He was prepared.

The air shimmered. His memory churned up a picture stored there from the physical realm, of wind running its hand across water, of dazzling sunlight dancing diamonds in its wake. It was as the light around him now. Sparkling. Alive. Tov pulled as much of it as he could inside, filling himself. He needed a store of it, would crave it and draw on it in the days ahead.

The jolt. He felt it. Concentrating, he turned away. A force pulled at his insides, an invisible thread tied to the pit of his stomach. It began to pull him in a direction that was unmistakable. A flap of wings and Tov pushed away from the wonder of his surroundings and into the shadows. He cleared his mind and set all his senses and thoughts on the pull. It was no great physical effort to travel to the other dimension, merely an adjustment in thought to move into time and space. This part he hated, though—the complete consuming dark, the vulgar empty territory between the ethereal and the real. He turned full, slow circles, trespassing into the cold, unwelcoming void, not seeing the black presence as he could feel it.

The invisible string tugged, pulling him on. The nothingness that worked to smother and squeeze him gradually took on shades of violet, then indigo. He was moving as a flash, lightning without thunder, heading for the dim yellow light radiating from a single source in the distance. He slowed to get his bearings, then looked down. Colour took on shapes below and he altered his course, obediently following. By physical standards, he was travelling at tremendous speed, all of his light totally contained within him. Land began to form as he shot along, the outline of mountains, trees, and water materializing as he descended. The parameters of a city planted past the rocky summits formed and grew as one single shape in the distance. He slowed again, and began a spiral downward, knowing no earthly glance to the sky would catch his presence.

A magnet unable to resist the pull of another magnet, he swept down across the treetops, reducing his speed yet again over a large metropolis. 'Welcome to Corrington' a sign said quickly to him, a blur in his wake. His pace was as slow as he dared now, to keep the thread that pulled him taut, yet allowing him to observe all he could. The awkward movement of this world never ceased to baffle him. Every action was a labour, not a thought as it was for him. These beings moved slowly, separated from their surroundings, unconnected to their environment, no existence outside their own thoughts. Hard to fathom. He was assaulted by the intrusive clamour of traffic, music erupting from car windows, a battlefield of sound making the most unpalatable buffet for his ears. He remembered to listen selectively, straining sound. The adjustment was always a series of steps, a putting away of instinct and plugging into little bits of gained knowledge. He frowned as the wisdom of this hit him. It was a saving grace that humans were created to live completely inside themselves. Without it this dimension would completely scramble one's brain.

Yet he knew that a few among the crowds below were somehow aware of him, of something out of the ordinary they could only feel. He could connect with their quickening of spirit, those that could reach past that wall of physical into spiritual. They continued on, left with a sensation of blessing, unaware, really, of what they were privy to.

The thread pulled, yanking him out of his thoughts.

◊

Ellen Whitcomb pushed hard, her back glued tight to the wall in the front entryway of her house.

"Do you hear me?" Kelly yelled. "What's wrong with you?"

Ellen's mind failed her, could not tell her what to say. Garbled words flashed, and then left her brain. Her daughter, inches from her face, pelted her with words, screaming animosity until her body was almost flattened against her. Ellen's legs were giving out. The pit of her stomach was churning. She could not even see the boiled anger colouring her daughter's face. Her head was turned aside to avoid the onslaught. There was pain. Such intense pain. It had been stalking her for months, claiming her, paralyzing the left side of her body. It stole her thoughts, her clarity, her sense of time. And in the worst moments, who she was. Her personal thief. She forced her head to turn, opened

3

her mouth against the anguish, and concentrated on the cold wall beneath her fingers while she could still feel.

"Say something!" Kelly spat. She stepped back and Ellen's arms flew instinctively to her head. She heard the crack of her daughter's hand beside her, again and again, exploding on the wall by her ear. It hammered the pain deeper, and deeper. A fuzzy realization shimmered in Ellen's head that her daughter could not bring herself to slap her.

"I... hate... you!"

The words were splattered against Ellen's cheek. She stole a fingernail of a glance over her arm and watched Kelly's lips form the words over and over. A razorblade of agony sliced through her head, grazing her eyeballs. She grabbed her hair, clutched for relief, and, unable to discern what was happening any longer, slid down the wall.

"You can't tell me what to do anymore. I hate all your religious crap. Do you hear me?" She was screaming at the top of Ellen's head, the lack of response fuelling her fire. "What's wrong with you?" Her fist slammed the wall above her mother. "Stand up!"

Silence.

"I said stand up!"

Nothing.

"Do you hear me?"

Ellen squeezed her face, her numb cheeks. She tried to lift herself, to speak. It was only a whimper.

"I'm leaving." Kelly grabbed her knapsack, and kicked the door. It banged open, found the wall, then ricocheted shut. Windows and ornaments shuddered. China in the buffet jumped. Seconds emptied into minutes, the clock puncturing the silence more deafening than Kelly's rage. Ellen sat in a portal where time did not exist. Seventeen years funnelled into a moment that didn't hold a word for her, not one coherent thought. She needed to move or be swallowed. As she tried to climb the wall in a white cloud, her eyes searched frantically for the living room. She staggered to the back of the couch, her legs buckling as she pulled her way around it. Surrendering to the floor, she planted her face in the cushions.

Two words. Over and over. Prayer smothered in pain, breathed again and again into the soaked fabric.

"Oh, God... Oh, God... Oh God..."

◊

Flying at the outskirts of the city, Tov observed the landscape thinning into small groupings of houses, bound together by a maze of streets and signs, separated by a network of fences. Over a grassy park he stopped at the sound of laughter, children busy on a slide and a set of swings. It captivated him, the little world of their park. He closed his eyes, as he had done only moments before in the presence of the heavenly choir, and their oblivious mirth lifted the corners of his mouth. Glimpses of home in this place warmed him, armed him. Amid even in the shadows of where he was, there were always such surprises for an angel.

Park and laughter fell to the distance as he pursued the tug of the string toward a little house of moderate means nestled in among more of the same. A low picket fence marked its boundaries, held tenaciously to a gate that rested at an awkward angle interrupting the sidewalk.

Paint had chipped and faded at its own pace, yet the lawn was cut and trimmed. Other than a few shrubs, there was nothing more the house said for itself. He flew closer, hovered under the roof, hesitated before moving in through the wall.

He was in the corner of a living room. Sunlight flooded a picture window, catching crystal ornaments, splashing rainbows on the wall. A clock talked from the mantle. A woman was on the floor, slumped over a sofa, whimpering, her face buried in the cushions. Tov descended. The thread dissolved. He placed his hands on the woman's head, and the two sides of the magnet desperately connected.

Her body shook, quivering at taking in breath. She radiated a hungry expectation, requiring no effort at all from Tov to release light through his hands into her. There was no resistance. Tov wrestled the shadows, overpowering and expelling them, slowly and steadily clearing her mind from its clamour, at first to a dull, throbbing static, and then to nothing. Exhausting itself, the storm inside her passed. Where her body had collapsed was far removed from where her mind was now taken. Her rocking slowed, the motions shorter and shorter. Confusion eddied from her like water into the angel as he stroked her brow, caressing her eyelids until her tears, too, succumbed, and then evaporated. Hands relaxed, she released her hair. Time left them alone as Tov sat in perfect company with the Spirit that inhabited her. He turned his face upward and smiled. A second glimpse of heaven here, in such a short time? Something, yet, needed to happen to make this feel ordinary. He was overly prepared for just this. The woman drank his peace, immersing herself in sensations that were so completely natural for the angel. Why did he get the feeling that there was so much more?

Chapter Two

The sun pouring through the living room window was no respecter of the scene playing out within its light. It passed the day, inching along the wall until it came to rest on the woman, dousing her. Her head lifted. Words began to flow from her, in soft, unending whispers, and Tov listened unashamedly. Prayers seeped from the relief she had been granted, yet her thanks, her every utterance, was for one called Kelly.

She asked that the peace and reason she had, everything that the angel had given her, would be delivered into the heart of one she called Kelly. Her pleas were for protection, for the hand of his Master to guide and guard, to rest on this one called Kelly.

Tov listened in awe. Her earnestness was no less genuine than her faith that all she was imploring would be answered. Hope radiated from her with each word. The angel was so deeply moved by her sincerity, her faith, but mostly for her love for this one named Kelly. His hand locked over hers. The two of them sat still and statuesque until the sun finished its routine along the wall. Weary of the day, it packed up its rays and slipped away unnoticed. From rose to orange, and orange to gray, the room eventually glowed from the streetlight that peeked into the window. The mantle clock rang midnight.

The last of her petitions faded. The room grew silent. She lifted her head, rubbed her cramping legs and rose, slowly, flicking on a small light on the side table. Sighing, she turned toward him. Even framed by the puffiness of shed tears, her eyes were gentle and full of what she carried on the inside. Time had not neglected to mark her with wrinkles, but they were soft, betraying the smile that formed their pattern. She stood straight eventually, and stretched, working her protesting body into movement again. She was not tall, but Tov could not see one hint of a slump in her shoulders. Hair the colour of charcoal and silver hinted at her age. Forty and a few, he guessed. The natural colour was a tribute to one who felt the comfort of her years, adding dignity to a countenance very much at home with itself. Tov felt the impulse to touch this face, as if the caress of a hand could absorb its tranquility. The countless prayers that heaven received belonged to, and fit exactly, this face.

She walked so quietly to the window, a silhouette watching, waiting upon the sidewalk that led into the dark.

"She hurt you," Tov said to her unhearing ears.

He witnessed it, many times, the love of humans lost in how thoroughly they could hurt one another. He could not understand it, but he would always be witness to it, because it was his to minister when they required his services. She walked through him to the fireplace and picked up a picture in an old wood frame. Intricate carvings of leaves and flower buds grew in an oval path around the photo inside. She held the frame with one hand and covered the face beneath the glass with the other and closed her eyes. Tov picked up the subtle breeze of her memory. She was caressing a freshly shaven jaw with her palm and fingers, her thumb free to move across the man's face. He peered over her shoulder. The bottom of the frame was engraved.

"Ben and Ellen Whitcomb," Tov said. "Nice to meet you, Ellen Whitcomb." When his glance caught the face of the man in the frame, the angel was taken back, surprised, flung into memories of his own.

He had seen this man, years before, on a dark night lit by the reflection of lights from a rain-drenched street. Tov and a small cluster of angels waited beside a mass of twisted metal, which minutes before were drivers in cars, totally unaware that they were living out the final seconds of their lives. The angels scattered to carry out their missions, and Tov found himself beside one of the cars, staring into the same face that Ellen now held in her hands. But then it was running with blood. Rain pelted through the shattered window, lining up the red drops across his skin. Tov watched them drip and fall, knowing the man was not in pain. There was no cry from his lips, no comprehension of the events that played out around him. With Tov as the only witness, the soul of the man slipped easily out of the physical and into the comfort and company of angels.

Transfixed on the photo, Tov was quietly and dutifully putting it all together. His mind was starting to grasp the unfolding events, sorting out feelings that followed him since he left home. Ellen's eyes brimmed at the picture. Tears splashed onto the glass and wound their way down the wooden frame in jerky movements.

"Ben," she whispered. "Ben..." She crushed the image against her chest. "I can't do this alone..."

Tov placed a hand on her shoulder from behind, and felt the cold fingers of hopelessness playing at her mind, pushing into the warmth of her heart. Only then did he become aware of a presence moving closer and closer as they stood, noiselessly stalking into the space around them. A chill travelled on the slightest draft, rode the quiet wave of despair that had begun in Ellen. Tov rose to the ceiling and opened his wings. A deep groan rolled through the darkness, accelerating the angel's already palpitating senses. A quick flutter of wings took him to the dining room. He froze, waiting, watching, his heavenly eyes penetrating the corners of the room. He saw only a hutch, table, and chairs. He slipped into the kitchen, the dim light giving him nothing but the outline of appliances and cupboards, every shadow determined to hide secrets.

Aware of Ellen alone in the living room, he hurried to complete a search of the house. Faster than sound he was back at her side, alarmed that he could be up against a force that he might not be able to see. Wings suspended, he took position above her as the sound of her suffering thickened the air of the room. Only heaven could see the burning within the angel, his form vibrating. He could feel the presence lurking, waiting. Ellen's sobs frustrated his attempts to hear, her sorrow giving cover to whatever it was that was closing the distance between them. Tov rose and held to the ceiling, his head moving side to side. He looked down with misgiving at the form below him huddled on the floor before he disappeared through the roof. Hovering over the house, he waited, quivering as an arrow on a bowstring, panic taking him.

Then he saw it—an inky shadow slinking flat across the ground, crawling from behind bushes and fences, covering ground at a cautious pace. It hesitated at the broken gate, for only a second, as it took in the form hovering above the house in its peripheral vision. Avoiding that side of the yard, the slithering form crept across the grass to the front window. There it stopped. Frozen, as the angel on the roof, it waited, listened. Ellen's muffled lament rolled through the silence, electrifying the air, sharpening nerve and resolve. Rising up on tiptoe, it peered through the glass. It raised itself up to hang off the edge of the window sill. There it dangled, watching. Then slowly, deliberately, the black body rolled back its head and looked into the face of the angel. Its mouth peeled back at the corners, and smiled.

Repulsed, heat and disgust swelling inside him, Tov strained through the dim light to see the bulbous nose, the mashed face of Grief. Large teeth directed threads of drool down its chin, the little body quivering and jerking in anticipation. It stole one last glance into the living room, simmering with glee for the rampage it was going to take through the old paths it had forged in Ellen. He was being teased and taunted into near frenzy. Grief turned back to the angel, and their eyes fused. Confidence seeped from every slimy pore.

Tov gripped the sword beneath his robe and tightened his hold.

Quicker than it moved yet, the shadow darted in through the window and was gone.

A cry curdled the air before the angel even moved. The speed of the creature took him by surprise, but as quick as the sound split the night he was back through the roof and inside the house. Screaming, shrieking, Grief was stopped dead before Ellen. Kneeling on the floor, words were flowing from her, a rapid succession of breath and placated sobs, her eyes closed in determined concentration. A stupid pride that only a heartbeat ago assured Grief that Ellen was his, now left him exposed to an angelic blade that vibrated with all the fury of heaven. The energy that cemented the howling form to the floor also prevented it from reaching across even the small space that separated them.

The sword jumped from Tov's side. The room went quiet. Cutting a glowing swath through the dark before Grief could turn to plead mercy, the blade sunk deep between its shoulders. The little body jerked, absorbing the pain, feeling the force of Ellen's words in the metal, the chill of a mighty power exploding inside. Tov held the sword in position. He let the writhing body dig the damage before he pulled it out, making Grief slump, twitching uncontrollably. It staggered across the room, groaning, feeble legs and arms scratching at the air on a path to the window, then plunged through the wall. Tov flew as far as the glass to watch the black skin melt into the night. He heard low mutterings, a rustling of the bushes in the yard, and then silence as Grief was taken and claimed by his own.

Tov stood between Ellen and what could have been for quite a while. His pulsating senses slowly pounded down to a calm, steady rhythm, yet he stayed at the window, staring down the night. Ellen eventually replaced the picture on the mantle, then left the room. He watched the dark until it played with his eyes, reflecting on the events of the afternoon, and wrestling with the idea of this "higher calling" to which he suspected from the first. He always escorted, kept these beings company in their passing. He loved being the first entity, the select one, to bear witness to so many first moments on the other side of life. He had been here to comfort, sit bedside vigils, privy to prayers and heart-wrenching requests from loved ones, into which he poured his light and tranquility, bled his peace into their pits of despair.

When he first laid eyes on Ellen, he'd been set to believe they would be leaving the physical together, inside the predetermined time frame that was hers. The power he left heaven with, and already yielded since his coming, was so much more than what was required for this. The tables were turning. He was standing in *his* first moments of a new awareness, of something in his existence that shifted. He could not stop re-living the battle with Grief in his mind, could not forget the instinctual timing that came to him, that fit like a well-made machine with the prayers of this woman. Excitement was spinning his thoughts into fast forward when he needed more than anything to try and make sense of this mission.

"His best tactics would have been no match for you," he stated simply to the woman somewhere in the house behind him. Yet he marvelled. He had been the missing piece. It was her battle to fight, but he was given the power to divulge as she asked for it. She was so familiar to him, the contrary virtues she displayed. Gentle, deep love woven securely with the strength of tested faith. This he knew in his Lord. It was the very essence of her life, a piece of the Creator inside her. A gift for the humans to have, but for him a concept only to discover and witness. The horizon of his expanding experience, the knowledge of what lengths his Lord would go for the love of His children incubated in his mind as the prayers Ellen uttered for her daughter dropped completely into place. They became as crystal. Clear. Untarnished by doubt and fully transparent. He could recite them, almost read them as his own, feel them planted deep inside himself. He suspected he was being given the chance to carry those deepest utterances, to bring them to light—a privilege he never thought would be his. He was sent so many times after others of his kind had put their effort and power into making them reality, but had never had the opportunity to carry what their hope and appeals had put into place in heaven.

He peered into the gloom outside. A tiny pull started in the pit of his stomach. Was he being called to guardianship? If indeed he was, then the same thread that pulled him to Ellen would lead him beyond the comfort of this living room.

◊

Tov bided his time on the edge of a precipice, waiting for the definitive tug that did not come. Disappointed, yet faintly relieved, he kept wondering if he was reading the situation correctly. His services were required here as he gave himself to be Ellen's shadow.

The days that followed were invested in wading with her through a quicksand of loneliness and grief, ministering to her when she stopped moving and the quagmire threatened to suck her completely under. Something was happening in her body that he did not understand, that he could not decipher, at times so incapacitating that it took her mind away. He would lay hands on her, feel her torment, but had no idea what it was or where it was coming from. He never strayed farther than her shoulder, and Ellen never ventured farther than her house.

They passed a lot of time in Kelly's room. Tov came to know the stuffed animals on her bed, all the pictures on her dresser and walls. His favourite was a snapshot of Ben and Kelly by a lake pretending to haul in a big fish. It was the diamonds on the water behind them that drew him into the frame. Ellen ran her fingers over pictures, a lot, held them close, went from one to another. After the first sleepless night in her own bed, Ellen moved to Kelly's room and stayed. She cuddled tattered animals, was comforted by the essence of Kelly in her things. Tov would caress her until she found sleep. He was thankful for the time. In some small way it was an answer to his own desires. He feared for her, was nervous to leave. She needed him to carry her over the sharp stones of a very difficult path. But this was not what she prayed. Her selfless heart and the will of the One who sent him were in tune with one another. He would do nothing short of obey.

Day and night blurred. Tov's frustration mounted at the limited influence he seemed to have. He could not make her eat, could not understand the pain that took her away. She was alone, drifting in and out of reality at times, needing more help than he was sent to give. She didn't answer the phone. Had made only two calls. One to the library where she worked, saying she was sick and needed time off. She offered no details, no explanation to any questions. The other was a call to a friend called Pat.

"It's good to hear your voice," Ellen said. Her knuckles were white against the receiver. Tov listened from the couch.

"No, no, I'm fine." She pressed her hand to her face. "I'm a little worried about Kelly. She's gone." Collecting herself. "She ran away."

A sigh of relief escaped the angel.

"No, I didn't. Let's give it time. I think she'll come home. I've been waiting..." Pause. "Oh, a few days ago. The same old stuff... you know the story..."

Tov flew to stand beside her.

"That would be wonderful," she answered. "I appreciate that. I'll try to make it to group this week. But if you would put it on the prayer chain anyways..." Shaking her head, "That's not necessary. I'm fine. I need the time."

The angel's shoulders dropped. She was fighting for poise.

"I promise, Pat, I'm fine. If I need anything, I will." She sat down, struggling with her balance on the kitchen chair. "No, I have enough to eat."

"For someone who won't eat," Tov interjected.

"I really don't know. I've never seen her so angry."

The pauses were getting longer. He could tell she was trying harder to concentrate. "Yes, it is... a tough age." She began to massage her eye with her thumb, shifting her weight on the chair. Tov hovered back across the room and took up his post at the window.

"We'll see what happens. I think she'll be home soon." The phone in both hands now. "Thanks Pat. It was good to talk to you." It was hung up with effort, and she sat until her breathing returned to normal.

Then as if she could see the angel, she came to stand beside him at the window, imitating his posture with crossed arms. There they stood.

At least someone knew, he thought. He drew a small ounce of comfort from that. Tiring after a while, Ellen retired to the couch, eventually lying down, fighting sleep until the small hours of night. The angel was holding a vigil at a distance, hope slowly draining from the room, when the thread tugged. He straightened, caught his breath in a small gasp, flew to Ellen in alarm. He put his hand on her cheek.

"Stay on your knees," he whispered. "Please. Just do that if you can do nothing else..." It pulled, but he lingered, imprinting the face of this saint into his memory. "I will fight for you until I can no longer stand, for you and Kelly..."

Ellen sat up, straining to see into a world outside her window that was hung in darkness, suspended before her like an empty blackboard.

Tov's words ground to inaudible even in his own ears. "*You have to stay on your knees, do you hear me?*" To leave felt like he was pushing her off a cliff to unreadable depths, but he could not change events as they were unfolding. He turned to the large picture window, set his sights on the black sky and deep shadows, and lifted off. Unable to resist, he turned one last time. Ellen sat, bathed inside the halo of a street lamp that reached in and touched her, looking more relaxed than she had in days.

"Peace to you," he said. A chaotic calm had taken the room, a restless expectation, like night around a fitful sleeper. He moved through the wall, and dread took a place in his stomach. Before he could change his mind, he gave a mighty push of wings and was gone.

The wrinkles on Ellen's face shifted, falling into place. She was smiling.

◊

Tov stuck low to the ground, as the pull was so faint. This was not going to be as easy as his mission to find Ellen. Judging by Ellen's prayers, he felt ominously forewarned that Kelly might not be open to his help. He followed the vague track, assuring himself that he would not lose the signal.

In the night musk of grass and flowers, the houses were asleep. Lights burned from behind a few closed curtains, illuminated slits like resting eyelids. He followed the streets and sidewalks as Kelly would have, his eyes roaming like a searchlight, penetrating shadow. He passed out of Ellen's neighbourhood and found himself moving through streets that silently screamed the names of stores and restaurants in neon. Other than the occasional car, he could hear the buzz of the streetlights where the moths had congregated for their nightly rendezvous. The smells were changing, from that of earth and growing things to one of fast food and fat garbage bins waiting for morning and the relief of the garbage trucks. The buildings grew taller at the mouth of the maze that was the city. He could see a distance to the left or right, but ahead loomed immense towers of cement.

Tov veered down arteries of streets that fed life to the heart of the city. More than the smells were changing. Closer in, the nightlife moved and breathed on its own. The air was as static on a TV screen, the ambience electric and dancing. It was a lure to excitement, Tov knew, a stimulant promising to awake sleeping passions—or it was for the humans. Hardly the case for him. He knew the territory on which he was trespassing, the forces that lived here to conceal life, to distract a wavering heart into empty pleasure. It could not masquerade as anything else to his heavenly eyes, daring the leery, swallowing the bold and the bored. Thinking Kelly could be here made him shiver. He almost stopped. Seconds passed, causing him concern. The thread was so thin, he needed to move or lose it completely.

Laughter and the thump of music surrounded him. From the sidewalk he watched groups of people gathered inside the windows that were thrown open for fresh air. Humans mesmerized him. His ability to be totally absorbed by them was matched equally by his inability to understand them. They did not share the same heart and feelings, as he did with his own kind. They studied each other, as he was doing to them now, took great pains to look and act identical, packaging themselves to be acceptable. How ironic, to cheat themselves out of the very imperfections that made them the same. He longed to collect them into his arms and fly them above the cement and asphalt, just to peek into the very gates of where he came from.

Windows beat with rhythms of multi-coloured lights; open doors blew cigarette smoke like jumbo lips. Tov peered into each one, searching faces, relieved that he was not being pulled into any of these. Further into the maze, the music dissipated. Monstrous buildings on both sides of him breathed differently. There were not many people here amid the structures that dizzied him. Walls of windows threw light on to the glass buildings standing opposite. Never extinguished, they refused the anonymity of the dark, even when rivers of workers left them every evening. Tov saw into them as easily as he had those who built them. The desire for money. For power. Vice was vice. It bragged of many aliases.

His nerves were fluttering. Where was he? The course was tenuous, and he was afraid to move any faster. One lone car passed. Then all grew still. Anxiety eventually merged out of his caution, and he chose to pick up the pace.

The thread became a string, then a cord. One great tug pulled him around a building to a space in the centre of the skyscrapers that opened before him. He stopped from surprise. A huge expanse of grass and trees stretched below, a park of impressive proportions covering two city blocks. He flew short circles at the periphery of the space, watching figures on the ground move about in the dull yellow of decorative lamps. He heard muted conversations here and there, but given the hour, it was the park itself that seemed restless. He flew over finely manicured flowerbeds and garbage cans chained to picnic tables and wooden benches. In the faint light he saw a stand of evergreen trees trimmed together to a point, and at the base of their trunks, rolled tightly in a blanket, someone was sleeping.

Curious, Tov parked above the heavy breathing. A head protruded from one end, the blanket twitching to a dream the angel could see. Tov leaned over the closed wrinkled eyes, the thin wisp of hair sticking from the top of the head. It looked like a sleeping sausage. He could not help himself. He knelt, put his hand on the forehead, and released heavenly light. It was quickly absorbed like overdue rain on parched clay. The twitching stopped.

"Peace be with you," the angel whispered. He looked across the open space, sensed the presence of many more, disheartened that he had to ignore them to continue his mission. Countless refugees of the city had sought solace here when the night left them to their own devices. As hard as it was, he left the sleeping sausage to new dreams and continued his surveillance of the park.

A conversation floated across the grass. Two figures stood on the outside bubble of a street light talking quietly. He watched one pick up a knapsack and hand something to the other, but his gaze wandered past them and fell on a solitary figure sitting on a bench under a light in the open, completely awake and quite erect. All else dropped out his mind. Moving through the two people and their conversation, he made his way down a tunnel that in that instant opened before him. The thread untied and floated away.

Her arms wrapped tense shoulders as she watched the two strangers out of the corner of her eye. Tov was taken by her face, delicate with the lines of youth. Her hair, black as liquorice, hung straight and heavy past her shoulders to cover her crossed arms. A light denim jacket, not as thick as her jeans, couldn't warm her as she was shivering. Her eyes were beautiful, the richest green he had ever seen. He took the liberty of searching them, but they gave him colour and nothing more. He knew her from the many pictures he and Ellen had spent hours pondering over. She was different now than in those photos. There was not a trace of life in her face, no illumination in her countenance. The tiny hope he had been clinging to dissolved. He was to receive no help from this one. He was on his own.

"Oh, Kelly." It was a whisper barely making it past his own disappointment. She was so tightly swaddled inside herself there was not one inlet he could pursue. Yet he found her. That was something. And she was safe. He did not fail Ellen in that. He didn't feel any real threat of danger, yet Kelly was edgy. He was at odds, wanting to do something for her, yet by her own will, she was not open to his help. Only when the two in the distance parted company and wandered away into the dark did she relax.

He sat beside her on the bench. "You choose this over home?" he asked. He thought of all the people he had passed over in the park since he arrived here. If they were what she was afraid of, then his vigil tonight was a matter of putting in time. There was the occasional rustle in the bushes, the odd car driving by. Tov would assess, and then relax with her before doing it again. His mind went to Ellen, how fragile she was when he had left.

"You're breaking her heart," he told her, then looked away. "But you know that, don't you?"

They were two statues on a bench, finely tuned into the slumbering park. Tov considered just sitting hopelessly, but quickly lost all patience. He could not offer her what she did not want, but he could work with what he had been given. One by one, he took Ellen's prayers and began wrapping them around Kelly, soft and soothing like electric blankets warding off the nip of night. He wound and tucked the velvet of her words tirelessly until Kelly's head bobbed to hang over the back of the bench. Arms slipped from her own caress, finding the cradle of her lap.

Fatigued, but at ease, Tov took a step back at the steady rhythm of her breathing, aware that there were no other sounds around them, as if he was being given permission to rest from his labours.

"This is going to be a long haul," he sighed. There was nothing more he could do but face the world beyond the circle of light surrounding their bench and defend her rest.

Chapter Three

The sun yawned over the horizon, vaporizing dew from the grass. From one end of the park to the other it began the work of painting trees from jade to brilliant green. The birds were the first to stir. Then the cars and buses ventured forth as the city awoke movement by movement, drinking the sun like a cup of coffee.

Tov stood his guard, watching the bushes shake as the assortment of people bedded for the night emerged from their cocoons. He thought of the sausage man under his tree, multiplying him by all the shrubs in the park. As far as Tov could see, a massed legion of the lost and homeless shuffled into another day. It was hard to be a silent witness, watching the routine of survival when he held the very essence of hope in his heavenly being.

In the distance Tov noticed a marble man astride a marble horse on a pedestal high above the people lounging at his feet, moulded forever into his moment of fame. What a funny picture, he thought, the lustre of the man stolen by the seasons, bird dung dripping where his glory used to shine. Only he, who lived in the absence of time, could comprehend it for what it was: that time was decay, not a clock or measurement invented to keep track of it. The marble man was no different than the ones who lingered at his feet. It was all passing away, as it was meant to.

Kelly groaned. Twisting, she attempted to move her neck to normal position as she worked out kinks. Tov smiled at her dance of waking as she opened her eyes. The reality of her life rose from the ashes of sleep and she went rigid, assuming the position Tov had found her in the night before. She passed on watching the park stir to life. Lips drawn to a thin line, eyes vacantly ahead, a comrade of the stone man on his rock horse. Despondency had her glued to the bench.

He crouched in front of her. "This is what you're going to do?" His hands on her knees, he was hoping beyond hope to get her to walk away from this place. But there was not a flicker of acknowledgment, not an inkling of response. Her arms enfolded her, sealing her off from the world and from him. He rubbed his face. A flutter of wings and he was seated again.

Kelly's stomach was complaining. Tov put his chin on his chest and closed his eyes, the crust of his frustration absorbing a granule of sympathy. She slipped into his heart.

"You're in a tough spot, aren't you?" From his storehouse of experience with humans, he mentally pulled the file marked "Patience." He could only help by giving her that. She was not open to anything else. Her intestines gurgled.

Those who came from the world of soft beds and hot breakfasts walked briskly along the asphalt pathways, heels clicking, briefcases loaded with purpose. Everyone moved toward the places they had to be. Air swirled around them as people passed, ignoring the girl made of concrete on the wooden bench. Tov was realizing this could be a marathon vigil with Ellen's stubborn daughter, so he settled back into his seat and took advantage of the gift that Kelly unknowingly gave him, the rare and wonderful treat of human watching, the chance to observe the beguiling creations of his Master.

$$\Diamond$$

She had dreamed of when she would walk out on her life, every waking moment of every day, but the fantasy never ended on a park bench. Kelly's mind was a video stuck on rewind, the last week playing out like a bad movie marathon.

She had always envisioned ending up with Gina's family, not as best friends, but as sisters. Around the dinner table, laughter that separated the business part of the day from the hours of a family evening bubbled and she was warmly melted into the scene. Kelly fit Gina's family. Gina's younger brother, Mark, tormented her as he did Gina, and she secretly loved it as much as Gina hated it. Family vacations, barbeques, dinners, she was always there, always felt welcome. Now she sat struggling to understand what had changed. Kelly showed up at their door and Gina's mom started asking silly questions, calling Momma to tell her where Kelly was. For the first time, she felt like an intruder in their house, Gina's mom and dad talking at her like Momma did. The more they talked, the more Kelly realized that they weren't even trying to understand. In the course of events of one inane day, the dream of her refuge turned to foreign soil. Just like home, she couldn't wait to leave.

The tape played on: standing on Gina's front step, Gina's mom acting concerned, sending her home. The end of the dream of Kelly's splintered hopes was the brass lion biting the doorknocker in its teeth, closing in her face.

The piece of paper was all she had. On the way out of the yard, Gina opened her bedroom window and called to her.

"What are you going to do?"

"I don't know. I'm not going home."

"I'm scared," she told Kelly.

"What for?"

"For you."

"Well, don't be." Something shifted between them. Kelly was on the other side of the window now. "Why won't they let me stay?"

"Kelly, you *have* a family…" Gina skidded to a stop at her mistake.

"Right. And you know that better than anyone, don't you?"

"I like your mom."

Sarcasm dripped from Kelly's mouth. "Then, let's trade!"

Gina looked at her out of the tops of her eyes. "Come on Kell, go home. Things can be like they were."

"I thought you knew how I felt."

"Kelly, I never dreamed you'd do it. Whenever you talked about it, I thought you were just blowing off heat."

"Are you turning on me?"

"I'm not. I never would."

"You just did." Kelly started to leave.

"I have something for you," Gina called.

Huffing, she walked back. Gina pulled out a corner of the screen and handed her the piece of paper.

"What's this?" It was a name, address, and phone number.

"That's my cousin." Gina cocked her head. "Remember I told you about her?"

"Your loser cousin?"

"Whatever," Gina mumbled. It was growing awkward. "She might take you in for a while. She's always looking for people to share the rent."

"You gonna give me rent money, too?" Kelly had lost her patience, didn't care much that Gina was too. "If your family won't have anything to do with her, why should I?"

"She's weird, not psycho." Gina's voice dropped. "I'm worried about you. I'd feel better if I knew where you were."

Kelly sneered.

"You can be stubborn. And unreasonable. Just don't get into trouble. Okay?"

"Fed up is higher on my list than stubborn and unreasonable." Kelly looked at the paper. "I'll call her if I have to."

"Let me know where you are."

Kelly flashed her the look.

"What? You think I'm going to tell?"

"Bye Gina." Before she was wishing again that she were on the other side of the window, she turned and walked out of Gina's yard.

She didn't feel like crying. She needed to kick something, to feel pain so she could believe this was happening. Never in her life had she had no place to go. The thought that she was crushing Momma hardened her jaw and quickened her pace. Momma was so weak; it didn't take much to do that. Momma would run to her church, to prayer group, to her Bible. Kelly was sick of it, of being bulldozed. She didn't have to pretend life was something other than what it was. How lame, to get sucked in to all that. Pretty dresses and Sunday school were childhood memories, good ones for what it was worth. But it was followed by Momma's questions, Momma's pushing and preaching wanting her to accept a life robbed of both parents. "It's God's will," people said when Daddy died. God's will? What kind of a God would leave her and Momma all alone? Momma went full force into it from there. Church was her home and the Bible was an extension of her arm. All she did was pray to a God who had put this crap on them in the first place. Momma disappeared into the church and Kelly was abandoned once again.

She was already thinking of leaving when Momma began acting weird. Kelly turned sixteen, ready to tell Momma she was done, but it was like Momma was sucked dry, no longer aware of Kelly or anything around her. She clued in one night as they were sitting at the table eating supper.

"I'm not going to church anymore," Kelly said.

"How about it?" Momma asked.

Kelly didn't know what to say.

"I'm listening," Momma said, smiling.

"I said I'm done with church."

"That will take some time," Momma answered. She didn't stop eating.

"Momma, what are you saying?"

"Things always work out in the end. It just takes time, that's all."

She felt nothing but anger when dealing with Momma. "You act as if you don't care," Kelly shouted.

Momma put her fork down. Kelly waited, expecting her to say something. But she didn't. She just stared.

"What's wrong with you?"

"I can still think. I can feel." Momma looked hard at Kelly before speaking again, almost angrily. "It isn't always so easy."

"What isn't?"

Momma put tiny bits of food in her mouth, going through the motions of eating, dismissing their conversation as if she didn't know what to say.

Kelly threw her fork at the wall and stomped from the kitchen, but the only place to go was the bathroom, the only room with a lock on the door. It was a waste of time to even be in the house.

Kelly remembered the silence from the other side of the door. No scolding. No knocking. It was so strange, like the conversation they had just had. She knew then that she was going to leave.

Kelly looked at the address on the paper, hated the thought of showing up on someone's doorstep, but she had no choice. She had twenty dollars plus change. When her fight with Momma had erupted, Kelly had indulged herself in rage, and what was in her knapsack determined what she had to live on. She had no idea where this place was. She stopped to ask directions, and a lady told her which bus to take downtown. Once there, she would keep asking. The ride went fast and she disembarked, feeling lost in the shadows of huge buildings and streets that teemed with cars and people. Gina's paper was a little, wrinkled ball in her fist. The skyscrapers looked at her through shining windows, dismissing her for the insignificant speck she was. Daddy would be so upset. He would never have driven her to the street like this.

The few souls that would give her the time of day steered her to an old building above a German deli and she stood in the second floor hallway, a horrible sour smell wafting through the floor. Her nose in her shirt, she gave the stench credit for the fading wallpaper that hung in shreds along the ceiling. She found door twenty-six and knocked, but footsteps from the other side never came. She kept knocking. Down the hall an old man yelled at her in a language she didn't understand. That, and the smell, sent her back out into the street. Kelly wandered for hours, window shopping, in and out of stores, never too far from the deli. Time dragged her through the afternoon and she checked her watch, deciding to go back. Her knocking turned to banging, a wish to disturb someone. The skin on her palm turned scarlet. The muscles in her arm burned. She slid down the wall, one tear pushing out her eye to wet her cheek. Her stomach was threatening to take recourse in the rotten smell, so she left.

The faint breeze of people walking quickly washed the odour from her nostrils. The sun was beginning to dip behind the towers, drenching the city in shades of evening, and in the stampede to get home Kelly stood alone and invisible, passed by and bumped. She let herself be carried by the tide, but when the torrent thinned to a trickle she was standing under a blinking street light at a complete loss. A vendor was closing his hot dog stand and offered her his last two for the price of one. She broke her twenty, reluctantly, but the food did nothing to make the queasiness in her stomach go away. There was nothing to do but keep moving, nowhere to stop. Somewhere along the horrid path of the day, her mind had fallen into a fissure. The endless wandering of her feet kept her brain from thoughts that threatened from dark places. Her feet hurt. Her stomach warned that it was going to give up the hot dogs.

That's when she saw the park.

Her memory told her it was there, only this time it was an amazing discovery for a weary body. She was here with Gina once, sipping cokes on a day filled with visits to shops that she couldn't even remember. She barely noticed it back then, but now she inhaled the fragrance of flowers and grass like the life-giving breath it was. Not daring to look at the faceless others who had taken the same invitation it offered, she spotted an unclaimed bench in the open, a lamp throwing a circle of light as if it had been reserving a spot just for her. Many were sheltering beneath bushes, deep in the shadows where Kelly didn't care to go. She sat for a long time before drawing a full breath. It was hard to see past the rim of light covering her, impossible to keep her head from bobbing for sleep. Eventually she stretched out, using her hands as a pillow, giving up a day that would, hopefully and mercifully, disappear in her sleep.

Her last thought was of her bed and a mountain of blankets.

As quickly as she had fallen asleep, she was awake. The sun lit the park and curious eyes felt no shame staring, making her uncomfortable. She was loathe to give up the bench, but did, the day being a carbon copy of the one before it, wandering numb. Gina's cousin was nowhere to be found, but not once did she court the idea of going home. Kelly had to find her own way, the same as everyone around her was doing.

That evening, and the ones after that, delivered her back to the bench. It was emptiness like she had never known, to approach it night after night and think of it as home. She sat for hours, for lifetimes, less inclined to leave after having sunk into the reality of what she had done. She invested a lot of energy silently screaming and swearing at Momma's God.

Chapter Four

Tov enjoyed people watching, but as the hours staggered by he grew anxious. Distracted, he spent more time observing Kelly, trying to decipher her. It was odd to observe her shut down tight, keeping in an emotional storm while those passing by walked in a gentle breeze. Out of nowhere, a deviate wind picked up and whistled around the buildings, gusting full force and feeding on the last of her warmth, the strong against the weak, it whipped strands of hair across her face. Tov could feel the hardening process at work in her, and it made him shudder. His hair stood as the chill blew through him, dimming his light as cold whisked in one side of his body and out the other. It felt like they were being watched.

Tov saw him in the distance, against the pedestal of the marble statue. He was older than Kelly, but not by much. Hands shoved deep into the pockets of his oversized jeans. A white T-shirt that had seen cleaner days poked through an open plaid jacket. His hair, shoulder length and fuzzy, gave him the appearance of an open umbrella sitting atop a long skinny neck. In a leaning pose he looked tall, but judging by his face he didn't seem muscular. He did look unmovable, resolute to a purpose. And he was staring at Kelly.

"Great," Tov muttered. He took a stance in front of her facing the stranger, prepared to defend his charge. On cue, the boy straightened in a moment of decision, walking with slow, easy strides, not taking his eyes from Kelly. As the stranger got closer, clearer, Tov's mouth dropped and his eyebrows shot up, and he spread his wings full to intimidate—not the cocky youth strutting toward him, but for what was perched on his shoulder.

Tov had heard of Addictions, but he had never seen one, much less had the pleasure of defeating one. Levelling his eyes with those of the boy, he met the surprised look of Addiction head on. Its unflinching acceptance of the angel's presence was matched by the grin on the boy's face. They came in all sizes, he knew, and this one wasn't large by any stretch of imagination. Size was a deception of power. The little blob sat, a useless array of long hairs protruding from the pimples on its ugly green skin, its bottom and feet on the boy's shoulder, bony knees around its own cheeks. The toes held on with flexed claws, digging into the flesh and joint of its perch. The danger did not lie in the few teeth that parted its lips, but in the scythed nails that grew out of bony fingers, and arms that far surpassed the length of its body. It allowed a reach of operation that made Tov uncomfortable.

Tov turned to see that Kelly's chest was thumping, trying not to let on that she saw him approaching, looking in the opposite direction when he came to a stand in front of her. Once he stopped, Kelly could ignore him no longer. One eye closed against the sun, she peered up at the figure casting a shadow over her space.

Tov studied the stranger's face. A sharp jaw and angular cheekbones were not particularly handsome, but not unattractive either. His eyes were as brown as his hair, his mouth hinting that it would break into a smile if Kelly would give it permission. She was looking into those brown eyes too, and they were working hard to tear down her defences with their sympathy.

Kelly smiled.

Tov pulled in his wings, deflated and disgusted that she gave him all the permission he needed. She might as well have tied up the angel's hands with a rope.

Addiction sniggered. It's fat, flubberous body rippling like jelly.

"You look like you'd rather be any place but here." His voice was low. "Didn't know whether I should come over, like you'd bolt or something."

"Nowhere to bolt to," she said.

Tov grunted. It was more than what this boy needed to know.

His head bobbed on his skinny neck like a dashboard pet with its head on a spring. He stuck out his hand. "I'm Steve."

"Kelly Whitcomb." She took it in a light grasp, shaking it loosely.

Smile's a little overdone, thought Tov. "This is going to be easy work for you, isn't it?" he asked. Not that Steve could hear.

"I knew it was going to be pretty."

She flashed him a funny look.

"Your name," he told her.

Kelly relaxed into the bench as Steve obliterated her walls, their eyes uttering conversations that Tov was not privy to. Words vanished while their souls spoke, searching for some ground of trust on which they could stand. Tov couldn't have felt more ousted if someone had physically pushed him out of the way. His annoyance fuelled the need to take matters into his own hands.

"Kelly, no," he said into her ear. "Don't talk to him. Walk away."

A spark of suspicion flashed across her mind.

"Look into his eyes," Tov implored. "See what I see on his shoulder."

Addiction, the only one who could hear, just stared.

"Please, Kelly…"

Tov's voice was a trigger. Indulging in exaggerated one-upmanship, Addiction wrapped one emaciated arm around Steve's head, embedding its nails into his scalp. With jerking motions it poked pin-sharp nails in again and again. Steve cringed, shut his eyes, attempted to stand firm against the familiar pain. Phlegm gurgled in the little monster's throat, drawing out the sounds in pleasure.

Pity shut Tov's mouth. His hands tingled as he thought of dismounting the parasite with his blade, but he stood his ground, hand on his sword, knowing the will of Steve was not in agreement. He could wait, trust the timing ordained by the One who sent him. Dismissing the temptation the creature dangled before him, he acknowledged the love that his Master had for this boy. He would wait.

Steve was waiting too, and as the pain started to ebb he threw it off with a few shakes of his head. The demon settled back into its perch, taking in the angel through the corner of its eye.

Steve was trying to focus on Kelly. "Hey, I know where we can get some good breakfast." His voice was soft. "I'm a good listener."

Tov prayed her lack of response was common sense.

"Let me feed you, and we'll take it from there." His timing and smile were perfect. Every pore in his body secreted charm.

The angel held his breath, until he saw Kelly throw off any hint of foreboding she may have been fostering. "That's the only offer I've had all morning."

A nod of Steve's head sealed the deal. Breakfast it was. He started walking backwards, motioning her to follow.

"I know this place that serves bacon and eggs for *cheap*..." He sang the last word.

Kelly shed her brooding like a second skin and left it lying on the bench. Her stomach growled, but only Tov was close enough to hear. Heaven alone could see this motley bunch for what it was. The fellow standing on the street corner glanced at two young kids absorbed in the business of making first impressions. He never saw the angel coming in behind, robes flowing full as he brought up the rear, no more than a few feet away from the lump on Steve's shoulder that was a little too close to Ellen's daughter for comfort.

◊

The silence of the moment and the holiness of the hour broke quickly as Hilda's nasal voice erupted from the rocker. "Well, let's have our coffee now, shall we?"

She rose from her chair, leaving the imprint of her body on the cushions. Steps that were anything but petite carried her to the kitchen to tend to the most important task of pouring coffee. The cake was her newest creation and the moment of reckoning had come.

Fitting into routine, Beth arose from her spot on the sofa and followed Hilda to lend her hands.

Ellen always found the transition hard. She would gladly dispose of the refreshment portion and trade it for another hour of prayer. But the years had slowly taken hold of their weekly prayer meeting and introduced the security of routine. The coffee and cake had become crucial, claiming the second hour of their gathering with a holiness equal to the first. Today the thought of opening her mouth and letting cake fall past her lips repulsed her. The conversation of the other three in the room flowed around her.

Gloria turned her coiffed head toward Ellen, mildly acknowledging that her detachment was leaving a gaping hole in their chatter.

"Don't worry dear," Gloria whispered. Delicately she patted Ellen's hand. "Everything will be fine, you'll see. Don't worry." With a final squeeze for sincerity, she turned back to the other two and continued the conversation.

Walls crashed into place around Ellen, separating her from the others in the room. Voices echoed faintly from the other side of the barrier as she crouched low and safe behind it, out of sight. Minutes passed. She sat tall, counting every single one. It was enough to put the others at ease while they discussed trivial things, such as the price of fruit, and how far back to cut an English ivy. They had prayed with her. When she was learning how to be a widow, they had prayed with her. This afternoon they prayed with her, and they meant well, choosing words carefully and uttering petitions sincerely when, in turn, they asked for Kelly's protection and safe return. Ellen grabbed solace from each word. Each one was breath to her now. She had stayed in those prayers for Kelly while the others had continued on with the afternoon, leaving Ellen behind. Their voices grew farther and fainter, and she found herself sitting in a very desolate place, on a path of bramble and thorn. Even the sun had left and followed the others, emerging in a clearing of green grass to pause for coffee and cake.

Pain burst into the left side of her head and shot down her shoulder and she went rigid, squeezing her hands. A muscle in her cheek twitched, her left arm tingled, and the room turned hazy. She fixed her gaze on a picture on the wall, her body braced. She heard voices in the distance, moving around the room, coming closer and closer until they came back to her head. By the time the haze shimmered away, no one in the room had even noticed she had slipped away.

She heard a sharp voice and looked up. Hilda was expounding on the adroit changes she had made to the recipe, her dialogue continuing through the ceremonial cutting as Ellen watched with a forced smile. In her mind a projector flipped on, and a movie in her imagination began to play to the sound of clicking film sprockets.

"Is this the one you've chosen?" she was asking Hilda.

The puzzled expression on Hilda's face echoed in her words. "What do you mean?"

"Is this the recipe you've decided on?" Ellen asked again. Hilda's face was blank. "The one you're going to take to heaven with you?"

Hilda's jaw dropped all the colour from her face. The sun was no longer shining on Hilda and her cake. She was now on the dark path, stuck in the brambles where Ellen sat.

Ellen startled. The projector shut off. "Forgive me," she muttered.

"What?" Gloria asked.

"Nothing." Ellen waved them off, her conscience sending a tremor through her, warning her of the spot where she sat, how quickly fear and loneliness could translate into anger. Ellen did the hardest thing. She looked into Hilda's eyes when she handed her a plate of cake, and forgave her. She gave Hilda permission to not understand.

Revenge was not Ellen's, but it was sweeter than the cake. Hilda had forgotten the sugar. Before she could stop it, the projector in Ellen's head switched on again, a dialogue to her own private movie. "Maybe you'll have better luck with this *incredible* humble pie recipe I've found," she was saying to Hilda. Ellen dropped a piece of cake into her mouth and tried to chew.

◊

Kelly inhaled steam from the plate the waitress put in front of her. Coffee was already flowing through her like new blood, and the food, hot and greasy, was the price of her soul. Tov watched her bow her head, out of habit, to say a word of thanks, but she stopped herself when she realized Steve was watching. She nodded to cover her blunder. Then she filled her mouth and chewed, becoming human again. The sting of hunger was not an experience Tov had ever been granted. Kelly was fully into the business of consuming, unaware of anything around her.

Steve sat back, arms on the table, hands around a mug of coffee. He was fidgety, wanting to talk. But like Tov, he had to wait. Kelly was doing some serious eating, and eventually Steve's face betrayed the enjoyment he was finding as a spectator. Tov sat in the booth for a while, and then opted for the aisle. Kelly was working every bite, and ridiculously, he felt in the way. Breakfast went on and on. At arm's length, he hovered. When nothing but the design was left on the plate, she sat for a full ten seconds, appearing distressed that the meal was over. Resigned, she pushed it aside and cradled the freshly filled mug in her hands. The air was growing heavy in the absence of conversation. She smiled awkwardly. Steve's cue.

"So," he said, "I need my curiosity satisfied. I haven't seen you around here. Are you from out of town?"

Tov crossed his arms. This was going to be good.

She shook her head. "You know everybody downtown?"

"Yeah. Pretty much. I have a place a few blocks from here that I share with a friend. Actually, he's more like a business partner."

Kelly perked up. "Really?"

Tov winced. She was a little too impressed.

"You have a place of your own?" she asked. Steve was fishing for clues, horribly amused. Her words were wrapped in gift paper and tied with bows. "That's great... more than great. You're so lucky. What business are you in?"

"We sell."

Tov looked at Steve through the top of his eyes. The comment left Steve's mouth and soared overtop Kelly. Addiction had nodded off against Steve's head, vibrating to the thrills of sleep. Tov took a deep breath, daunted. This was not unfolding to his benefit.

"You still haven't told me where you're from," Steve persisted.

"From here, but not this part of the city. I've lived most of my life in the suburbs."

"That would explain why we've never crossed paths."

Kelly's expression changed. Tov saw she was debating on taking Steve into her confidence. He put his hand on her cheek, the light in him warm though his skin, releasing pictures of Ellen, of home, snapshots clicking behind her lids, jumping to her mind. Kelly put her hand on her stomach, fighting for the courage to turn her back on it all again.

"You okay?" Steve asked.

She didn't answer. Tov entered the table, standing an inch from her nose, taking her face in his hands. A glow emanated from his fingers as he focused on Kelly. She looked around, puzzled, but saw nothing. Tov delved into her eyes, and saw the same.

"I left home seven days ago," she said.

Tov's arms dropped.

"I left in a hurry, without any place to go. I ended up in the park because I don't have a lot of money." She paused. "I don't have any money. I don't know what to do."

As she spoke, the hope Tov had felt moments ago died. He stood in absolute unbelief at how ineffective his heavenly power was.

"Daddy was killed when I was nine. I live with my Momma."

"I would've given anything if my dad could have been killed when I was nine," Steve said.

It got the reaction intended. Kelly's mouth dropped.

"He beat me and my mom." Steve returned the horrified look he was getting from the other side of the table. "What? Your dad was great, right?"

"That's awful. I've never met anyone…" She stopped. "I mean…"

"It's okay. I left home when I was twelve. I've been on my own ever since." Steve didn't talk again until Kelly relaxed. "So, why did you run?"

She took a drink from her mug, then played with it, fitting it into dried coffee rings on the table. "I felt trapped."

"Trapped?"

"Momma. She's so intense about stuff. She has this wonderful faith that is such a crock of crap. I finally told her I don't buy it."

"You're a church kid?" Steve grunted.

"I was. But not anymore."

"Guess not, hey?" The blob on Steve's shoulder woke as if summoned when Steve laughed. Knocked off balance, it buried one needled claw into Steve's head. Practice alone gave Steve the ability to take the pain behind a curtain. Addiction eyeballed the angel, challenging. Removing the claw was the furthest thing from its mind, and Tov guessed the pain was there to stay, that Steve was going to have to make his move.

"I need to meet someone." Steve made the pretence of looking at his watch. "I have to go, but I don't feel good about leaving you here. I'm wracking my brain to figure out how I can help you."

Steve was playing Kelly, hard, but Tov already knew what she was thinking. There was no way she was going back to the bench. She had yet to figure out what Steve was offering. All he had to do was ask.

"You can crash at my place today, only because you have no place to go. I won't be there. It would give you time to think. I've got work to do, so you're more than welcome."

Kelly looked uneasy.

"No," Tov said in her face. She was weighing her options. "Please Kelly, no."

"Yeah," she said quietly. "Okay. But just for today."

Tov moaned.

"Great!" Steve's voice was overly cheerful, camouflaging his agony. "My place isn't much. Don't expect a lot."

Kelly drained the lukewarm coffee from her mug, not noticing Steve's fight for balance as he stood to throw money on the table. He was face to face with the angel, in extreme pain, and Tov could see his brain cooking up plans that Kelly had given him permission to conceive.

Tov didn't wait. He flew ahead into the street, circling above the pavement, around and around, hating the helpless moments of this strange calling. What could he possibly achieve in the face of such disregard towards him? Why would an angel be sent to dispatch the powers of heaven if it wasn't even wanted? What he needed was help. There were so many layers in the spiritual realm, unlike earth that had only one. Tov's chance of running into another heavenly in this exact plane was slim. Not impossible. Slim. So far he had only encountered Grief and Addiction. Scanning the street, he squinted. Flying higher, he strained to stretch his vision as far as he could, but there was not a glimmer of heavenly light to be seen.

The restaurant door opened. Steve was guiding Kelly by the elbow, pointing up the street. "It's about fifteen blocks," he was saying. Tov watched them blend into the kaleidoscope of people walking. The mighty angel could stand it no longer. He turned his back on Kelly and shot up into the sky. It was the only thing he could think of to do.

Chapter Five

Tov soared upward until people below were but dots moving over a miniature landscape. Before losing sight of them completely he came to a graceful halt, stationary, hovering, his magnificent wings spread, his eyes closed. The physical fizzled away as he turned his thoughts to heaven. A gentle breeze blew faint music through him, making him instantly homesick. Peace touched him, not unlike the peace he had felt at Ellen's side. His thoughts were received as fast as he could think them, and the pull of home, the impossibility of his mission, his cry for help, all blended together into one laboured breath.

He shifted slightly in the invisible realm to another plane, the view below slipping in and out of focus. A movement in the distance caught his eye, wings growing larger as they approached. He watched intently to see what form his request would take, eventually making out a body that trailed long slivery strands of hair and beard on a face deeply embedded with lines. It slowed, came to a stop in front of him. Massive billows of robe, radiant with light, settled gently around the newcomer, then fell still.

"I am Malheev. By the request of our Lord, I have come." He held out his hands, which Tov took, holding them in his own.

The face was ancient. Power pulsed from the old hands into his own, awe and reverence stymieing words.

"Malheev," Tov repeated. The angel of inspiration. "I am glad our Lord has realized that an angel of your capability is needed for this task." The expression on the older angel's face did not change.

"My heart is pure, and I carry the love of our Lord well, but I have come against the impenetrable will of a human. My influence seems to have no effect."

Malheev dropped Tov's hands and clasped his own together inside the arms of his robe. He nodded, the burden of mission familiar to him. "I have not come to relieve you of your task. You are the one our Lord has chosen. I am here only because you have asked for help."

Elation withered. Tov pulled back, his hope eclipsed. "So we will work together."

Malheev looked long at the younger angel then shook his head. The peace of moments ago folded and fluttered away.

"I am at a loss," Tov declared. "Please say that you will tell me what to do."

"There is one thing I can give you," Malheev said. "It is a reminder of knowledge that you already possess." Tov merely blinked. "Your biggest challenge is their greatest gift. That is something you cannot change. Acknowledge the full choice that they have been given in all things, and you can use your power to full advantage. That will be your success."

"I know she makes her own choices," Tov agreed. "I want to know what insurance my presence makes that all the prayers given for her will be answered. What am I to be doing, other than pouring the power of those prayers into thin air?"

Malheev took a second before replying. "Waiting."

It was not what Tov wanted to hear. His mind fell back to the revelation of love that came to him as he attended Ellen, so powerful it had led him to think all things would be possible. He had felt it, believed in it. His mind strayed to Ellen, the image of her on the couch, on Kelly's bed, in the dark, waiting. A much harder wait than any he was being be asked to endure.

Malheev spoke into his thoughts. "Be there when the opportunity comes. Wait for it. You hold the prayers for optimum power when that situation arises. When it comes, fulfill your purpose. In that you cannot fail."

It was what he knew, but it was buried in doubt, swallowed by intense frustration. The simplicity and wisdom of the angel's reminder began to soothe his racing mind.

"Remember that we are made with the ability to mimic the humans in all things," Malheev clarified. "You will find yourself pulled into their unbelief and scepticism."

"Regardless of what I feel, she could always choose against me."

"Yes. That is her failure, not yours." The older angel let his words find their place in the young one before he repeated the message he was sent to deliver. "Just wait. In that you cannot fail."

There was no easy way, as Tov had been hoping. "To know how our Lord has the patience for this," he whispered, "would be the crowning glory of all knowledge."

Malheev chuckled, stating the angelic mantra, "All things are as they were meant to be." He touched the cheek of the one called to guardianship. "If you need the help of others, rest assured it is in place. Do not make yourself weary with what cannot be changed. It is a mighty calling that will require much of you, and in this dimension it is easy to become discouraged. Set your mind to that which falls into the light of eternity, and proceed in that purpose alone."

Tov looked down from where they were hovering and set his eyes on the pinprick that was Kelly. Wait? Yes. He could wait. For Ellen he could wait.

Malheev lifted his hands in the gesture of parting, Tov's heart plunging as the angel of inspiration backed away. He liquefied into the clouds and disappeared, traces of Tov's growing confidence vanishing with him. "Goodbye then," he muttered.

◊

Ellen sat on Kelly's bed waiting for the room to appease her emptiness, for one of the photographs to swallow her back to a simpler time. The stuffed animals stared at her with glassy eyes. The digital clock relentlessly ran its digits, never stopping as time seemed to. Through open closet doors Kelly's clothes hung, giving the scene a false sense of normalcy that was ghostly. The room was becoming smaller every day, closing in on her, pushing her farther into the knowledge of her failures. Kelly was gone. She needed help.

How many times had she stood by the phone, picked up the receiver, put it down? If she didn't call, it somehow kept Kelly from becoming a "missing person." The words stabbed her mind as she wrestled with them. How could she bring herself to say that she was the reason for her daughter's disappearance? Wasn't it only abused kids that ran? Would people think Kelly was one of those?

She pushed her face into her hands, pain biding its time in the back of her head. Days had passed and she was sinking deeper into unwanted thoughts and intense anguish. Kelly's five-year-old face smiled at her from the dresser, cuddled between her and Ben in a hug. Ellen's heart was thumping long before she stood up from the bed. She made her way to the kitchen and picked up the number on a pad of paper. Pain stalked, lurking, surrounding her foray into reason. She picked up the phone.

On the third ring a man with a gravelly voice answered and said good morning, told her the precinct number, asked how he could help.

"I need to file a missing persons report." There. She said it. Papers shuffled in the background.

"How long?"

"Pardon?"

"How long has the person been missing?" he asked.

"Eight days."

"Eight," he repeated. "Name?"

"Mine?"

"Yeah, okay."

She spelled her name, gave her address and phone number.

"Who is missing?"

"My daughter, Kelly." Yes, she has the same last name. No, she has never gone missing before. No, there wasn't anything unusual in her behaviour lately. No, she didn't just disappear. They had a fight and Kelly left.

"What did you fight about?"

His lack of expression made Ellen uneasy. How could she tell a stranger about her faith, about what her daughter thought of it? She could imagine him thinking her a fruit loop, as Kelly did. "Does that make a difference?"

"Could be a clue where she is. If it was a boyfriend you were fighting about, that's who she'd be with, for my guess. If it's curfews or something, she might be at a friend's house where the parents don't care what their kids are up to. Yeah, it helps to know."

A voice in her head and a sickly feeling in her gut steered her away from his probe.

"I've heard from her friend's mom. Kelly did show up there, but they sent her home."

"Do you fight a lot?"

Yes, thought Ellen, too much, enough to keep their home from being one. "Over the past year it's been more than normal." What was normal?

"Social Services ever been called in?"

There it was. Her stomach churned as she digested the insinuation, completely alone in this world of police procedures and raised eyebrows. "Look," she said, "Kelly is rebelling, not abused. If anything, I've pushed her too hard with my expectations, but never with my hands." She kneaded her forehead, prayed to be understood. "I'm sick with worry. I've had no sleep. My emotions are a little high."

"Yes ma'am," he replied automatically.

Of course. Dealing with her was a part of his job, too.

"Is there a father in the picture?"

The question surprised her, tugged her heart. "He died eight years ago."

"Single parent," he muttered, maybe writing. "Can you give me a description of what she was wearing?"

"A light blue denim jacket... jeans..." The pain surged, jumping from the back of her head to the front, piercing her eyes so quickly she almost fell out of the chair.

"Ma'am?"

It shot into the top of her head, down her neck, into her ears. Her throat rasped a barely audible cry. The breath she had fought to control was caught in her open mouth.

"Lady, are you okay?"

One hand clutched the phone, the other the seat of her chair. Muscles went rigid against the torture. Ellen turned to stone. Her eyes rolled as her body stilled. She held tight as she was flung into a labyrinth of dizzying numbness.

Then a faint babbling. "Lady, do you need help? What's happening?"

Slower than it had come, it began to recede. She became aware of the kitchen as the white sheet that covered her eyes dissolved into spots. Needles ran her scalp. Pain settled in her eyes.

"Are you okay, lady? Do you need someone over there?" The voice was clearer now.

Quietly, "I don't think so. It's going away now."

"Is someone there with you?"

She was coming down, gaining her mind. It took a few seconds to comprehend. "There's nobody here." Then she realized what he was asking. "No one is hurting me."

"I can't hear you," he said loudly. "Do you need someone?"

"No. No one is hurting me. I was in pain, but it's going away now."

"Do you need a paramedic?"

Ellen shook her head gingerly. "No. That's okay. It comes and goes." It had never come like that before.

"We can do this another time," he offered.

"No, I want to do this now. The sooner you have the information, the sooner you can find her."

He went silent. "Well, ma'am, we don't actually go looking for her. Bring in a picture and we'll keep our eyes open. We check out leads, or the young offender's centre, or the hospitals. Other than that we don't have the manpower to look for every kid that goes missing."

"But she's never been out on her own before." Wasn't this their job? Isn't this why she phoned? "What if she's hurt, or in trouble?"

"That may be the only way we'll find her."

His words siphoned all expectation through the receiver. Reality, clear and cold, cinched her gut. There was no way to fathom that things were going to stay much the same as they had for the past eight days. The phone call wasn't going to make a bit of difference. Days like the one she'd just survived stretched out before her, and she could not imagine existing sick with worry anymore. "What am I supposed to do?"

"You would be the best one to find her."

"I don't know where to look. I don't know where she would be."

"They can disappear pretty good if they don't want to be found."

Silence. That was all she was going to get? "You said you needed a picture."

"Yeah, it goes out on a bulletin. If she's on the street someone may recognize her." The nonchalance grated on her nerves.

"I'll drop off a picture. Do I leave it with someone at the front desk?"

"That'll be fine. We'll need a full description of her clothes. Do want to give that when you come in?"

"I'll be in shortly."

"I'll take her file up front then."

Kelly's file. She sat unmoving after hanging up. Kelly was now a file.

Pain nudged her, crawled along her consciousness. There was one more call to make while she was still able, to James Ramer, her long-time family doctor and her dear friend Pat's beloved husband. She had been putting it off, even though the pain had been warning her long enough. She wasn't able to crawl out from under it anymore. But the police station came first. Gratitude for an errand to run steadied her nerves.

She dug out Kelly's last school picture from a frame and tucked it into her purse on the way to the bathroom. Deceived that a dab of make-up would sufficiently hide her dilemma, she left the house for the first time in days. She would call James when she got back.

◊

Malheev faded into the sky, and the burden of Tov's mission settled heavy on him. He looked to the bustling mass of people, then to where the angel of inspiration had been. "Fine then," he said. "If I was chosen..."

Urgency set his wings in motion as he saw Ellen's daughter being guided through the streets, and he descended to watch the two of them walk at a pace set by conversation. Above the streetlights he followed, much more comfortable on top of the noise and chaos than in it. Steve was pointing Kelly toward a doorway, one hole among many along their route. Steve walked in but Kelly stopped on the sidewalk. In a heartbeat Tov was behind her. The light inside the passageway was dim. He could make out a long flight of concrete stairs between two cement walls, cracked in places and incredibly filthy. Old litter was compacted on the floor while new garbage was forming piles in the corners. Kelly wrinkled her nose at the smell of urine and the thick tang of alcohol.

"Sorry," Steve said from the top of the stairs. "I didn't know you were coming or I would have cleaned."

The urgency in the boy sent alarm up Tov's spine. Two pinpoints of green light radiated from the eyes on Steve's shoulder. Addiction was quivering, feeding on the emotions churning inside its perch. The legs jerked out, causing it to teeter before it threw an arm around the boy's head and did one complete go around, landing back on Steve's shoulder like a rotten apple, losing chunks of flesh and bodily fluids on impact.

"Don't go," Tov whispered to Kelly. Staring at the twosome at the top of the stairs, Tov moved in front of her and spread his arms to cover the doorway, the sleeves of his robe sliding from wrists to elbows. "Listen to me, Kelly. Walk away."

Kelly looked up. One step into the doorway and she stopped inside of the angel. The hair on her arms stood. She squinted, whipping her head around to the bright sidewalk behind her, but saw nothing. She was listening, heeding the tickles of warning in her gut.

"Turn around and walk away," the angel pleaded.

Kelly looked up the stairs, then down the street in the direction of the park.

The angel went instantly cold. She walked through him and climbed the stairs. Tov's chin dropped to his chest. He glared at the garbage on the floor, listening as she made her way to the top, then followed. Tov took a position behind Kelly's shoulder on the small landing where they stopped in front of a wood door. The sun fought to get up the stairs from below as Steve removed a brick from the wall and took out a key, sliding it into a padlock hooked onto the outside of the jamb.

Tov turned to Kelly, dumbfounded. She was anxiously waiting to see what was inside. Steve pushed the door open, gesturing for Kelly to go ahead while he switched on a light.

It was a long room with three open doors on the opposite wall. To Tov's left was an old TV standing on a plastic milk crate. A balding beanbag chair suggesting a memory of fuzz sat on the floor in front of it. To his right, on the same wall as the front door, a kitchen counter was decorated with garbage beneath a row of cupboards. An old fridge stood at the end of the kitchen, and a poor excuse for a table with two mismatched chairs finished the décor. Clothes were scattered everywhere over a hard flat rug that was doing a good job preserving years of smoke and foot odour.

"Oh," Kelly said. "It sure is small."

"Don't need more than this. There's two bedrooms"—he pointed—"and a bathroom on the left."

Tov and Kelly ventured into the rooms. Double mattresses on the floor in each room were in no better shape than the beanbag chair. A few blankets and more clothes covered the floor. This mess must be Steve's laundry system, Tov was thinking, merely a rotation of what was the cleanest. Even to the angel's untrained eye this place didn't look lived in. But after sleeping on a hard bench, this stinky place probably looked better than home to Kelly.

"Who else sleeps here?"

Steve shrugged. "Mostly me. Sometimes my partner. But it's mainly my place."

"Uh huh…" said Tov, pointing to the key in Steve's hand. "That's why you store that in the bricks, right?" There wasn't anything he wouldn't give right now to throw his voice into the physical to startle the idiot.

"So," Steve asked, "you'll take it?"

Kelly was sifting answers, trying not to be rude. Gross as it was, Tov sensed her extreme gratitude at being rescued. Never again, the set of her mouth said. "Yeah, I'll take it."

"Great!" Steve smacked his arms to his sides. Addiction chuckled, a sound that could have come from the boy's own mouth. The putrid thing was jumping, working itself into a frenzy. Wrapping around Steve's head, it grunted and squeezed, contorting Steve's face as its greasy bottom bounced up and down. The domination this thing had over the boy seemed complete. Steve had been fighting for control all morning as it directed the human's thoughts, feeding on his body and mind. Agony was just a part of Steve's face.

Tov put his hand on his sword, ran his fingers over the grip. The ugly face taunted, spewed aplomb at the silent angel. Wait, Malheev had said. In that he could not fail.

"I have to go," Steve said. "I'm late meeting my partner. Make yourself at home. If you're still hungry, there might be something in the fridge. I'll bring supper back for us, okay?"

Kelly nodded. She stepped over a mound of clothes to put her knapsack down on the kitchen table.

"Bye," he threw over his shoulder as he went through the door and closed it in one motion. It was not shut before Kelly dashed for the bathroom.

Tov looked in both directions, deciding to follow Steve. Expecting the landing to be empty, Tov passed through him on the other side of the door. Steve was closing the triangle clasp over a hook on the door in slow motion, as quietly as he could. The demon gurgled, gouged at Steve with its nails. The lock clinched together with a soft click, and he pocketed the key, taking the steps two at a time.

The bathroom was minuscule—a tiny sink with a small mirror on a medicine cabinet, a toilet, and one very small tub. There were towels on the floor under the sink, and to Kelly's relief a few squares of toilet paper on the roll. She was more than done with her morning coffee.

She scraped a sliver of soap off the bathtub and washed her hands, savouring the sensation of water running cold to hot on her skin. "I can do this," she said to the mirror. An apartment this size must be cheap. There had been so many signs in shops and restaurants looking for help. If Steve wouldn't mind her crashing here until a first paycheck, she could envision the person staring back at her putting a life together for herself. She had done it. She was actually on her own.

There was no cupboard under the sink, no shelf in the shower. The medicine cabinet had nothing in it. She'd thought there would be a toothbrush, deodorant, anything. She couldn't remember that Steve had smelled, yet there was no accounting for the personal hygiene of others. The towels were in desperate need of laundering, as was everything else in the apartment. Her hands smelt worse for the use of them. Doing the laundry would be a small price to pay for the walls that would give her privacy and protection from strangers. A kitchen. A toilet. A mattress. It was heaven.

She flicked off the light and retrieved her knapsack from the table. Since she'd set eyes on the mattress, she had wanted nothing more than to curl up on it, no matter how dirty it was. She kicked the clothes to the floor and folded a blanket into a pillow, shaking another blanket over her body as she lay down. It hugged her as it settled, and she drew one very deep breath. Seconds after her eyes were closed she was no longer in Steve's stinky apartment.

Chapter Six

Kelly wasn't going anywhere, and no one was getting in. Tov glared at the padlock, deciding to follow Steve. He flew into the daylight, spotting the bush of hair high above other heads as it approached the corner and stopped at the lights. Tov took a vantage point above him and they started back in the direction from where they'd just come, Steve's fists shoved deep into the pocket of his jeans, walking for blocks with the demon on his shoulder holding his head in a vice of claws. All Tov needed was the slightest hint from the boy that the company of the wretch was no longer wanted, and he would gladly appreciate the chance to dismount it. Addiction was nothing without the will of its victim. It was only taking what was up for grabs.

Steve eventually jaywalked across the street and turned onto a road lined with two-story buildings. Stoops of three short steps and iron railings framed the doorways on either side of the street, the buildings all made of the same brick, but each stoop boasting a different colour door. Window boxes filled with struggling flowers attempted to brighten the view. There were fewer people here, and virtually no traffic. Children played and hollered, running on the sidewalk while adults watched. Steve walked past it all and jumped the steps to a green door. Tov found him pushing buttons on an intercom inside.

"Yeah?" the box asked.

"It's me." Buzzed in, Tov followed him down a long hallway that had successfully trapped the odours of many a cooked meal. Black lanterns with gold windows emitted barely enough light to see the hint of design on a carpet lost to a well-worn path.

Steve stopped and banged on a door.

It opened slightly. A face peered over the chain and then retreated. The lock fell, a bolt retreated, and a man in a sleeveless T-shirt and tattered jeans filled the frame.

"Where have you been?" The man's voice matched his features. Pockmarks erupted on his face everywhere there was skin. He had hair on his lip and chin, but the attempt at hair on his head was exactly that, fizzling out before a few stringy strands reached his shoulders. A handful of years older than Steve, he was a good head shorter, his T-shirt doing little to conceal a barrel stomach.

Over the man's shoulder appeared the head of a snake, taking in the two at the door before making its way down the man's body. It flicked and jiggled the long tongue of a reptile, but had the nose and eyes of a human, silently observing Tov as it slithered shoulder to shoulder and across the man's neck. Tiny sets of three-fingered hands along its body held and clenched, gripped and let go as it made a circle down one leg then up the other. There was no question as to what it was. A cohort of the one on Steve's shoulder, only this one much more mature. This Addiction had the look of years in its size and eyes, form and power accumulating the longer they had claim of a victim.

"Had to start delivery myself this morning," the fellow rasped. "What's up with that?"

Tov could imagine his breath by the colour of his teeth.

"I got one, Reese," Steve said, smiling.

"Got one what?"

"My ticket to paradise."

Reese shrugged.

"A girl."

Reese's expression changed. "Really?" A laugh blew his wispy moustache. He slapped Steve on the shoulder and stepped aside.

"Just a minute…" Steve muttered. He rushed down a hall to a bathroom, going directly to the toilet. The face of Addiction was pure restraint as Steve reached behind and pulled out a needle, bottle cap, lighter, and a baggie. A line of drool ran down its face onto its legs.

Stepping aside in disgust, Tov opted to observe from the living room as Steve and his sidekick joined Reese in the kitchen. He sat down at the table, took white powder from the bag and mixed it with water in the bottle cap. Hands shaking, holding it between two bent tines of a fork, he cooked the concoction with the lighter. Tov's stomach lurched as Steve injected, his head rolling, and it wasn't a minute before his hands relaxed and the needle rolled to the table. He slumped into his chair. Addiction groaned, massaging and caressing the boy's scalp, slobbering into his face, following him into the abyss of dangerous pleasure.

Reese waited until Steve opened his eyes. "So, give me the details. Where is she?"

"At the clean house."

What Tov heard was not Steve's voice. Raspy and abrasive, low and slow, but it was coming from Steve's mouth. "It was the easiest take you could imagine. She followed me like a puppy."

Reese slapped the table. "How are you going to work it?"

"She's so green… man, I don't know." Steve put his head against the chair. "Help me decide."

"Where'd you find her?"

"It was classic! She was sitting in the park, just waiting for me… a first-time runner, and a looker too. Man, I couldn't believe it when I laid eyes on her." Steve's eyes bugged. "She was so scared… I could have given her a sucker and asked to look under her skirt and she would have done it."

"First-timer?" Reese played with the handle on his mug. "She's got no clue?"

"Not a one."

Reese smiled a weird little smile, somewhere between a wince and a thought. "What's she look like?"

"Oh…" It came out as a moan. "Black, black hair, long and shiny. And these gorgeous, green, terrified eyes." Steve's head lolled to one side. "Great body. A little too skinny maybe."

"What you got against fat?"

"You, man!" Steve reached over and slapped Reese on the shoulder.

Thankful for the distracting view out the patio doors, Tov turned away while the two tousled, knocking things over, punching and slamming each other across the table. He didn't know how much more he could stand.

"You are trying to figure out the years of captivity this Addiction has over this human, are you not?" asked a voice.

Tov swung around. A figure like his own stood in front of him, wings to his sides, head tilted. Shorter than Tov, his pudgy cheeks gave the impression his body would be as round, when it was not. He was wide in girth, but by no means as round as his cheeks suggested. His grin begged forgiveness for the surprise entrance, and Tov's impulse to fly or fight dissolved. Complete irrational delight overtook him and he held out his hands to be taken in a grasp of salutation. They stood with locked hands.

"Oh! Oh, my!" Tov spurted. "It is so good to see you!"

"And you!" The angel pumped Tov's hands up and down. "It has been so long, I was beginning to fear that this dimension would not hold company for me." He bowed slightly. "I am Chaver."

"Greetings, Chaver. I am Tov."

"Tov," the angel repeated. "Greetings, Tov."

They stood in shock, eventually releasing hands. Chaver glanced to where Steve and Reese sat, blissfully unaware of the angelic meeting. "Is that your mission?" Chaver nodded to Steve.

"No. He is a hindrance. But the other, is he yours?"

"Yes, yes he is. I have been here five years, by earthly time, and I have nothing to show for it but the fruit of my patience." Defeat wrinkled his face. "His father is a minister who took grievous pains with prayer at their parting, but I am afraid that the father is losing hope. I spend more time with him than the boy. With a heart that broken, my power seems limited in the face of his growing doubt. His faith is being tested, and I am finding it to be a little thin." Chaver went quiet. "My ministrations are but a small comfort in the face of such loss."

Fear tickled Tov. He recalled his own ministrations to Ellen in her living room, the praying saint on her knees. How wonderful it had been to fill her with a power born of her faith, a power that had pulled him into this world. He could not let Chaver's words into his mind. He refused to think of anything but a reunion as the end for his own mission.

"I, too, have been called to guardianship, by the prayers of a mother. But I have only begun my task. It has been days, in earthly time." Chaver was listening intently. "Her name is Kelly. This one named Steve has taken her to another place and locked her in. She has less of an idea than me what his intentions are."

Chaver clasped his wrists under the folds of his robe. "No, this isn't good. Steve has not been with Reese long, a little more than a year. But I think I know what he is planning. Is that why you are here?"

Tov nodded.

"He is learning from Reese. I have seen him take ones like Kelly and use them for his gain."

"How?"

"He will sell her to others for money."

Tov's voice was a whisper. "Sell her?" Conversation filled the kitchen behind them, broken by spurts of laughter, but Chaver's words shut it all out. "He will sell her?"

Chaver hesitated to answer. When he did, his voice was unveiled disgust. "Others will pay him to use her for their pleasure."

Tov stared.

"He will take the money and feed Addiction with it," Chaver finished.

It was becoming repulsively clear, but he rose to defend what little he knew of Kelly. "He may try to lock her up to take her freedom, but she will not allow herself to be used."

Chaver looked at the beady eyes of Addiction watching them from Reese's stomach.

The one on Steve's shoulder wasn't able to focus, eyes sunk deep into its face.

"The boy will break her will," he said under his breath. "He will introduce her to Addiction."

The eyes of Reese's demon slowly changed from black to green, narrowing to slits, listening.

"Do not despair." Chaver touched Tov's arm. "You said you have been here only days. This is to your advantage. I am sure that you have the full power of someone's faith behind you yet."

Yes, thought Tov. The power he had been sent with was vibrating inside him, the reason he was having trouble settling into this dimension. It was enough to blow the four at the table into oblivion. And it lay at Kelly's feet, sent on the wings of a mother's love.

"I can help you," Chaver offered. "The minister has a heart for all children, and his prayers come much easier for them—and with more faith—than they do for his own son. I do not know why. But I have been sent, by his requests, to others like Reese."

"Know I will call on you then." The thought was wonderfully fortifying. "What must I do when I need you?"

"If you are in the force of battle and call to me, I will find you. If there is a clash in this sliver of our dimension, I will feel it." Chaver drew breath, appearing to debate. "I have also experienced the physical, altering it with my hand." He nodded at Tov's astonishment. "And it was not subject to the will of any human."

Tov had heard stories about their Master allowing them to touch the physical. It took incredible power, changing the course of events without the will of any being able to interfere. He could not keep his voice from shaking. "I would like to do that."

"And I again. It is nothing I had control over, save that I had been diligent in waiting. It was given to me in the instant I required it. I am afraid that if I had the power myself, I would be meddling continuously without proper knowledge of what I was doing."

Meddling would be his first intention, but Tov had no intention of letting his new friend know that. "How did it feel?"

"I felt flesh. An incredible compulsion overcame me to take his arm, so I did. He turned at my touch, even though I could not be seen, and he took my pull as a sign to turn away from where he was going."

"But what did it *feel* like?"

"Amazing! I cannot explain it." Chaver disappeared into his memory, savouring it, then remembered Tov. "I wish it for you. The physical will not be here forever, as you know. It will pass away, and the opportunity will pass with it."

Reese went to a closet and came back with a knapsack, which he threw on the table in front of Steve. The angels turned to each other, foreboding anchored between them.

"Steve will be delivering now," explained Chaver. "This is how he pays his rent. Reese buys from the dealers, sets up customers, and Steve delivers. It confuses me as much as it does you. Will we ever understand fellowship for the purpose of destruction?"

"It is hard to witness."

"I don't know if I'll be back here tonight," Steve was saying. "I'll see how things go."

"Don't push her, Stevie. If she's as green as you say, you can use her trust to your advantage," Reese warned.

"Why wait?" Steve studied his friend's face. "What, because she's a first-timer?"

Both angels turned, drawn into the sudden silence from the kitchen.

"Yeah, cut her some slack."

"Since when? Since it's money in my pocket and not yours?" Steve pushed him on the way by.

Reese was struggling. "Get out of here. Go earn your rent."

Steve stopped, hand on the doorknob. "Are you going to help me or not?"

Reese got up, leaned against the counter, his answer a little long in coming. "I'm here if you need me."

"All right then." Steve went over and slapped him on the back. "All right."

Chaver squeezed Tov's shoulder, then pushed him away. "Go, my friend. I'm here if you need *me*."

Tov laughed. It was such a horrible impression of Reese. The thought of leaving his new companion made him feel wretched, and he could not take his eyes from Chaver as he left silently through the apartment wall.

◊

Kelly rolled over, pulled from a dream. Snuggled deep into the mattress, she kept her eyes closed, content to wallow in the aftermath of the soundest sleep she'd had in days. Her surroundings began to penetrate drowsiness, and she opened her eyes to the pigsty around her. Light seeped through a rectangle of glass block high up on the wall. She checked her watch only to find it had stopped.

In the living room was another window made of glass block she hadn't noticed before. It let in light, but she couldn't see out—a small price to pay for the privilege of privacy. She could live with that.

Her stomach was telling her it was time for food. A stove clock in the kitchen that lacked hands peeked through a layer of grime, displaying a circle of useless numbers. She looked tentatively at the fridge. "What wonderful surprises do you have lurking inside?"

The fridge shuddered as she peeled the door open. The smell was strong, but her curiosity was stronger. She discovered two cans of open beer, a coffin of a pizza box with dried remains, something green she guessed was once a loaf of bread, and a mountain of ketchup packets. She leaned on the door to reseal it, waiting for the smell to dissipate before taking a breath. Faring a little better in the cupboards, she found a box of crackers, a can of soup but no can opener, some hard peanut butter, and a vast collection of fast food napkins and plastic cutlery. Didn't he eat? The crackers were stale but the lesser of the evils. She drank from the tap, surveyed the room, and decided to start earning her keep.

She picked a corner and started sorting laundry, making a separate pile of socks that could stand against the wall by themselves. Undaunted, she sifted dark from light, a layer of grime rubbing off on her hands that she could scrape with her fingernail. She hadn't really thought about clothes until now. All she had were the ones on her back. This mess held some possibilities if it could meet up with a washing machine, but maybe that was pushing the limits of Steve's generosity. How much can you ask of someone you don't know? The piles grew, as did her spirits. How wonderful it would be to have a place of her own to clean. Momma would absolutely die to see her daughter doing laundry. Momma. It was going to take far more work to rid herself of Momma than it would to clean up this mess. How far away did she have to run to get Momma out of her head? If only it were as easy as sorting her into a pile of light or dark and carting her off to the laundromat.

Momma's ghost fluttered in her thoughts. "Leave me alone," she begged, throwing the last of the living room wardrobe onto a pile. The bedrooms beckoned.

Pulling arms out through shirtsleeves and legs through trousers, it felt like she was invading Steve's privacy. Too bad he was such a slob. Steve's face jumped into her brain in place of Momma's and she let her mind play. He wasn't bad looking, in a rough sort of way. It struck her why she was so surprised to find his place such a mess. He was clean. His hair was washed and bushy, and his clothes, other than being oversized, were clean. This place didn't fit him. The clothes were such an odd array of sizes. She held up a sweatshirt. Maybe these weren't even his.

Her stomach was talking, shrinking. "I hope he remembers the food."

◊

Tov's patience was splintering. Other than what he'd learned from Chaver, Steve had given him nothing but a tour of the inner city, some of which he wished he had never seen. The knapsack hung empty on Steve's shoulder, and he guessed they were headed back to the apartment. Tov flew ahead to check the distance, then returned to find Steve gone. He ducked in and out of walls and found him standing in line at a burger shop, sorting through a mound of change in his hand. Sick of the boy's company, he parked himself outside the window. He would catch him when he came out.

The sun was dropping from the sky, pulling shadows from the buildings, pushing people off the sidewalks and nudging them home. Home. He was starting to worry about Kelly, if she discovered that the door was locked. As the day had unfolded it wound him tighter and tighter, helplessness taking a hold of him again. Malheev's visit had drifted in and out of his mind as he wandered with Steve, grounding him to contend with the contemptible chore of the deliveries. Nothing could make him feel lower than what he was feeling. The longer he was here in this place, the darker it became.

Dazzling colours of the sunset caught him off guard. He could feel His Master's touch upon him as it changed hues and intensity, and it made him think of Chaver and his long-endured mission. His new friend must be made of stronger stuff. Tov could not imagine earthly years of delving deep in the depravity of what existed here, of witnessing the destruction of something as beautiful as life, especially without being able to deliver the power and peace he was sent with. As desperate as Tov was to find help for his mission after only days, he was beginning to imagine what his presence here must have felt like to the other angel.

The door opened and closed below, ripping Tov from his musings, but it was not Steve. He scanned the thinning crowds and picked out the fuzzy head a ways down the block. Tov caught up to him at the doorway of the apartment and flew through the wall. Kelly was sitting in the beanbag chair banging on the TV, fiddling with the buttons. Like a hand sliding into a well-worn glove, he took up his position behind her and waited for Steve. She seemed fine, no inkling of being imprisoned. On the contrary, she seemed rested and relaxed. Things were feeling a little like normal until minutes passed and Steve didn't show. Reluctant to leave her again, Tov went back outside.

Steve was sitting on the landing, a cup of soda between his legs, a lid and a straw on the ground beside him. He pulled a baggie from his knapsack and dumped white powder into the cup, stirring it with a straw, watching it dissolve. Popping the lid back on the drink, he threw the empty bag down the stairs and fished the key from his pocket.

Chapter Seven

The demon was crouched deep into the boy's neck, timidly watching the angel, quite unlike the foolish, slobbering idiot it had been all day. Steve opened the door, leaving Tov rooted to the landing in stunned silence.

"Whoa" Steve cried, stepping into the room, seeing Kelly in front of the TV. "That's what the floor looks like!"

"I would have cleaned more, but there isn't much to work with." Kelly's voice betrayed her pleasure that he was back. She was about to say something more, but caught sight of the bag in Steve's hand. Arms outstretched, faster than the angel, she jumped to rip it from his fingers.

He was outwardly amused. "Sorry I took so long." He set the cups down on the table, taking her assault in stride. Tov took up position between Steve and Ellen's daughter, nostrils flaring.

Kelly was giving Steve no mind, completely missing his attempt at sincerity as she unwrapped a hamburger and buried her nose in the foil. "I forgive you, but only because you bought food." She peeked into the bag, groaning as she pulled out fries. Caressing the burger between mouthfuls of cold oily potato, it was much the same as it had been at breakfast this morning.

"Is there enough in there for two?" Steve asked.

She pushed the bag toward him. He slid the soda cup at her.

Tov raised his face to the ceiling. "Now, Lord," he implored. "Now would be a good time to touch…" He put his hand on the cup, swiped at it fast, then slow, waiting for a voice, a feeling, something.

He fixed his mind on it, concentrated his light into it, tried to smash it flat between his hands. But he moved right through it.

"Looks great in here," Steve complimented. "Was it boredom, or disgust?"

"Both. I would have done laundry if I had some soap and a machine." She cocked her head. "Where do you do laundry? Or is that like asking you where you cook?"

Tov stopped swiping.

"There's not a whole lot of stuff around here," Kelly said, waited politely for a response. "I thought you said you lived here."

Steve was nodding, chewing vigorously.

"Your time is up," Tov whispered to him. Maybe he had given Steve too many credits for smarts. It was obvious the boy was scrambling.

"This isn't my main place," he said. "I share an apartment with my partner. I use this place when I need to get away."

"Get away from what?"

"From things. People." Steve busied himself with his burger. "I need my own space, time to myself. This place is small, and cheap. It's one luxury I give myself."

Tov huffed. "Hardly."

"Why don't you just live here, then, not share with anyone if you need the space?"

Steve chewed, forever.

"Not too quick on your feet, hey?" Tov goaded.

"I do it more for Reese. He's my partner. I have a room at his place and he charges me practically nothing. Reese needs people around him all the time. He comes from a large family, can't take the quiet." Steve settled into his chair, chin up, a little smug.

"How long have you and Reese been partners?"

"A little more than a year. He's helped me a lot. I was in the same position as you are."

"Is that why you're helping me now?"

"Exactly." Steve smiled.

"Some help…" Tov mumbled. He swiped at the cup from under the table.

"You said you left because of your dad," she stated.

Tov stopped. The boy was going to buy her over with the kindred spirit ploy, the "pity me" party. He braced himself, knew what was coming.

"I was having trouble in school. Dad was down my back about it. He liked hitting me. Made him feel big, I guess."

"Did he hit you hard?" She was struggling. "A lot?"

"Yeah. He loved his beer more than he did his family. I knew when to take off, when to come home. He beat me so much, sometimes I couldn't go to school." Steve snorted. "Stupid idiot…"

Tov straightened. He put his hands on Kelly's shoulders to gain her thoughts, imploring her to ask the questions. It was important that she hear this, but she wasn't speaking. Warmth radiated through him, and Kelly, almost absent-mindedly, received. Thoughts of Momma came. The angel poured out the comfort of her memories, sitting her on Ellen's lap, nestled her in the crook of Ellen's arms, the hum of familiar songs resonating through her Momma's chest.

He was doing it. He was reaching her. "Yes!" he whispered. Ellen was in his fingertips, the power of her prayers moving through him into this precious spirit that embodied her love. He concentrated, immersing himself in the first chance Kelly had given him to touch her.

"Where was your mom? Didn't she help you?" Kelly asked.

"My mom? I never saw her stand up to anything in her life. If she even thought about it, she got it worse than I ever did." Steve was wading, carried by thought, caught awry by reminiscence. "She must have thought about it a lot." He returned to Kelly momentarily, reacting suddenly to the pity on her face. "What? You never got hit?"

Kelly was slow to shake her head. "When I was little they spanked me sometimes, but it never hurt. I can't imagine my parents hitting me like that."

He sneered. "Well, lucky you. I see why you had to leave."

Kelly pulled back. "Are you mad at me?"

Steve changed his tone and regrouped, working for self-control. "No." He took a breath, tried again. "If your home was so great, you shouldn't have left."

Tov felt his hands grow warm again, felt her confusion. "I told you Daddy was killed. It's been Momma and me for a long time. Forever, almost. Daddy died and Momma changed. We both changed, like we didn't fit together anymore. It makes me mad that she would accept losing him so calmly. How can she be okay with that?"

"Maybe she didn't love him."

"No, she loved him. I remember snuggling between them when I was little, when I saw them together. I wanted to feel what they had."

"So...?"

"Then he died. End of life. All we did was go to church. I quit going, and Momma spent more time there than she did with me. She became somebody else. I hated her, pushing me, preaching at me. God took Daddy and that's who she went running to." Kelly leaned over the table. "How can someone give their whole life to some stories in a book?" She sat back. "I'm stronger than that."

"Sounds like our moms are the same."

"How?"

"Neither of them can stand on their own two feet."

Tov was pleased to see her jaw clamp, her offence.

A long, bony arm reached slowly from Steve's shoulder across the table, testing the waters, needling the angel's already undone nerves, and retreated. Then it started a rhythmic thunking on Steve's head, rapping hard with bony knuckles. The angel alone could hear it, could see the buggy eyes taunting him while it hammered on the boy's skull, hard then soft, hard then soft. Steve took a sip of his drink, squirming, and pushed the other cup closer toward Kelly.

She picked it up and drank.

Tov gasped.

"If you don't live here full time, maybe you wouldn't mind if I did, until I get on my feet," Kelly said. Steve sat mute. "I don't want you to get sick of having me around, so maybe the fact that you have two places works great. I'll pay you rent as soon as I get a job."

Steve was running his finger up and down the side of his cup.

"That's all I need. Oh, and I would have to borrow clothes from you so I can wash the ones I'm wearing, and I would do your laundry as payback…" She took another drink, tried to interpret his changing moods, his weird silences. "Are you listening?"

"Yup."

Tov was tuned to her thoughts, sensing her fear that Steve had changed his mind. She was too much trouble, an intrusion on his solitary life, she would cost too much until she could pay her way. Her tongue was running her teeth and her lips. She tried again. "I won't sponge off you, I promise. I'll get a job."

Steve nodded, settled back, still playing with his cup.

"What? Did I make you mad again?"

"No."

"You don't like me, do you?"

"Why do you say that?"

"You're acting like I'm not here."

"I'm glad you're here. Really." He smiled.

"I appreciate what you're doing for me. You don't know how grateful I am to have a place to sleep." She studied the room like she had never seen it before, slaking the awkward one-sided conversation with a break. Kelly picked up her cup. Tov watched in horror as she drank it down to half.

Steve was watching closely, pretending not to, putting in time, the stiffness in his body thawing. "I can sleep at Reese's," he finally said.

"That would be great." Kelly put her cup down, spilled a little.

"So, what kind of job do you want?"

She was attempting to focus, her head veering to one side.

"Do you cook?" Steve asked. "That would be a bonus, if you know how to cook."

Her head was starting to bob. She fought to keep it level. Steve shifted his weight in the chair, his eyes oscillating between the cup and Kelly.

"Something's wrong," Kelly murmured.

Steve was calm. "What?"

"I don't know... I don't feel good..." Her head was swaying, rolling freely on her neck. She rested it on the table.

Tov was rigid, anger pelting into rage, feelings that had never been induced before in the realm of his missions. If the gift of touch were his, this beloved boy of his Master's would have been breathing his last.

"Steve..." Kelly muttered, grabbing her middle.

"What's the matter?" he asked, sweetly, sarcastically, grinning. She was past picking up on innuendo.

"*I* can still hear you, moron," Tov said.

"Oh, geez..." She straightened, hand over her mouth, and sent the chair tumbling as she scrambled for the bathroom. It was impossible to navigate the corner without balance and she collided with the wall, spraying the contents of her stomach as she fell against the doorjamb.

"Oh, great..." Steve groaned.

Convulsion after convulsion wrung her, squeezed her dry until she was left gasping for breath. It was a few minutes until the heaves grew further apart. Tov was on Steve as he took her arm to guide her into the bathroom. He pushed her down to the floor in front of the tub and stood back, hands on his hips.

"That's all you're going to do?" Tov asked. The angel rushed through the boy's body, burning Addiction as they touched. It screamed, recoiling as it claimed ownership of Steve with its claws.

Tov dropped to the floor, falling into the strange afflictions surging through her as his body and robe consumed her, as his wings wrapped her. Electricity ran her nerves and muscles, stealing her away. Flying high, rocketing recklessly into a steady climb, she was a feather released into the wind, weightless, but made of rock. She could not lift her head, was fused to the floor, the feeling of having no body. And there was no fighting it. She let herself go, floating higher, then deeper, into a fog of horrifying sensations.

Addiction groaned euphorically, rolling its eyes. Lost to the promise of perverse thrills, it reached a talon for Kelly, rubbing her spine, hurling the hitchhiker further into the bottomless canyon of her fall.

Tov exploded. The burn was instantaneous. Charred flesh stuck to Tov's hand as he grabbed Addiction's scrawny arm and pulled it out of its socket. The air ignited as they connected, the demon working to free itself, reaching for the safety of Steve's shoulder. Full force, Tov struck Addiction with the back of his hand, flinging him into the boy's body, embedding claws so deep into Steve's skull that the angel could no longer see them. They fell backward as one, a shrieking, rolling mass, grappling at each other for consciousness. Tov cringed at the pain he was capable of inflicting. Never had he had to navigate such a dangerous minefield of emotion, or felt the flammable affront of such supreme rage. He struggled desperately to push feelings away, placed his arms around Kelly, rested his head on hers, bound on saving her from the destiny that the two on the floor were determined she would inherit. Their screams receded from his troubled spirit as he called up the power given to his disposal and rushed headlong into the abyss where she had fallen to try and bring her back.

Chapter Eight

Pat Ramer was Ellen's faithful friend, wife to Doctor James Ramer, receptionist for his practice. As far back as Ellen has ever needed them, James and Pat had been her friends. When Ben was alive they dined out, played cards, celebrated weird holidays they found recorded on odd dates of the calendar. It was a friendship that needed no maintenance, their gatherings complete with comfortable laughter and serious talk. When Ben died, they had been her strength, her wailing wall, the family she no longer had, being an only child whose parents had passed. No longer four, but three, the group still felt secure.

Ellen had put the call off for so long that the knowledge she could gain from a visit to James seemed formidable. Pat would be on the other end of the line, and that gave her the courage to mechanically dial the numbers. That, and the need to hear her voice.

Their small talk over other lines ringing in the background was a solace that knew no distance, Pat apologizing for the chaos, telling Ellen of a cancellation tomorrow. It was hers if she wanted it. She did, at the time. But leaving the house the next morning, apprehension undulated her gut like birth pains. Sidewalks and streets stretched beyond her car windows, beckoning her to change her mind and go searching. Everyone looked like Kelly. Everybody that moved held the secret of where Kelly was. Gas pedal forgotten, her car crawled the pavement as she gawked, fighting the impulse to roll down her window and shout the impasse of her life to anybody who could hear. Pulling into the parking lot and turning off the car was a relief. The sun touched her through the window, faint birdsong from a nearby tree kept her anchored to the seat. Let someone else fill in the cancellation, she mused, to receive whatever news fate had in store for them. Ignorance could be a very warm blanket. Ellen relished the moment.

It was a forced march through the office door, but inside Pat threw her arms around her—long, leggy Pat, who towered over her. It felt so good that Ellen held on. Pursued by the phone, Pat waved her to the waiting area and plunked Ellen's skinny file on top of the desk. Ellen was so out of place here. Doctor's waiting rooms were filled with the very old, the very young, and the occasional middle-aged tourist like herself. Nothing to do but put her in time here, the waiting room game, observing others without them knowing. Out of the corner of her eye, Ellen was drawn to a little girl with long, dark hair at the toy box. She tried hard at first to avoid it, but the childish chatter enticed her. The hair was not as black as Kelly's, and when she looked up Ellen could see the girl had freckles, but she was a close enough ringer to trigger a foray into memory. The little girl pulled them out for Ellen as easily as she pulled toys from the box.

Her little body a movie screen, complete with sound and snippets of conversation, Ellen sat watching herself, Ben, and Kelly at the ocean jumping waves that pulled them in and spit them out. The next minute they were beside the twinkling lights of a tree Christmas morning, Kelly's eyes reflecting the magic. Scenes changed, rapidly, randomly. Walking home from Kelly's kindergarten play in the late hours of afternoon, the spring leaves and greening grass a fragrance Ellen could still smell. On a whim they had entered the flower shop at Ben's suggestion. A bouquet was needed, he informed them, to place on the mantle in honour of the success of the budding little actress who stole everybody's hearts and lines. The shop was muggy with flower perfume. Kelly had picked red carnations. The bouquet was dried now, in a vase on Kelly's dresser.

Startling Ellen, suddenly back in the waiting room, the girl's mother stepped in front of her to snap puzzle pieces into place before taking her chair again. Sadness touched Ellen, hung a cloud over her and coloured the air. She envied them being in the middle of the years one lives too easily, believing all the best times are still ahead. Hard to imagine she had ever sat in that mother's chair. But here she was, on other side of the room. She had tried so desperately to hang tight to the handlebars on the ride of her life, worked to keep Kelly safe in the seat beside her. But where had she taken them? What happened that Kelly would leave, as Ben had?

Oh God. Every nerve in Ellen's body was cut by the child on the floor. *My life has turned into a journey down a funnel. If you push me through the end, I think I will disappear.* A tear slipped out the corner of her eye and held her eyelash. *Whatever your will is, I try to accept it.* It made a slow descent to her chin. *But please, please, hold my little girl. Don't ever let her go.* It jumped from her chin to her shirt, made a dot on the collar. *Engrave her name on the palm of your hand, God. Never erase it.* She touched her other eye, taking another tear on her fingertip before anyone could see.

Ellen looked up, felt Pat's concern through the pressure in her fingers. She had her hand on Ellen's shoulder. "You can go in now."

Ellen gathered her purse, let Pat lead her down the hallway, arm around her. Pat put the file in the holder and opened her mouth to speak, but changed her mind. She opened the door, touched her hand to Ellen's cheek, and left. Minutes were like thin, fine crystal, fragile and hard to hold, brittle seconds thrown from a clock on the wall.

James knocked and entered. "I don't get to see you professionally too often," he said. He sat to flip open her chart. "What can I do for you?" He was talking to the paper in front of him, reading a minute before looking up.

"I should have come in a long time ago, James."

"How long have you been putting it off?"

Ellen looked sheepish. "A year, maybe."

James didn't say anything, leaving Ellen to continue.

"I have headaches. They're getting worse. Well, they were headaches at first, but now I get dizzy, and the left side of my body goes numb."

James took a pen out of his pocket and started to write. "How long?"

Ellen tried to calculate but shook her head. "It started small, and I didn't realize it was a pattern until it got worse. A year maybe, probably more."

"Uh huh…" He was encouraging her to keep talking as his pen moved.

"The dizziness feels like when you get up too fast, but it's there all the time now, whether I am up or not. I just walk slower and closer to the wall."

James frowned. "I always knew you were one of those."

"Those what?"

"Those who are more afraid of what they'll find than what they don't know."

"Now you know my darkest secret," she joked.

"Ellen…" he said, quietly exhaling. "Let me have a look." He patted the examining table and went to the paraphernalia on the wall. Ellen sat while he poked, shone, peered his way over her body. He asked her a barrage of questions that left her drained, made her uneasy with his intent concentration and face of stone.

"Well…" He took a seat. "I would like to run a few tests, book you for an MRI. I need to see inside of your head to give us a clearer picture, tell us what we need to know."

Ellen was trying to read his expression and his voice. "Tell me what you're looking for." She smiled to encourage him.

He acknowledged, a slow nod. "There is the possibility of a tumor." He waited until her face registered what she'd heard. "The MRI will show us a map of your brain and tell us if there is anything there. It isn't painful. We put you in a scanner and take pictures. I wouldn't normally reveal my suspicions without proof…" he glanced at the floor, "but I also know what you're going through with Kelly. We can't ignore this. You have to start thinking about it so I can help you. Not knowing is a heavier burden." He chose his next words. "Aren't you learning that?"

Ellen's eyes filled. They swam in her lids, distorting James. "Yes." It was the smallest of whispers.

"You haven't heard from her?"

Ellen shook her head.

"I'm so sorry." He stood and put his arm around her.

Her lips moved words but didn't speak them.

"Stress can aggravate what we may be dealing with. It may accelerate the progress of any physical problem you might have."

Ellen had her head down, tears rolling freely into her lap. Barely strong enough to stand, she faced two battles now. Her life was suddenly someone else's, far from anything even lucidly familiar.

James held her. It was the catalyst she needed. Grabbing his chest, she gave her burden to him in sobs, the heaviness that had been sitting on her draining into the vessel he made of himself. And he took it all, held on until she let go. Then he reached behind the desk and pulled out some tissues.

"What am I supposed to do?"

"I'll walk through this with you. You know I will do the best I can, don't you?" He waited for her nod. "Okay. My first order of business would be to bring Kelly home. But that is out of our control. So, we act on what is within our control."

Ellen pushed her fingers against the pain growing in her temples.

"We'll get a diagnosis, which may come after the scan, and possibly after some other tests as well. Then we'll look at treatment." He took hold of her hand, aware that she was checking out. "I'll have Pat phone today for an appointment, okay?"

"Yes."

"I will give you something for the pain." He scribbled on a pad, ripped off the sheet and put it in her purse. "The MRI will be done at the hospital, so we have to wait for an appointment, or a cancellation. If you have any questions or unbearable pain, promise you'll call me right away."

"I will."

"Promise?"

"I will, James. I promise." She raised her eyebrows.

"Okay. Fine." Silence took them both to the same place. "She's a good kid, Ellen. She needs time to figure things out. She's not fighting you as much as she is finding out how she's going to cope as a grownup. It comes on them so fast…"

Sam and Darcia, James' girls, both older than Kelly, looked at them from a frame on his desk. "Darcia gave you and Pat some problems," Ellen stated.

"Oh, yeah." His voice rose on one word, fell on the other. "She took us for one heck of a ride. I will always remember that sick feeling waiting up nights… the incredible string of yahoos she found to date. I don't envy you. But it does look different on the other side of the fence after they find their footing."

The concept escaped Ellen. It was only words. They did nothing to comfort, to fix the play button of her future that was stuck on hopeless.

"Ellen, you've raised her well. All the good you've invested in her will come out eventually. Don't blame yourself for the choices she's making now. She's entitled, as an adult. She'll test out a few and arrive at the right ones."

Ellen wanted the remedies now, wished she could spare him telling her what she worked so hard to avoid knowing. It wasn't fair, but she planted her eyes into his. "Will I be here for her, James, if she needs me?"

He studied his hands. "I can't answer that. I will do everything I can to help you. And I would choose a specialist who would do the same. We just have to take this one decision at a time."

Fair was fair. "Just give me permission to ask the hard questions when I need to."

It surprised her to see mist in his eyes. He agreed.

"I'm so glad to have you and Pat."

They stood, no intention of ending their visit in a doctor-patient handshake. James hugged her, opened the door, and escorted her into the waiting room right to the front desk.

"If you need anything… you promised," he reminded.

"I did. And I will." Ellen returned Pat's wave before quietly closing the door on her other life.

◊

The apartment was fatally quiet. All he could hear was Kelly's fitful breathing from the mattress. Tov stood in the corner opposite her, hands clasped, wings flat and still, the hours he had put in uncountable. Steve had left in the early hours of morning after he'd checked on Kelly. He had cleaned the bathroom doorway, rinsed Kelly's ordeal down the tub, and collected the garbage from their dinner the night before. Then Tov had heard the lock thump into place outside the door after. It had been quiet ever since.

A faint light peeked through the glass block, steeping night into morning. There was no decision to make, whether to stay with Kelly or follow Steve. The thought of leaving her panicked him, delved him into the terrifying spiral of last night all over again. Following her to such a horrible place required all the power he had, to be the presence that kept uninvited intruders away from her that were slinking in the corners. Fear gave him the stamina he needed to stand guard now, alert to any presence that may have lingered in search for a home.

Hour by hour the light in the room was brightening, changing the colour of the walls. Tov tuned into the faint ebb and flow of traffic, hazarding a guess that it was late afternoon.

There was an intake of air, movement under the blanket. He got to the mattress as Kelly opened her eyes, wrinkling her nose at the smell of vomit, the crust cracking under hand as she reached to her hair where it was matted.

In the bathroom she flicked on the light and scraped the sliver of soap off the sink, making quick time to scrub her hair into suds, coming awake under the wonderful ministration of hot water. Slowly she raised her head and looked at her reflection. The intensity in her eyes made Tov's breath quicken. He pivoted, putting his face over the Kelly in the mirror, working her thoughts, standing inside them, pushing the truth at her.

She had vague memories of things that made her insides chill. Hair dripping, she was staring at the mirror. What the heck had happened? She had been fiercely ill, then remembered falling asleep, carried into a dream of violent and magnificent imaginings. But she'd had the feeling, the surety that she was actually there. It had been too real. She had been heavy, and at the same time floating, a balloon of concrete riding the breeze, a string dancing below just out of reach of someone chasing her, jumping to try and pull her down. The thought slipped into her mind. Her mouth fell open. The initial suspicion touched her, and left. She couldn't get her mind around it before it came again. Eyes in the mirror were daring her to accept what she couldn't fathom.

"Yes, Kelly," Tov said. "You were drugged."

Kelly picked up the soap and flung it at the tub where it stuck. "No!" she hollered, grabbing the door, throwing it against the wall. The knob left its imprint before bouncing back and slamming shut. "No!" she screamed. Then a whimper. "No..." She slumped against the wall, head in her hands.

Tov raised his face. "Thank you," he whispered to heaven, hope flickering.

She cried herself empty. "Okay," she said, sniffling. "Okay." She was speaking to the Kelly in the mirror, drying her hair. The towel hit the wall where she had thrown the soap and plopped into the tub.

Tov followed her out of the bathroom, stopping when he realized she was headed for the door. Kelly grabbed the knob. It turned in her hand, but the door didn't budge. She took it in both hands and yanked. Frenzied, she kicked it with the flat of her foot, over and over. When nothing gave, she leaned against it and yelled. "Let me out!" Her ear against the wood, she waited. "Someone let me out!"

Tov flew through the door. "Now, Lord?" He kicked at the lock, his foot passing through.

The door was thick, absorbing Kelly's fists, muting her screams. Tov looked down the stairwell at the shadows of people passing. He floated down the stairs only to realize Kelly's screams were disintegrating into the noise of the street. There was nothing to do but go back.

She was standing in the living room glaring at the door, the look on her face the same feeling that was simmering in his stomach. She became surprisingly quiet. Walking backwards, she stopped at the wall and slid to the floor, arms holding her knees, her eyes trained on the doorknob. The angel dropped into position beside her.

Chapter Nine

Kelly tensed. The lock was being undone on the other side of the door.

Steve peeked through as it opened slightly. He didn't notice Kelly on the floor against the wall in the twilight, but two sets of eyes, seasoned to evening shadows, were locked on him. He made his way to the table, put down what he was carrying, and went back to the light switch. The bare bulb above the table flickered to life and he turned immediately to where Kelly was sitting. There wasn't surprise on his face, or none that Tov could see. His expression was fixed, ready to face what he could read in Kelly's demeanour.

"Are you okay?" he asked, dipping his toe, testing the water.

She wasn't answering, was as silent as she was still, determined to test the water herself.

Steve put his hands in his pockets and leaned against the door, a heel up to hold it closed while he studied his other shoe. Tov noticed that the demon on his shoulder had changed. The arm he'd wrenched from its socket hung limp, a condition the angel secretly hoped was permanent. It swung with Steve's movements, making Tov's heart thump at the memory of the stinking flesh in his hand as he pulled the gangly thing out of commission. But that wasn't it. Addiction was bigger. The resolve of both Steve and the pet on his shoulder had been fuelled by what the angel had done. He had only succeeded in making his enemy greater.

Steve broke the ice. "It was a mistake. It was in the drink you had. Yours got mixed up with mine." He glared at her, challenging.

Kelly's breathing didn't falter. She didn't blink.

"So," he stated simply, "you know I do drugs." He waited for acknowledgment, anger, anything. "Would you have let me help you if I walked up to you and said, 'Hey, I'm Steve and I do drugs?'" Not bloody likely." He huffed, indignant. "I sat with you after what happened. I even cleaned up your mess, and I didn't leave until I knew you were sleeping. What can I say? It was a mistake."

Kelly's voice was level, controlled. "Was locking me in a mistake, too?"

"I didn't lock you in. I was locking them out."

"Them?"

"Yeah. Notice with me, if you will," he said, playing the door like a hand model on a game show, "that there is no way of locking the door from the inside." He moved his hands gracefully up and down the parameter of the sill. "The only lock I have is for the outside. Notice there is no keyhole here. There is no other way to lock the door."

Tov grimaced at the 'I told you so' on Steve's face.

"I didn't know I would be having company, and that the present means of security would be unacceptable." He put his hands on his hips.

Condescending smile in place, Kelly walked to the door. Tov flashed the same look and flew into step behind her. She went through and stopped on the landing, looking back at Steve. He raised his shoulders and shrugged.

Hand on the wall, Kelly descended the staircase to the third riser. Half a dozen pairs of eyes stared at her from the bottom. In the dark, silhouetted against the street opening, she counted six men blocking the entrance, some sitting, some leaning on the wall. Cigarette smoke hung thick. One of them let out a catcall, and all of them guffawed, sending waves of alcohol up to where she'd stopped. Her hesitation was only brief. She continued on.

"Come on, baby! Bring it on down here for me!" one called out. She was close enough to make out his features as he grabbed for her. He knocked her backward, sent her stumbling.

"You get your pick tonight, honey. Ain't you lucky?" This voice was lower, his hands quicker. He went for her wrist, squeezed it until she cried out, anticipating resistance. But Kelly moved to him rather than pulling away, and slammed her knee into his elbow. She heard his arm crunch as she connected, and the sound of shattering glass as the bottle he held in his other hand smashed to the steps. The language that spewed from his mouth sent her scrambling back to the top.

Tov was watching one who hung back from the crowd, standing almost on the sidewalk, leaning on the corner of the wall inside the entrance. He flew down and stopped in front of Reese, a thought flashing in his mind as he rushed to the street, searching the sidewalk and above the lights. No Chaver. Perturbed, he stayed to take in the view from the bottom of the stairs. Steve was guiding Kelly back through the door, and she was going without a fight. The door slammed shut and Steve stayed outside, joined them, slapping the closest one on the back.

"Thanks guys." They punched knuckles, shook hands, carried the charade on and on.

"No problem." The words were slurred as the fat one rustled Steve's hair with dirty fingers. "It was fun... good for an evening's entertainment."

"Fun for you," the low voice growled. "She almost broke my arm." Someone laughed. "Suck it up."

"Think you'll have any trouble convincing her to lock the door now?" They dissolved into drunken hysterics. Someone fell off the bottom step and fresh laughter broke. Their attempt to keep it quiet made it all the more funny.

Steve was smiling, but sober, completely outside the hilarity of their comments. "Can you stick around awhile and make some noise?"

"Our pleasure," said fingers, bowing with a theatrical sweep of his arm. As he touched the ground he farted, which sent them all sideways giggling until they couldn't draw breath.

"Right," Steve muttered. "Thanks." He opened the door. It banged hard on something blocking the way. "Kelly, it's me," he said through the slit.

Tov went to look, found the table pushed against it on the other side. Steve braced against the wall and pushed with his feet, squeezing through the opening as the table scraped the floor. He slithered through the crack and closed the door. The stairwell went dark.

Tov took in the bawdy gathering of imbeciles that thought nothing of Kelly's demise. Their delight sickened him. He turned as cold and metallic as the blade in its sheath beneath his robe.

One squinted, looked up to where the angel fumed. "Do you see anything?"

"Where?"

"There." Eyes followed his finger as he pointed up the stairs. Some moved to get a better look. The closest to Tov took a step up, stuck out his face. "What is it?"

"I don't know. Some weird light or something. Don't you see it?" They had their sights locked on the angel.

Their idiocy and Tov's anger merged. Electricity bolted through him. "Get out of here!" he yelled. Tov startled as he felt the words in his throat and ears. The whites of every eyeball in front of him doubled. There were double-takes, expletives shot at the light that shimmered and shouted from the top of the stairs. Someone swore. Another bolted. The best was the six of them running for the doorway at the same time, pushing each other back, thwarting any attempt at a quick escape. One by one they broke free, swarming to scatter down the street. Their running petered out in the distance before the corners of the angel's mouth lifted into the biggest smile. He let out a laugh that rang off the walls. Reaching his arms to heaven, he clasped his hands together, shaking them over his head.

"YES!" he shouted. He flew to the sidewalk. "YES! YES! YES!" He hollered at the buildings. "Oh my!" Spinning circles of delight, he clapped his hands in time with his dancing feet, heaven bent on making the most uncharacteristic fool of himself.

"Congratulations!"

Tov stopped, dizzy. Chaver was standing at the entrance of the stairs.

"Where were you?" Tov flew at the other angel, grabbed him by the arms. "Were you here? Did you hear it?" Tov pulled back, looked him in the face.

"I didn't, but your enthusiasm is certainly infectious." Chaver laughed. "Judging by what I passed down the street, I gather you made your presence known."

"Oh, did I! You were right Chaver, I didn't ask for it to happen." Tov fought for breath. "The power, the emotions, they grew to such unmanageable proportions in me that I couldn't contain them. How does it all of a sudden happen, when you're not expecting it?"

"I don't know. But tell me what it was that was required of you."

Tov shook his head, hard pressed to give up his smile. "I spoke!" He nodded vigorously, in case Chaver needed the affirmation. "I opened my mouth and it came out. All the times I speak here and it is only to myself. But it came out of my mouth! I felt it in my throat and ears." Tov dropped his arms. "That's how it must feel for them when they speak, do you think?"

"I imagine," Chaver mused. "Our bodies were prototypes for their physical ones. They mimic us in the physical the same as they will one day function in thought like we do in eternity."

Tov's mind raced. "So when we speak to each other, you and I, would it be to them like their thinking?" Chaver looked blank. "We know the words we say, but we can't feel them in our throats. Our talking is like their thinking." He stopped. "But we hear it when we talk."

Chaver was trying to follow. "I would think so."

"Where were you? I looked for you before it happened. Reese was among them, so I thought you would be, too."

"Reese was with them?"

"Yes. You didn't see him?"

Chaver shook his head. "I shot rather quickly over the stamped-ing mass."

"When I saw Reese I thought for sure you had shown up to help."

"I was at the place where they take in kids like Kelly when they end up on the street, with one boy the preacher sent me to with his prayers," Chaver explained. "I felt you when you transcended into the physical, and left him rather abruptly, I'm afraid. I switched into our pure form..."

Tov's face registered the proper alarm.

"I know, I know," Chaver agreed. "We're not supposed to do that here, but I wanted to get to you as fast as possible. I did it only for speed."

"You could feel me? Where I was?"

Chaver nodded. "It is very powerful. Remember what if felt like when you were sent to your mission here?"

"You're talking about the pull to destinations?" Tov asked.

"Exactly. I felt the power given to you when you were pulled momentarily into the physical. It was a burst, such a quick surge that I was afraid I would miss it. I don't think I gave myself away." Chaver looked around. "Nothing unwanted seemed to have picked me up."

He had Tov looking, too. They both listened, wary and guarded, until they were sure nothing undesirable had detected Chaver in pure form. Advertising their presence to forces that did not want them here was dangerous, absolutely perilous to their missions.

"I needed you. I was searching for you only moments before." Tov squinted. "How are we supposed to determine if the power will prevail, or if we need to call for help?"

"That's the point. It is not within your control. You just have to be willing."

Knowing beforehand would make it so much easier, Tov thought. As exciting as it was to experience the physical, his feelings toward the humans in the staircase made him wonder if he wanted to know all that his Master needed to have control in this place. The humans were so disturbing, so hard to understand, that a part of him was secretly relieved he was delegated to the waiting and not the knowing.

"I'm glad you're here to share it with me," Tov said.

"Oh, I know. You understand, then, how I feel as well." Tov saw the years of Chaver's mission blow across his thoughts. "We are fortunate. It can be so long between connections down here."

"I love that our Master would consider the bigger picture and put us together. How much fun would it be with no one to share this with?" They stood apart but locked together by affinity under the streetlamp in such a foreign place, bound by the comforting touch of the eternal that they were to one another.

Chaver stepped back. "I have to go. There is a young man who I left suddenly in a moment of receiving comfort. Until we have the privilege of meeting again, my friend," Chaver said.

Tov was at peace, full and fortified, not troubled with the parting. He felt his true power, believed things might go right for a change. Chaver lifted his wings and beat them in a splendid and graceful rhythm that carried him down the street. He turned at the corner and waved to Tov before he was gone again.

◊

Steve was clearly provoked, attempting to control his temper, his face pushed against the locked bathroom door. Guilt toyed with Tov for leaving Kelly to celebrate with Chaver, but the boy's position absolved it. The angel made a wide sweep past Steve out of pure disgust and joined Kelly in the bathroom. She was sitting on the floor, face blank like it had been when Tov found her on the park bench.

"If you're scared they'll get in, you don't have to worry as long as I'm here," Steve assured her. Silence. "I'll put the lock on the door tonight. You'll be safe." Nothing. Steve shifted his weight. The wood groaned under his arms as he leaned on the door. Tov wasn't surprised at the change of tactics before the next words were out of his mouth. "I bought some food, but it's probably cold by now. It's pizza, so I can heat it up in the oven."

He walked away. Kelly relaxed deeper into her slouch. For the next twenty minutes they listened to Steve banging in the kitchen. Her eyebrows joined. The noise outside grated on the angel as much as it was torturing Kelly. She ran her hands through her hair as the table scraped back across the floor. Her stomach growled, and she shifted to ease the needles in her backside. The smell of bubbling pizza eventually seeped under the door and she stood against the sink, inhaling, biting her lips. Tov grunted at the sorry state that would again put her at Steve's disposal. She debated, wrestled with her hunger, her knuckles white on the sink before she unlocked the door.

Steve was standing by the table set with paper plates, plastic cutlery, and two cans of Coke. "Madame," he said, gesturing to the chair.

Kelly clinched her jaw and sat, arms crossed. Steve took a napkin and flicked it open by the corner, placing it elegantly across her lap.

"Welcome to Chez Steven's," he said in a raunchy French accent.

From the bathroom door, Tov shook his head. Steve opened the oven, and for lack of oven mitts took the pizza out with his hands, dashing to the table before throwing it on the burnt spot where others had been dropped before. Tov just about fell over when Kelly's eyes closed and her head dipped, for the briefest of seconds, saying a silent thank you for the food. It was so quick. Addiction curled its lips, holding the look on its face so long that its lips stuck to its fangs. Then it turned to Tov.

"Get used to it," the angel muttered. He hovered to the table, placed his hand on Kelly.

"You don't like pizza…" Steve declared. Kelly acted like he wasn't there. She took a piece and dropped it on her plate, gave herself over to the most wonderful ritual of eating.

"You do like pizza…" Steve said, undaunted.

"You're going to play this even if it kills you," Tov said to deaf ears.

Steve helped himself and the two of them ate in dense silence.

"As you can see, I brought you a sealed can of Coke." Steve pointed. "You can drink it without worrying." Kelly ignored him. "I feel bad about what happened. How many times do I have to say I'm sorry?"

Guttural noises bubbled from Steve's shoulder. Addiction was growing agitated, its good arm wound around Steve, working hard to transfer its fussing into the boy. Steve threw his food down, squirming like his chair was infested with ants. He wore the demon and answered to it like a wristwatch. And he gave it one more try. He reached in a bag and pulled out a magazine and put it on the table in front of Kelly. She glanced at it, wiped grease from her mouth, took a Coke and popped it open.

"I'm sorry, Kelly," he said. He pushed the magazine toward her and got up.

By the antics on Steve's shoulder, Tov knew that he wasn't going to last here much longer. "If it's so painful to have me around, then I'll go."

Tov rolled his eyes. "Oh, pleeeease…"

"I'll stay with Reese tonight. You can have the place to yourself." He walked to the door. "You don't have to worry. I'll put the lock on again. No one will get in." He opened the door, stuck his head through with the pretence of looking down the stairwell.

Tov couldn't resist. He flew to the door at Steve's intake of breath and realized the stairs were empty. "I think they're all passed out," Steve said. And he left.

This time Kelly heard the lock scraping against the door. The click. She pushed the food aside, let go of the tension holding her body rigid and put her head down on her arms. She cried, sucking air hard. Deflated her body vibrated, a rhythm of misery.

Tov knelt, put his arms around her, rested his head on hers, and watched her tears puddle on the table and drip into her lap.

◊

Ellen closed the book she'd been trying to read and looked at the clock in the circle of Kelly's reading light. Eleven thirty. Eleven thirty, and dark again. Another night alone. She had made it through the horrible day, the day of her appointment, the day of her knowing. She should switch off the light, bring it to an end, but her arms were aching. She hugged them to her chest.

"Wherever you are baby, this is for you." She could feel Kelly's hair against her cheek, breath on her shoulder, the deep, dark anguish of her own heart. Tears came. She cried, rocking, pouring out her torment. A dull pain pounded in her head, warning her, and she had no choice but to stop. She could not bear it again. Her only comfort, her only connection to Kelly, was prayer. She knew with all her heart that as she prayed, Kelly would feel it. The numbers on the clock counted the stamina of Ellen Whitcomb.

Tov began his work, drawing on a faith and love that knew no limits. As he received, he gave, placing what he could into the small cracks of Kelly's disintegrating confidence. Enabled, commissioned, he worked hard for such little gain, stealing into the tiny cracks opening up in the girl. Wrapped, held, her mind slowed and her chest grew still.

The numbers on the clock beside Ellen's bed flipped to one o'clock as heaven mercifully took the day away from each of them.

Chapter Ten

A single car drove by, shining its headlights through Tov before moving on. He was on the sidewalk outside Steve's apartment, wondering how many times he would come to standstill, not knowing what to do. His impulse was to find the place Chaver had told him about, where they took in kids from the street. He would love nothing more than to get Kelly there, but he had no idea of where to look. Images of this place haunted his thoughts as Kelly slept, then they had pulled him out into the street. And now he stood in the dark, wondering. He had to find Chaver.

He followed the same path Steve had taken him on the day before, but glad at the hour. The empty streets were far less stressful than the commotion of the day. But he hated the dark. If there was one thing he could not abide, it was the dark. Lamp lights formed a pattern of circles alternating left and right as far as he could see, but they only deepened the shadows outside their sphere. And it was such a pale light, not a whole lot different from the darkness.

He was going from memory, making great time until a movement caught his eye, stopping him in a circle of light. Hovering at an alley entrance, he saw it again. On the ground beside a dumpster lay a large dog, a study of mange and hair as surely as the heavens were a study of the eternal. He was brown, with ears, feet, and tail dipped in black. Tov wasn't sure if that was colour, or dirt. As he approached, the dog followed his every move.

"I won't hurt you," Tov assured him. He was in front of the dog, and it was looking back. "You can see me?" Tov whispered. The body didn't move, but ears lifted. The angel reached out, and to his profound dismay his hand passed through the mountain of hair. "Can you feel that?"

The ears shot up.

"You can hear me?"

The hairy head tilted left, then right.

Tov cupped his mouth, in complete disbelief that they were communicating. "What wisdom would give you the senses to know I'm here?"

The eyes questioned. Then the dog did something that pleased the angel immensely. The long, shaggy tail thumped the ground, then the dumpster, tentatively at first, before it erupted into full-scale wagging.

Tov threw his head back and laughed. "Oh, you are amazing! What an absolutely wonderful creature you are! Would you like to walk with me?" Tov backed away. The tail stopped. He moved again, his voice was more hope than confidence. "Come?"

A huge tongue dangled looking like a smile, but the dog made no attempt to get up.

"Maybe you have work of your own? I would not ask you to abandon your responsibilities. The decision to come or not is in your capable paws." He reluctantly turned, glancing back once before he reached the corner, only to see his new friend lying where he had left him. The picture tugged at his disappointed heart as he took the corner that erased the dog from sight.

Forcing himself on, he traveled quickly to the street lined with brightly coloured doors. Through the green one he breezed past the intercom, down the hallway and into Reese's apartment. A dull glow radiated from between the drawn verticals in the living room. He followed the only noise to a bedroom, finding Reese. Two pinpoints of light popped up from behind his sleeping body, Addiction startled at the sudden presence of the angel. It hissed warnings, winding possessively around the man. Uninterested in the mock display, Tov checked the apartment and found it empty. In the living room he was in the same situation as on the street outside Steve's. There was no use bothering the scum he'd awakened in the bedroom. It would only rob Reese of sleep. And Chaver was probably at the place he was trying to find. Waiting here seemed as ridiculous as a building-to-building search.

"What now?" he queried, face up. Divine guidance or personal revelation weren't banging at the door. He was fighting the urge to act, rather than wait as he'd been instructed. The apartment was so dark and quiet, save for snoring. It twisted his nerves. He didn't like being by himself, the need for companionship as much a part of him as his wings. He could never live so separated and detached from any living thing. He looked at walls designed to keep the humans from one another, altogether stumped at how they could bear it.

A key sounded in the lock. The door flew open and the wood on the sill protested as the chain jerked tight. Forced to its limit again, it closed with a bang. The voice gave no thought to anyone in the building. "Let me in! Come on, open the door!"

The bed squeaked. Unsteady footsteps shuffled down the hall. Reese flicked on the light beside Tov, rubbing his face. "Hold your shorts," Reese said under his breath. He slid the chain from its track.

"Keep it down!" someone yelled, swearing before a door slammed down the main hallway.

Neither Reese nor Tov were surprised to see Steve leaning against the wall in stoned and drunken glory. Reese shook his head. He went to the kitchen, turning on another light, and picked up a package of cigarettes. He lit one as Steve came in, pulling the door hard behind him.

"Problems?" Reese asked.

"Bigtime."

"What now?"

"You guys left."

"Yeah," snorted Reese. "Something weird was going on."

"Weird like what?"

"We were hanging out, and someone told us to leave."

"Since when do you listen to anybody?"

"Stevie, there wasn't anyone there."

Steve held up his hands, inviting explanation.

"There was a voice, but there wasn't anyone there."

"Yeah, well thanks anyway," Steve said, teetering on the belief he could appear sober. "You guys scared the crap out of her, but I don't think I'm going to be able to keep her there."

Reese smoked, took his time exhaling. "Well, in case you didn't hear me, something creepy happened. Hanging around your door all night isn't an option, okay?"

"So what am I supposed to do?" Steve sunk into alcoholic thought, Addiction on his shoulder savouring the euphoria. Tov looked on from the kitchen doorway, leaning against the jamb, resigning himself to such low-grade diversion.

"I'm going to go for it," Steve said. "I don't feel like playing these stupid games with her. She needs me, right?"

Reese shrugged. He went to the fridge, took a beer back to the table.

Steve did the same. "So, do I have to start from scratch, or can you help me out and give me some of your old customers?"

"I still get a few guys asking. I can send them your way." He played with the end of his cigarette in the ashtray. "It's a lot of work, you know, kind of like having a dog. Ever had a dog?"

"Never."

"Well, it's a little like that. A dog needs food and water, and as long as you give 'em that, they're happy. A girl... well, depending on how bad she's needin' her dope... she could have a mind of her own. They get demanding. A real pain sometimes."

Tov bristled. What was going on?

"I gathered that. She gets choked about everything. Can't stand the mess, cried when I told her my old man beat me... didn't know what hit her when I slipped her some."

Reese quit messing in the ashtray and went still.

"I polluted her virgin veins," Steve laughed.

Reese's head bowed slightly, the tiniest of movements. Tov would have missed it if he hadn't been watching so closely.

"I mean, what was she thinking, coming down here? It's like she was dropped from another planet," Steve said.

"I'm from that planet," Reese reminded him. "Not everyone got their lumps growing up."

Steve leaned across the table, theatrically thrusting his hands toward Reese. "So, why are you here?"

Reese didn't look at him. "One foot in front of the other, I guess. It's not where I ever planned to be. It's a surprise some days after I wake up, when I realize where I am, what I do." His voice dropped. "All the decisions that didn't seem important just kind of added up."

"There weren't many decisions for me. I only had one. When to leave." Steve thought that was funny.

Reese pulled a long gulp from the can. "Is that why you hate her?"

"What?" It had the desired effect, draining Steve's hilarity.

"It's going to feel good bringing her down, isn't it?"

"Why would you say something like that?"

Reese was suddenly placating. "Sorry. Forget it."

Something was stirring in Reese, confusing the angel. Tov fixated on him, and beyond his belief the tiniest magnetic force began in his belly, pulling him toward the table.

Steve's next words were bullets in a gun, and he shot them at Reese. "Think I'll double her up, give her enough to push her over the edge."

"Watch it, Stevie. You're the one who's going to pay if she ends up in a bag."

Tov's insides stirred, the force in his belly growing. The grotesque creature, usually stuck tight to Reese, was sticking out from his body, little excuses for hands clamped tight, holding itself out in midair. The slug on Steve's shoulder was roused from its stupor.

The angel backed into the living room, the eyes of both demons upon him. He regarded Reese, head down, eyes averting the boy across the table, and saw a man falling apart. Feelings, that by practice Reese could usually squash and ignore, found the man's face. He was groping for something, as the demon clutched at him from the outside. Reese was stirring the magnet in Tov, and Tov was aware of his presence doing the same for Reese. Addiction started to flail, the contact with Reese a growing sting to its flesh. Unwilling to relinquish its grip, it thrashed frantically, growling, scaring the little one on Steve's shoulder.

Tov readied his sword, astonished at the sudden turn of circumstances. The light inside him began to pulse, preparing him. Ear-splitting curses pierced his nerves. He thought of his blade penetrating the neck that was straining to reach out and strike. "Please," Tov pleaded, picturing the pronged tongue hanging out at the end of a severed head. "Please Lord…"

He was pulling the sword out of its sheath, but it was not the sudden jump and thrill of battle. He was fighting with every muscle in his body, pushing hard against a force pushing back equally hard against him. His body burned with effort, the strenuous movements taking a toll on the initial rush of adrenaline. He knew it to be Reese's struggle that he was engaged in. For some reason, Reese was calling upon Tov to help. Surprised yet ready, as laborious as it was to Tov, every feeling rising up in Reese was just as heavy and filled with power for the man as it was for the angel. Tov fought the force that worked to keep him away from Reese as the human fought against the good rising in him, attempting to bury again what had been buried for so long.

Only it was not so easy. Something was bringing it to the surface, driving it into his mind, tugging him from the depths of apathy to which he had sunk. He was being forced to choose.

Tov knew the conflict for what it was, and there was no way was he going to give in. He strained against the force, using every ounce of his strength to gain an inch of headway. Ignited, he cried out at the pressure needed to move the wall of dead weight. Through the smallest crack in Reese's armour, what had been entombed there for so long was seeping out, slipping through. Tov forced his light, his will, into the opening, determined to rip it apart, to bring the long-worn barricade to rubble.

Exhausted, Tov's weapon was painfully freed. With the same effort it had taken to remove it from its sheath, he forced it above his head, clutching it with ferocity. He would not make a mistake. He would not let up. He advanced, moving the sword lower and lower, lining up the blade with those green eyes. The demon reached with scrawny three-fingered hands, lashing its oblong head. Tov pushed, making contact, searing flesh. Addiction screamed, whipping its head, beating all its arms against its body, exposing its belly, and Tov kept moving. Sluggishly the steel pierced the skin, punctured the stomach, then stopped.

The sword had gone as far as Tov could push. The weapon jerked in his hands as Addiction, drunk with pain, twisted on the other end. The angel pulled back and the tip dropped to the ground. The demon clutched at Reese, the lower half of its body almost completely severed from the upper, which was hugging the man's shoulder, straining for a hold.

Tov saw a tear on Reese's cheek. He watched it fall, a tenderness growing in him for the man who stood his ground and decided to fight. He sheathed his weapon, filled with an overpowering impulse to hold the little boy inside of Reese, the little boy who had gone sideways, who patiently stored the secrets of freedom saved for this moment. Tov felt drained, completely used, and absolutely wonderful. He closed his eyes, said a prayer of thanks. When opened them Chaver was there, his arms around Reese. The angel looked at Tov, gently put his head on top of Reese's, and cried.

Addiction fell into the man's lap, grasping for a hold on his legs. Steve sat motionless across the table, the wretch on his shoulder hiding behind his neck, shaking. Even in his state of mind, Steve saw that Reese had checked out. He fidgeted, eyeing the broken man crying at the other end of the table, studied his beer, took a few drinks and lit a cigarette, smoking the whole thing before Reese stirred.

"I'm tired," was all Reese said. He walked out of the kitchen. Addiction howled at the movement, dangling from his knees.

"Whoa," Steve mumbled. He sat drinking, smoking, and then finally walked past the angels, turning out the light.

Tov and Chaver stood motionless in the dark.

"I never saw it coming," Tov whispered. "It happened so fast, I never saw it coming."

"After all these years... all the prayers..." Chaver was choked.

"What was in that moment that was different?" Tov asked. "Why now?"

Chaver shook his head. "I don't know. I wish I did, but it's not for us to know. Like you, it has taken me by surprise," his voice cracked. "A welcome, welcome surprise."

"You felt me in battle, didn't you?"

"Yes," Chaver said, struggling. "There seems to be great use for you down here. It appears that you are given to accomplish much in a short time."

Tov chided himself for insensitivity. "Chaver, your mission is a call for many. You said so yourself. The prayers of the preacher bring you that privilege. The comfort and hope you have brought over your span of years here are beyond measure. We both know once you invest your heavenly power into one heart, most reinvest it into another." Tov bent down, level with Chaver. "How does that make my mission of hit and miss look bright by comparison?"

"It doesn't, my friend. It just makes mine look especially dull. But I wouldn't have traded my moments tonight with Reese for anything in heaven." The corners of his mouth moved. "For anything."

They celebrated the miracle, quietly partaking in the ethereal peace that surrounded them. Tov allowed his friend that space to settle into the idea that after so many years he was standing in the wake of answered prayers. It was not over for Chaver, he guessed. But the wonder of tonight wrestled with the sadness for his friend that he had not been the chosen instrument.

Chaver broke the silence. "So. I need to know what brought you here in my absence."

"You," Tov answered. "I was looking for you."

"Needing my help when you really didn't need it. Again."

Tov revelled in the lightened mood. "No. Just looking for you when you are not to be found. Again."

"Ah hah…" Chaver rubbed his chin, nodding.

His antics drew the required smile from Tov. "Yes, I was on the trail of the elusive angel of comfort, waiting for you to show."

"So rather than wait, you decided to call?"

"Precisely."

"Well, now you have me. How may I be at *your* service, great and mighty Tov?"

Tov let it pass with a raised eyebrow. "Take me to the place where they help kids like Kelly."

"Glad to return the favour. Nothing would give me greater pleasure to share with you the one spot on earth that makes me truly happy, where I would always choose to be."

"Maybe that place is your mission here more than Reese."

"I'm beginning to think so." Chaver was thinking. "My focus on the preacher's son has felt like a failure to me... until tonight." His eyes twinkled. "Now I am torn. Is it because of Reese that I have been called to all the others who share the same struggle? Could there be the one mission without the other?"

"I hardly think so," Tov assured him.

"If my Master trusts me with more than Reese, then I am content and thankful for the responsibility. He cares for so many... I will embrace all that I can." Chaver held out his arm. "Ready?"

They went through the kitchen wall in no great hurry, chatting, moving as easily as dust on sunshine. Engrossed in conversation, they passed through the lobby and out the green door. Rearing simultaneously, wings instinctively blooming to full span, they covered a shadow scurrying out of their way on the sidewalk.

Tov's heart vaulted. He tucked in his wings and knelt in front of the furry face. Chaver stayed where he was. "How did you know I was here?" Tov asked the dog.

"He can see you?" Chaver asked, incredulous.

"It appears that way." Tov glanced over his shoulder. "He can see you, too."

"I passed him on the way in. He didn't even blink."

"Here, I'll show you." Tov pushed Chaver down on the sidewalk. The angel looked up at Tov, unsure what to do.

"Talk to him," suggested Tov.

Chaver peered into the funny face, his motions guarded. "Hello dog," he said. The lolling tongue made it appear that the dog was smiling, but the brown eyes never left the angel standing over his shoulder. "I said," Chaver tried again, "hellooo."

The tail stopped, the head twisting in question as Tov backed away. The dog followed his movement, whining. Chaver put his hand out as he saw Tov do, passing his fingers through the shaggy hair. Amazed and disappointed, he turned to Tov. "I don't think he knows I'm here."

"How can that be?" Tov spoke, and the tail started again, the dog offering him one giant paw. Nothing could have moved them to greater depths of pleasure than to see the dog wanting to touch them, too.

"This is astounding," whispered Chaver. "Maybe you and I aren't in the same dimension here at all. Close enough for us to perceive, but obviously far enough apart so the animal cannot discern mine." He looked at Tov. "How did he know you were here?"

"I met him on my way over, tried to get him to follow me, but he wouldn't. I have no idea how he figured out where I was."

"They are supposed to have special senses that people don't have. They can follow trails that humans can't, but I never would have imagined that they could see into the spiritual."

"I wonder if he sees me, or just hears what I say."

Chaver picked up on the thought. "Do you think he is responding to your feelings?"

"Maybe."

"Well, this is totally amazing." Chaver went quiet, toying with possibilities. "Let's see if he follows you now." Chaver took his friend's arm and led him down the sidewalk, their heads turned back in anticipation. Almost at the end of the block, they hesitated at the corner and the dog got up.

"He's coming!' Tov shouted. "Look, he's following!'

"I know!" cried Chaver. "I know!"

Chaver stopped, jerking Tov. "Do you know what this could mean, a contact with the physical world that anyone can see, and that *you* can *lead?*"

The angels each swam through the tide of potential, silently imagining the possibilities. They turned at the same time, regarding the animal sitting on the sidewalk with curiosity. "This is surely getting interesting," Tov muttered. Sparked with the current of unforeseen adventure, impatient to see where their discovery would take them, he held out his arm and pointed down the street. "Shall we?"

The convoy took off into the night, the click of canine nails on the sidewalk giving voice to their mission.

◊

Chaver led them into a house where they waited in the corner of a bedroom. The dog at the front door was making enough noise to wake the deaf. Covers flew and a woman sat upright, dazed at the sudden departure from her dreams. She turned on a lamp. Short, dark waves of hair hugged her head from sleep, while others stood to attention. Tov saw her face as it popped through the neck hole of a housecoat. It was narrow, lent charm by a slender nose with a bump on the bridge, giving her face a shot of personality that Tov decided he liked very much.

"Tov, meet Jennis Croft," Chaver said as she sped by them on her way out of the bedroom. He pointed at a snoring lump beneath the comforter. "That, is her husband, Carl." Chaver pulled Tov into a hallway where Jennis was turning on lights. To Tov's left was a spacious kitchen filled with a large country table surrounded by at least a dozen chairs. On his right a rock fireplace slumbered in the living room, watched by an eclectic cluster of furniture. Jennis stood at a large wood door, peering out its window before she flicked on a light that brought a huge porch to life.

When they had approached this home, Tov noticed the large porch that wrapped itself around the house like a pair of arms. It was a big two-story, elegant and old, dwarfed by surrounding buildings. Any other setting would have granted it the charming impression it deserved. But it sat saved from a wrecking ball that had obviously taken others like it to make way for the structures that stood with their toes along its grassy yard. It looked out of place, but Chaver said that most of the residents inside could lay the same claim. As much as it didn't fit, the porch that pulled you into its front door looked as inviting as Grandma's lap.

The noise that awakened Jennis stopped. She waited, hoping she had scared whatever it was away. Claws and a monster head burst into sight—there, and then gone. She caught her breath, and it registered. She laughed as the scratching that had pulled her from bed started again.

"What are you doing, getting me up in the middle of the night?" she chastised the repentant face that greeted her when she opened the door. Ears down, tail on the move, the dog was making it impossible for this collector of homeless hearts to resist him.

"He's good," Tov said. Chaver agreed.

Jennis ruffled his ears and did a quick inspection of his body to determine what brought him to her door. He had no collar, no blood, no wounds she could see, and no food for a while by the feel of his ribs. "You on your own, boy?" He put his paw into her hand and Tov felt a twinge of jealousy. "What are you?" she asked. "You look like your German shepherd mother was cornered by a hairy giant." She rubbed at the layer of grime left on her hand. "You need a bath and a meal, but not necessarily in that order." She stepped to one side. The dog immediately entered and sat at Tov's feet.

"What is it, boy?" Jennis knelt, looking up, inspecting the plaster on the ceiling that had his attention. "What is it?"

"Can you believe this?" Chaver asked. "She is looking right at us." He leaned into her face.

Tov was pacing. "I was scared to even hope for this." He turned to Chaver. "The dog could take Jennis to Kelly." He looked at Jennis, then the dog, clapped his hands and continued pacing.

Jennis took two bowls from the cupboard. "I'm sorry, it's leftovers," she apologized from behind the fridge door. She dumped out a mess of gravy, vegetables, and meat into one bowl and filled the other with water. She put them on the floor in front of her, and the dog could not resist. One long, beseeching look at the angel warned him to stay where he was, and then it bolted faster than a dog his size should move.

"You like my stew?" The animal stopped, flashed a gravy snout at her before resuming his banquet. "No one else around here does."

She laughed. "You're a first, you know. You should be honoured for that." Jennis studied him. "Now, what do you look like? Rover... No..." She knelt to enjoy him devouring what everyone else in the house had barely touched.

Chaver tapped Tov's shoulder, pulled him down the hallway into a bedroom. Someone was asleep on a bed Tov could faintly see against the wall. "This is the girls' floor," Chaver explained. "This room has one bed. The other has two. They are usually full. Jennis says that if God gave her this many beds, then that's how many kids they should have."

"The kids live here," Tov observed.

"For a while. Some leave of their own free will and disappear. Those ones break her heart. Some stay until she can get them to go home. Some have no place to go, and just stay."

"How many does she have?"

"Three beds for the girls on this floor, and three for the boys upstairs."

"Do their own children live here as well?"

Chaver's voice went soft. "They don't have any. They can't." He took in the look on Tov's face. "I know, I know, but they have more kids than they could ever have imagined."

No wonder angels were dispatched here, Tov thought. In the presence of such benevolence, Tov understood the draw this place had for his friend.

"I worried at their heartbreak, but there are just too many kids that need them so desperately."

Tov smiled. "Our Master knew the length of your mission here and provided you a home away from home."

"It does feel like it, doesn't it? They minister to me as much as to the ones they take in," Chaver confessed.

"Where is the boy you were called to?"

Chaver motioned. At the back of the hallway they approached a large old staircase. Wide at the base, it narrowed following the wall to the second floor. Carved spindles held a thick railing, shiny from years of the caress of hands. They took it to the next floor, which was like the one they'd just left, dotted with doors on either side. On the end wall, a window level with a streetlight brazenly shone its probing eye through parted curtains. They went through the last door on the left, and Chaver pointed at one of the two beds, the quiet one. Snoring came from the other. Tov edged closer, surprised to see the boy's eyes open, fixed on the window across the room.

"This is Travis, who I think will be going home soon." Chaver spoke tenderly as he knelt, putting his hands on Travis' forehead. "Sleep now. It will be all right. There's no need to work it all out tonight. Just rest." He stroked the boy's face, speaking quietly until Travis' eyes blinked, then closed. Chaver held him until he was fully asleep. "Travis prayed with Carl tonight. It seems that Travis has known our Master since a very young age. Tonight he has come back to rest in those arms that have waited so patiently." He was breathing in sync with the sleeping boy. "What a privilege, to bathe him in memories, dry him in the prayers of the preacher."

"Reese's father?" Tov asked.

Chaver nodded. "I am tempted to follow Travis when he goes home. How can I resist a reunion?"

"How can you?" Tov looked at the boy asleep, longing that it could be Kelly. He thought of Chaver following this boy home. He pictured Ellen, in the dark, weeping.

They heard the faint rhythm of toenails taking the steps at breakneck speed. The sound grew, skidding to a stop outside the bedroom. The dog scratched at the door, and in a mad dash of whispers and tiptoe, Jennis was in pursuit. "What do you think you're doing?" she fumed.

"I think we are in trouble," Tov said, never dreaming this could turn into a nuisance, much less a mistake.

"Why in the world do you want in there?" Jennis whispered. His claws took to the door again. "You are so weird. This is so weird..."

The doorknob turned. In came the dog, its attention on the bed. Gently, the animal stepped up and sniffed the boy before curling up inside his legs. He settled, rolling his eyes apologetically to Tov.

"I'll be darned..." Jennis went to the bed. "What do you know that I don't? I'd give anything if you could talk."

The animal didn't lift its head, making clear that he was going to stay exactly where he was. Jen tugged his ears. "So, you aren't the underdog. You just have a heart for them, like I do. Okay then, but tomorrow you hit the showers. Understand?"

The dog burrowed deeper into the nest of luxury.

"Maybe he *is* on a mission," Tov mused.

Chaver shot him a look, warned him not to go there. "I agree with her." Chaver nodded to Jennis. "This is bizarre."

Tov had hoped the dog would follow him to Kelly. Presumably now, that was not the plan, given the animal had a mind of its own. He had to rethink the situation, the creature being so unpredictable.

"I am going to Reese," Chaver declared.

Jennis ruffled the furry ear one last time and let herself out.

"I know where to find you now," Tov said. He had no idea how to express a gratitude that so completely filled him. "Thank you, Chaver."

"I know. Believe me, I know." Chaver flew quickly, sliding along on the faint fingers of early light, and disappeared.

The dog was now oblivious to Tov's presence. "So we part company, but I know where to find you, too." Tov put his hand on the boy, whispered his own prayers of blessing and peace, and then followed Chaver out the window.

Chapter Eleven

Ellen had both suits on the bed and was leaning toward the navy one. It was his best colour. The only problem was a tie, the green suit having a nicer tie than the navy. It was difficult to decide. Maybe she would let Ben pick for himself.

She stopped at the closet and took out a full apron, tying it over her dress. The coffee was percolating, giving the house the smell of a restful, relaxing morning. All that was left was bacon, eggs, and toast. It had been a tradition since the first week they were married, the best breakfast of the week happening on Sunday. She adored Sunday mornings working in the kitchen and her family knew it. When she was content and preoccupied she would hum, absent-mindedly. The linen tablecloth billowed, exhaled, and came to rest on the table. She ran her hands over the cloth, memories woven deep into the threads. Sunday dinners. Christmas. Easter. The best family times were shared over a meal around a table as far as she was concerned, and she revelled in the pride that she provided that.

The doorbell rang as she was turning the last piece of bacon in the frying pan. She grabbed the dishcloth, wiping grease from her fingers. Her left leg was being especially difficult this morning, not moving as it should, more pain than help.

Pat was standing on the porch. "Good morning Ellen!" Her voice was up and cheery. "Thought I'd pop by and see if you wanted to go for coffee on my day off." She took in Ellen's dress. "But I see you have plans already."

Ellen regarded Pat's jeans. "Aren't you going?"

"Going where?"

"Church?"

Pat hesitated. "Today?"

"Yes."

"It's not Sunday."

"Of course it is," Ellen assured her. "Stay for breakfast, now that you're here."

Pat stepped in to smoke rolling across the ceiling into the living room. Pushing past Ellen, she ran to the kitchen to a red hot frying pan belching bacon grease over the stove. Smoke curled and dodged her flurry as she grabbed a dishtowel and lifted the pan to throw the crackling mess into the sink. She turned off the burner and opened the window. Ellen watched her from the doorway.

"Don't you have a smoke detector?" Pat asked.

"Ben has to change the batteries."

Pat's eyes narrowed. Her gaze went to the dining room, beautifully set. "Who else is coming to breakfast?"

"Just you."

"But you didn't know I was coming. You have three places set." Pat lit up. "Is Kelly home?"

"Of course she is."

"Oh Ellen, that's wonderful!" Pat giggled, hugged, elation emptying when Ellen went stiff in her arms. "What is it, Ellen? Is she okay?"

"She's fine. Why wouldn't she be?"

Pat went quiet, confused. "Can I see her?"

Pat went into Kelly's room, peeked in the bathroom, then offered her words distinctly. "Who else is eating with you this morning?"

"Ben," she said.

Pat put her hand to her mouth.

"He's changing in the bedroom."

Ellen followed to the master bedroom, protesting. She hobbled to the door, touching the tears on her friend's cheek. "What?" Ellen asked. "What is it?"

Pat had no words. She pulled Ellen close, hugging all she could not say. Distressed, she held tight, took Ellen's face in her hands and caressed her cheeks with her thumbs. "How are you doing this morning?"

"Not so good. My leg is giving me trouble."

"How about if I call James?" Pat wiped her nose on the back of her hand. "Would that be okay?"

Ellen nodded, relieved.

"He's at the hospital today. Would you let me take you to see him?"

"Yes." Ellen stood like a child, waiting for instructions. It felt good to quit. The breakfast was tiring her, and she didn't know if she had the energy to finish. Remembering was hard, the food looked funny, and she couldn't think why she had invited so many people anyway.

"Come," Pat urged, putting Ellen in a chair. "Don't you worry about a thing."

Ellen closed her eyes, hearing Pat far in the distance. Her right arm rested in her lap, her left dangled by the chair. She hummed a tune that showed up in her thoughts. It had been so long... she was so familiar, but so far away. Why had it been so long? Why didn't she do this before, let her mother handle it? She always knew what to do. She had almost forgotten what it felt like to have her here. Why didn't she come sooner? Why had she left her alone for so long?

◊

Tov hovered over the morning rush outside Steve's apartment, stopping at the entrance to the stairs. He chuckled, conjuring the image of terrified men scrambling out the doorway, a memory he was looking forward to sharing when he got home. The kitchen and living room were empty, the mess of dinner from the night before on the table. No surprise to see the pizza box empty. In the bedroom Kelly was sitting on a mattress leafing through the magazine.

"I found it Kelly," he said to her deaf ears. "I found the place you need to be. The problem is how to get you there." He sat beside her, resting his elbows on his knees. Her eyes moved from page to page, taking in the pictures, ignoring the print.

She jumped at the sound of the door, throwing the magazine.

Steve closed the door with his foot, his hands preoccupied with bags and coffee. Steam escaped through a lid, drifting past his nose in uninterrupted spirals. He was holding his breath.

"Let me out," she demanded.

"No problem." He held up bags. "Our solution." He offered the coffees, which she ignored. "Fine." He put the cups down. "Fresh muffins for breakfast…" He grabbed another bag. "Toothpaste, toothbrush, deodorant, brush, shampoo, some kind of make-up…" And another bag. "A lock for the inside of the door so you can come and go as you please. Anything else the little lady will be wanting?"

"Awwww, no Kelly," Tov groaned. She picked up the bag of toiletries.

"You're welcome," Steve said. "Are you going to eat breakfast while it's still warm, or get ready for your first job interview?"

She picked up a coffee and the muffins and cleared a place on the table, trying not to watch as Steve dumped out the contents of the other bag. Screwdriver, screws, and a lock bounced on the floor and settled at his feet, and he busied himself with the instructions.

"Not willing to leave your post at the door?" Tov scoffed.

Steve made pretence of positioning the lock on the jamb. He fumbled the screwdriver and dropped it, resorting back to coffee and instructions before Kelly put an end to the charade when she took all her stuff into the bathroom and locked the door. Steve dropped the paper and sat down to drink his coffee. Before the shower could drown him out, he yelled he had forgotten something. He was going to the hardware store and would finish later.

Tov watched, feeling sick as Steve locked the door from the other side.

$$\Diamond$$

It bothered Ellen that Pat wasn't driving to church. She wondered if she was pushing the envelope of good manners when she kept reminding Pat of the directions. She hated being late.

"Don't worry, I'll get you there," Pat said.

But it didn't feel like they were going to church. She did trust her friend, uneasy as she felt. Alarmed now, she allowed Pat to lead her through the front door of the hospital. James met them, and one on either side they took her down a long hallway.

"Can I go home now?" Ellen asked. Walking hurt. It took a lot of effort and concentration. She kept looking at her leg, checking to see if it was still there. They were not in church. Confused, she stopped in the heavy foot traffic and refused to go any farther. She closed her eyes and listened to voices blowing around her. Suddenly she was sitting, on the move. Flashes of light played with her, her body shifting from side to side in harmony with changing directions. She never wanted to open her eyes again. A click of wheels beat out a rhythm and she started to hum.

The touch of many light hands lifted her body then lay her down. She went limp with relief. A light settled upon her eyelids, promising kisses of a summer sun, the prickle of grass as surely as if she were sitting on it. It was okay to be where she was, to go where she pleased. Her body was moving, but it was not of her doing. Layers of clothing were peeled, chill touching her flesh before it was covered again. The weight of blankets fell on her, and a tender hand touched her forehead. She had to stay where she was, far away, where it was simple. Easy. She let go. It was okay. It was time.

Tov watched from the living room as Steve prepared for his rounds at Reese's kitchen table. Steve had taken a little powder from each bag, making a new one, and put it in the cookie jar, patting the head of the ceramic pig after he replaced it. The ugly pig grinned at the angel with gaudy red lips. How appropriate. Wasn't the pig a symbol for greed and gluttony?

"Oh, stop!" Tov cried out. He was weary of deciphering the plans of twisted people, sick of witnessing repugnant behaviour. Why didn't Kelly stand her ground and leave this morning when she'd had the chance? The question persisted, rankled, sucking him into emotions that Malheev warned him about.

Someone came in the door. Tired, Tov didn't care to move from the patio doors, waiting while they rustled bags and banged dishes before they made their way into the living room. The easy chair beside him sunk under the weight of Reese, a mug of coffee in his hand. Wrapped loosely around Reese's legs was the top half of Addiction, a gaping wound where its bottom had been. Skin hung in dry, curled strands. Eyes, dark and empty in their sockets, barely acknowledged Tov's presence. Reese lit a cigarette, taking big drags, holding the smoke. His eyes were sharp and clear, intent on a thoughtfulness born of distraction.

Tov touched the man sitting so peacefully.

Reese's hands started to shake, his breathing accelerated. He butted his smoke and lay his head back. Addiction was grabbing for handholds, fighting to climb to his knees. Sweat filled the pores on Reese's body as he pulled at his meagre strands of hair. "God! Help me!" he moaned.

"Reese..." Tov whispered, aware he was causing the war within, angering what was left of the worm clinging to him. "Reese..." The angel moved through the chair, and from behind wrapped his arms around the suffering man.

Reese was suspended, struggling to sense which road of pain his body would take. Determined to fight, his fists were white. The angel was sinking with him, connecting, fighting to keep him swimming above the depths below his feet. Tov alone could see the sky, distorted above the surface, just out of reach. The angel stretched his arm, felt the ripples as his hand emerged. Clinging to Reese, he resisted the pull to descend deeper. Tov was locked around his body, a buoy until temptation relinquished, floating him to the light above.

"Follow it," Tov whispered, "trust where it takes you." Words, breath, serenity, prayers, all radiated from Tov, and layer by layer the angel negotiated crevices in the cold wall that pulled Reese down like cement, reaching places that had been shut down and locked up for many years. Faint recall, long forgotten dreams, the downy embrace of forbearance oozed through cracks, and the heavenly minister shone his beacon into every single one.

Tov knew the instant that the human was taking in more than he could bear or understand. Reese's hands fell from his head. Tov touched his eyes, his ears, chest, arms, relinquishing his hold when he knew the man was soothed and strengthened. He was breathing with silent, heaving breaths.

"You have help," Tov told him. Reese opened his eyes. "You won't go through this alone." Addiction was withering, blood slowly draining from its severed body, the noise of asphyxiation muffled and subdued. Tov was the serene hush that surrounded them, the sense of well-being that filled them. He was the vessel emptied only to feel completely full.

Reese took a cigarette and sat a while before lighting it, his head resting on the back of the chair. Tov stepped away, suddenly realizing he was possibly looking at the answer to his own dilemma. Reese had made himself a receptacle, privy to the angel's thoughts and ministrations. And it had happened for the man when he acted on his empathy for Kelly. The knot in Tov's stomach returned as he thought of putting any hope in the precarious whims of a human. But what he could see in front of him was an advocate for Kelly. The longer he pondered, the more he knew it was sadly necessary. His Master knew a prevailing goodness in people that Tov always questioned. Nervously, he suspected his attitude could be imperative to any success, the equivalent of a human's doubt in prayer. If he would be the hindrance in a lifeline to Kelly, then he had only a short time to balance his trust and offer this man, with such a tiny faith and miniscule grasp of the spiritual, every benefit he could.

"Show me, Master," the angel asked. "*Show* me what you know of his soul..."

It was uttered, and done. The human and the angel fused, silent and searching companions, the only witnesses to what began to unfold in Reese's apartment. Earth had no hold on the eternal, hushing clocks and hours in the divinely constructed classroom. They jelled in thought and question, aware of a guiding presence giving them permission to explore and ask. In one brief, unexpected chance, heaven was planted on earth, and earth into heaven.

◊

Steve dropped his knapsack on the floor and headed to the pig on the counter. He pocketed the bag of white powder seconds before Reese came around the corner and punched him on the shoulder. "What's up?" Reese asked.

"Usual."

"Way too casual," Tov said to Reese. "You stink at this."

"Going to stay and have dinner?" Reese asked.

"Naw. I should get some food to Kelly."

Tov braced himself, put a hand on Reese's back and implored him to keep going.

"Then what?" asked Reese.

Steve shrugged, looking everywhere but Reese's face.

"She still at the safe house?"

"Yup."

Reese threw down the glove. "Don't do it, Steve."

"What's it to you?"

Tov was squeezing Reese's shoulder, his head vacillating back and forth between them. He could almost hear the click as they locked into combative positions.

"It's nothing to me. But it could be everything to her." Reese was treading lightly.

"Since when do you care? What's wrong with you? You tellin' me I can't count on you?"

"Tell him!" Tov urged.

"How many times have *you* done this Reese? How many?"

Reese didn't answer.

"How come when *I* get the chance, you jump on some stupid high horse to rescue a piece of white trash that was looking for it in the first place?"

"Whoa…" Reese held up his hand. "No one deserves it. You got that? No one."

"Shut up!" Steve yelled. "Just shut up!" Addiction had his mouth on Steve's temple, sucking and blowing, stirring the anger, spitting it into his head with a force that made its little body backfire like a gun.

Tov gripped Reese, worried the turmoil in Steve was pushing him further than he would have gone without resistance. Fine and dandy to goad Reese on for his own cause, but not if Kelly would bear the consequences. If only the worm on Steve's shoulder would have his fill and explode.

But Steve was drinking it in, hungry for it. "You said you were going to help me! I depend on you. What now? What?" He slammed his hand on the counter, not registering the slightest reaction to pain. "You're just like everyone else."

"How did I help you, Stevie? All I did was drag you down with me."

"Drag me down? What do you think my life was before? I actually like what it's turned out to be." Steve worked his jaw. "For the first time I can ever remember, I'm actually happy. Don't you bail on me now, Reese!"

"I can't do it anymore." Reese shook his head, apologizing. "I can't."

"What then?" Steve pushed. "You're a druggie… an alcoholic. Gonna' put that on a résumé?"

Tov heard the unspoken. Reese had a place to go. If he needed help, his dad had always told him to come home. How could he say that to the kid in front of him?

"I don't want to bail on you, Stevie. We can clean up together."

Steve flew at Reese, stopping short with his fist. "Go then!" he yelled. "Go ahead!"

"Steve…"

"Don't you preach! You think you're better than me?" His chest heaved. "We're the same, Reese. We're scum. Changing your ways doesn't change anything you've done. Don't you dare look down your nose at me!" Steve grabbed the knapsack.

A step behind, Reese took hold of his arm. "Steve... don't."

The knapsack hit the floor. Steve threw his fist into Reese's face, flattening him against the cupboards. The angel watched, horrified as his body crumpled in slow motion.

Steve regarded him for a second, then went to the bathroom, Tov an inch behind. He retrieved the needle, bottle cap, fork, and lighter from behind the toilet, not once looking at his friend on his way out the door.

Chapter Twelve

Tov took one helpless glance at Reese and left, intending to follow Steve's fading silhouette. Not halfway down the hall his feet planted, the thread tugging him in another direction. He watched the knapsack walk out the door. Baffled, he cried out, hearing once again the words of Malheev. *Be obedient. Wait. In that you cannot fail.* He passed through the second floor, out of the roof to search the street, but Steve was gone. He could not believe what he was going to do, that he was going to go against his heart. He flew in the opposite direction.

Between buildings, skimming the streets, the power pulled him farther away from Kelly. He had no idea where he was going, his fear for Kelly stronger than his concern at what he might find at the end of this detour. Life below wasn't registering as he manoeuvred at a speed that suggested obedience, not willingness. Looking back in dismay at downtown, he quietly and compliantly followed.

◊

Ellen was aware of touch on her skin, of voices speaking, but she had no desire to leave the quiet place. Nothing was able to call her back to the dark. Wheeled and moved, she no longer concerned herself with her body. She walked in dreams that echoed childhood, and then in moments when she realized she was not in those places at all. A vague idea came to her that they were only dreams. But it didn't matter anymore. She lost the feeling of the needles, of hot and cold that touched her by the ministrations of a pair of hands no longer even attached to a person. Her mind attended to all that she needed. In flashes she had memories of her body, of searing pain. Funny she had the choice to leave it now, like it didn't exist. She was shrunk to the size of her memories, living in the absence of time, the folding up and winding down of a life with as little effort as it had started.

◊

Tov could see a hill far off, a sprawling building built on top and down the sides. He covered the distance quickly, slowing to hover in front of it. People moved everywhere, doors opening and closing. A parking lot surrounded the building, while other vehicles fed numerous entrances with their passengers. Glass doors opened of their own accord, and he chuckled. This is the closest the humans could come to the experience of moving through a wall.

He was swept along into a lobby where the air was flavoured by coffee brewing in the coffee shop. Three women sat behind a front desk, directing the masses into various halls and elevators. The thread picked him up again, pulling him through the ceiling into a hallway that ran the length of the building. He went through two more floors before being drawn down another hall, the rooms filled with people in beds, attached to machines, watching television, sleeping.

He entered a door and approached an elderly woman lying on a bed, switching channels with a remote control. He was puzzled until the thread yanked him through the wall and pulled him alongside a bed. Then it loosened and fell away.

He was standing by Ellen. Motionless under blankets, her face was pale, her breathing slow. He approached the bed, expecting her to open her eyes, her body to move. She was attached to a machine that beeped methodically, with wires that seemed to hold her in place.

"Ellen." He touched her, ran his hand across her mouth. He refused to believe what he was seeing, faint with regret that he had ever left her. "What happened?" Her cheek in his palm grew warm, and he quickly moved through the bed. He cupped his hands on her face and felt the light leave him. She was receiving, holding herself out for the grasp of heaven, calling for the power he carried. Tov released his comfort, his succour. Connected now, he could feel and picture the place where she was, the scene fluttering into focus. She was in a garden of sorts, sitting in the company of plants and reaching flowers, taking in the smells and serenity. Peace filled her. As he was given the picture of the garden, he was standing in it, one of the most beautiful sanctuaries he had ever seen. He was behind the bench where she sat still and calm, emitting no emotion. Not happiness, or sadness, or fear. She was occupying space. Waiting, almost.

Waiting?

This pull to Ellen was different than the one that had brought him to her before. How could he not recognize the difference? This one lacked urgency. It was the call to escort.

This was not how it was supposed to be. Why would he be called to a mission that would end like this? "No…" he pleaded, "not like this, not without Kelly…"

Ellen turned and looked at him.

"No," he begged, bracing himself. She was neither surprised nor alarmed to see him. They didn't speak. He didn't explain, and she didn't ask questions. The power was not there for them to communicate. "Oh, thank you," the angel breathed. "Thank you…" It was not yet time. She turned on her bench, settling back into the tranquility of her surroundings.

There was something else in this space, something in the garden that did not fit. Like the wall between them that prevented them from speaking, it was holding Ellen here, preventing her from leaving. Ellen seemed unaware of it, but Tov could see it. It was in her brain, growing, reaching with long fingers to hold new flesh. Sickness. The ultimate curse, he knew, for anything with a physical body. It was why she was here, lingering in the physical. Why had he not been shown before that this was her source of pain? Her body was now transparent to him, and he regarded it as clearly as the garden she occupied. The mother, the friend, the flame of a believer was fading into the first adventure of eternity. Kelly was going to lose that light, left in this place to fend for herself. The bitter mingled so harshly with the sweet that Tov struggled to hold them both in his heart.

Ellen turned, was watching him. This was quite a time for her, he knew, her soul still in the physical, witnessing what was to come. He was sent to let her know that she could wait. In this beautiful, amazing place, she could wait.

$$\Diamond$$

"Sorry! I'm sorry!" Steve's mouth was going as he came in the door before he realized Kelly was still in the bathroom. He didn't know if she had been waiting, but he guessed that shampoo, scented soap, and a long hot bath had passed her afternoon. When the door opened there was a difference in her demeanour. She looked radiant.

"We missed lunch, so we're eating lunch and supper together tonight. It's cheaper." His mood and good fortunes lightened considerably. "I call it *lupper.*"

"Maybe we should knock meals down to one a day," Kelly offered. "I feel bad that you're spending money on me, even though that's going to change. When I get my first paycheck I'm going to take you to dinner."

"My choice?"

Kelly shook her head. "No. Mine. You've picked so far." She sniffed. "What is it? Smells Chinese."

He bowed, presenting the banquet.

"Oh, *yum.* I *love* Chinese."

They sat at the same time, hands fishing in bags and pulling out containers, dishing and trading, a comfortable space between them.

"You know, if I get a job waiting tables we could get leftover food. It would help our budget."

"Ever waited tables?"

"No. I've never had a job."

Steve felt—but hid—disdain. Things were going well. He wasn't about to ruin it. "Well, you're in for a shocker. Working with the public is a real treat."

"Have you ever waited tables?"

"Sure."

"Where?"

"No place fancy. If you want big tips, you have to work in the fancy places."

"My wardrobe puts a limit on that. I could start at a coffee shop, work my way up."

She was fiddling with her food. "What the heck is this?" On her fork was what looked like a mushroom smothered in mucus, the token sprinkle of broccoli for colour.

Steve inspected it. "Not sure, but don't be scared. The rule with Chinese is that you always have to try something new. I think that's it."

Kelly shrugged.

"You like mushrooms?"

"Love 'em. Just never had them cooked in snot before." She dissected it with her eyes, then put it in her mouth. "Not bad, if you can get past the look of it." She grabbed the container and put more on her plate. "Want some?"

He shook his head. "I was trying to guess what you would like. Figured you've probably had every kind of takeout there is."

"Why?"

He knew that he shouldn't, but did anyways. "Coming from a life of privilege..." He'd caught her off-guard. Again. "Ambition. It's a good thing," he mumbled.

"What's wrong?"

"Nothing. What you're doing is good. Stick to your plan. I hope it takes you places."

"Really? Are you making fun of me?"

He didn't answer.

"It seems like you're always mad. I said that I'll pay you back."

"I know." Steve pushed his plate away, put his elbows on the table. "I'm not used to looking after anybody but myself." He succumbed, dying to play this thing to the hilt. "Actually, I like having you here. I'm just not used to someone like you."

"Someone like me? What am I like?"

"You're decent. And I'm not."

Sympathy painted her face. "Don't say that."

"Why not? It's true."

"You've had it rough. You're doing the best you can. I don't put you down for that."

Steve pointed at her. "See? You're decent." Rustling through the plum and soy sauce, he picked up a packet of screws. "Found the parts I needed." He went to the door and picked the screwdriver off the floor.

"Steve..."

"What?"

"Why do you think you're not decent?"

He ignored her.

"Are you okay with me being here?"

He still didn't look. "More than you know."

Kelly pulled back. "Why is that?"

"Because I think you're going to end up helping me." With his back to her, he couldn't keep the grin off his face. There wasn't a thing he'd said that wouldn't appeal to every decent, useless bone in her body.

"I'd like that."

He did turn to her now, all dolled up, ready to follow her foolish dream that was never going to happen. "Me too," he said. He had the imbecile in the palm of his sweaty hand. Back to work, he moved the lock up and down the doorframe. "I have two keys for this lock. You get one, I get the other."

"That's fine." Her hand rested on the table, a fork balancing loosely in her fingers before it fell to the floor. She yawned. Steve resisted noticing as he fiddled, screwed, hammered. When he did, she was sound asleep, face to the ceiling. He banged and clinked for a while, then put everything down.

"You're so stupid," he said aloud. "So stupid..."

◊

Tov and Ellen rested together in solitude, not yet connected, apart from the world. She was at peace, the Spirit strong in her. With just a thought, Tov was back in the hospital room standing beside her body. It was going to be much harder to leave her now, but it would go against her needs and wishes if he stayed.

"I'm so sorry, Ellen. I don't know what to do." He was a comforter. He was praying to be her escort. Guardianship was doing a great job of tangling his loyalties.

Her face was void of life. The desire he'd had in their first meeting came strong upon him, to touch the wrinkles of her smile, to absorb the strength that seemed to radiate there. He put out his hand. The skin firmed beneath his fingers. He pushed, and it resisted. He pulled, and it moved.

What was happening? Astonished, he traced every line of her eyes and mouth, marvelling at the limits of his hand. His senses were riveted on the soft, elastic texture. He caressed the confines and imperfections of her skin, gradually understanding the limitations of her body. This was flesh, created by the same Master that had given him a body that transcended dimensions and moved at the speed of thought.

The machine beeped. Ellen's chest laboured. His hand passed through her cheek and the spell was broken.

He raised his face in agony, conceding that he did not have the capacity to understand how the One he served could love them all like this. "Master, this is going to be more than I can bear. I need your strength. I can't abandon her now." He sought the eternal face, the beautiful emanation of mercy. As he gave the burden of his sorrow up, his concern for Ellen dissipated as a thread took hold of his stomach. His Lord had shown him what he needed to know.

This was it. The next time he would see Ellen, he knew what the call would be. Her prayers set his wings in motion, a tear blowing across the angel's face in the flurry of his departure, seen only by the One who understood the courage it took to leave.

Chapter Thirteen

Steve put Kelly's arm around his neck and lifted her out of the chair. Her feet pulled against the carpet as he dragged her to the bedroom, her body folded and flopped as she was dumped onto the mattress. Steve went into the next bedroom and rummaged the closet, emerging with a ball of sheets. He dropped their faded flowers by her head and rolled her onto the floor, trying to remember the last time he had made a bed.

"You should feel honoured. Nothing but the best for Momma's girl, hey? Wouldn't she be proud? You're gonna be a working girl, pay your own way for once." He tucked the last corner and pulled her back on the bed by her arm and leg, laughing as her head bumped over the side. "Momma never tucked you in like you're gonna get tucked in tonight."

Apprehension crept silently around the preparations. He had anticipated groggy, easy to handle, but not limp. He checked the mushrooms left in the container, realizing she had eaten four of the ten sleeping pills he had pulverized and stuffed inside. Initially figuring odds, he guessed she might choose one or two that were spiked. There was no time to let her sleep it off now. He had her booked for the evening.

Steve took the knapsack to the bedroom. The tiniest shred of sense made him think twice. She was out of it, enough to be used. He didn't have to take it any further. Bringing in customers this early was a bonus. But his purpose was to shoot her up at every opportunity until her body demanded it, considering he had no idea how long he could keep her here. He checked her breathing and decided it was a gamble he was willing to take. Maybe he could use a little less, but how much was too much now? He swore, thinking about Reese. He said he would help.

He touched her cheek, the smooth skin, her face so white against his hand. He stroked her features, loving the thought that he could kiss her lips, or break her nose. Play with her eyelashes, or cut off her hair. He was calling all the shots now, and he knew exactly what he wanted. His heart was pumping blasts through his ears. Adrenaline revved him into high gear, forcing him to concentrate to keep his hands steady. He pulled the lighter, bottle cap, and needle out of the knapsack, then took out the bag of white powder. He slid an elastic band over her wrist and tightened it on her upper arm. Her veins jumped, and he measured, trembling. How much? He looked her over, trying to figure how much she weighed, but all he could imagine was the liquid coursing through her veins, kicking her into overdrive, spinning her senseless on a trip he himself was craving.

"Settle down, get a grip…" he muttered. He put the bag on the floor before it spilled and took some deep breaths.

$$\Diamond$$

The scenery below blurred at the angel's speed. He was rushing between walls that crashed in behind him, urgency a string tightly wound in front of him. A weight rode him, pushed him down, a combination of agony and dread as he raced on. Reeling from the constant fight to keep his emotions at bay, he could stand it no longer. As if a ramp had been placed in front of him, he shot up into the sky, arms and wings flat against his body, a bullet of light slicing the clouds. He stopped explosively, wings and robe rocketing above his head. Suspended, he offered his anguish to the heavens in the surreal silence. He emptied. The magnet, the grief, the tightrope of suspense. All internal chaos shattered at his breaking point and dropped into a pile of smoking ashes.

His arms dropped at the touch on his shoulder. He turned to face Malheev, utterly weak and deplete before the mighty angel.

"You have a sense of what is to come?" Malheev asked. Tov nodded, as did the other angel. "You are not afraid, but need to be sure of what it is you are called to do."

"How can I be sure when events take control of me," Tov confessed. "I am hurting. Angry."

"Angry?"

"Yes."

"Why?"

Tov hadn't known until it was out of his mouth.

"What thoughts will not leave your mind?" Malheev asked.

Tov had felt it when he was with Ellen, the realization that her prayers might not be answered. It had grown stronger after he'd left her in her garden. Aware now of the sickness taking her life, loathe at having to leave her again, it intensified as the distance between them did. Now he was running a cold hard road that may lead to what might be his own prayers unheeded. "Things are not..." He tried to find words that wouldn't sound like what he suspected he was going to say. "Things are not... right."

"What things?"

"The lives of those I was sent for."

"And what is right?" the elder asked.

"Right is the assurance that their prayers will be answered."

"Are they not being answered?"

Tov surged through his torrent of uncertainty, sifted confusing events, threw his hands in the air. "I don't know."

Malheev tried again. "What is it that makes you angry?"

There was no point guarding his words. "Heaven has the power to intervene. Why am I here? To bear witness to all that can go wrong? I have the power of creation at my disposal, and I watch as their lives fall apart. Is that fair?" He debated on continuing. Malheev waited. "I am angry that things on earth cannot be as they are in heaven. Ellen needs to see her daughter again. Why can't her prayers come to pass?" Spoken, the words threatened. His throat tightened. His voice fell to whisper. "That's not going to happen, is it?"

"I do not know," Malheev answered, throwing a question into the same breath. "And what is the difference between earth and heaven that you see?"

The answer was simple. "Heaven is perfect. Earth is not."

"Yes," Malheev confirmed. "So is the imperfect disadvantaged if that which they inherit is perfect?" He leaned into Tov. "I think I am a reminder to you once again, my friend, to keep your focus on the end of all things. All that you are involved in will always… *always* play to the purpose of eternity."

He knew. How stupid, how weak to continually fall prey to the battle of emotions. Why did he keep losing his sight?

"You are very privileged," Malheev told him. "Keep your eyes up, but keep them open. What you will learn of our Lord here is far more than the perfection of heaven. Trust me."

"I do. But I don't think *I* am strong enough. I sink too easily into this conflict."

"It is hard, especially after we have already fought and won our battle in the heavens, when we know our place in eternity."

Tov thought of Ellen, of Kelly, the acceptance and rejection of what he, Chaver, and Malheev lived and knew. "Why does it have to be so difficult for them?"

"Remember our battle was, too. Watch these people closely, and you will see something of our Master that is the most wonderful thing in all creation…" His voice drifted. "But, you are needed," he spoke loudly, back in the moment. "You cannot delay. Do you feel the strength to continue?"

Tov hesitated, then nodded.

"Without the experience of their struggles, you would not appreciate what you were sent here to learn."

"What *I* was sent here to learn?" Tov pulled back.

"Yes." Malheev said, letting the question pass. "Keep your mind set to the end of all things, but keep your eyes open while you are here."

Tov nodded, his body tense.

"Good. There is nothing left to say." Malheev touched his cheek. It was the signal that their talk was over. He withdrew his hand, let the other angel take the initiative of parting.

Tov offered the thankfulness in his heart, given to the other angel by thought, absolved of all but the purpose of his presence here. He wished the elderly angel would stay, accompany him to the ends of his mission instead of leaving him to juggle feebly with the message sent once again. So simple, but what was needed in place of his feelings of ineptitude. The magnet pulled at him, and he looked desperately, deeply, into the eyes of Malheev, trying to secure for himself the instinct and wisdom of years.

◊

Tov was focused. Anything but calm propelled him into a foreboding so great it was hard to enter Steve's apartment. The living room was empty, quiet. Drawn to the bedroom, he hovered in the doorway and went cold.

Steve was sitting against the wall running his hands through his hair, the needle and paraphernalia on the floor in front of him. White powder coloured the rug where the bag had dropped. Addiction was on the mattress beside Kelly, its dead arm sprawled across her stomach, the other wrapped around her head, talons embedded. In a moment of awareness it sat up slowly and turned to the angel in the doorway.

Scrambling, the fat slug attempted to leap over the airborne sword. The blade caught its foot, slicing skin before the weapon dropped to the floor. Tov was there to pick it up as it landed. The wretch screamed, threw an arm around Steve's neck in flight, circling his head, then planting claws into his shoulder. Tov approached, expending a hatred he could not control. The point of the sword came to rest on Steve's chest and the boy clutched at his shirt in alarm. Tov felt Steve's breath rushing through his body. The angel trembled, suddenly afraid of the sword in his hand. Steve's eyes were wide, blind with surprise, no comprehension of the force against him. Tov urged the sword on. The demon goaded, told Tov the boy was his. All the angel wanted was to drive the blade home. "Help me!" Tov cried out.

"Can you not remove the evil?" Addiction taunted. "Can you not stand victorious over your foes?" The voice sputtered. "Make him pay... make him pay... make him pay..."

"No!" Tov yelled. He looked into Steve's eyes, Malheev's voice rising through the mist of frenzy. *We have already fought and won...* Tov turned his face to heaven and set the scene before him into eternity as he had been told. He was a power the human did not understand. Without the light, how could he know? How could this frail being fight against the likes of him, or the demon? No. Steve did not have to pay. His Lord had already made provision for that. Tov did not remove his sword but stood firm. Anything that happened now would not be of his doing. Addiction peeked one beady eye as it grabbed Steve's neck and pulled him back against the wall. They rose slowly. Tov didn't sheath his weapon until they left the room.

Tears took the angel's face, sorrow shredding him as if he had been a victim of his own sword. At the mattress he fell on his knees where she lay so still. He touched her forehead and felt nothing. Nothing. Her soul had cried out for him the last time, and Tov had walked into her nightmare. Where she was now, he did not know. His hands upon her told him nothing but the struggle of her body to keep its functions going. He lay down beside her, feeling her fight to live.

$\Diamond$

Tov roused to voices in the apartment. The kitchen light filtered into the dark room and he checked Kelly's breathing.

"In business for yourself now, Stevie?" a voice asked.

Tov went to the bedroom door. A man in his fifties, well dressed in a shirt and tie, had a suit jacket over his arm which he smoothed over the back of a chair. He turned to Steve, wringing his hands. "What you got for me?"

"You'll be taking her for her first ride," Steve said.

The man raised his eyebrows. "You out to double the price?"

"No. I swear."

"How young is she?"

122

"Younger than me," Steve answered.

The man's eyes lit. "It's been a while. Where is Reese? He no longer in business?"

"Nope."

"Too bad. I always feel better sticking to one or two I know rather than take chances with what's on the street."

Steve half-heartedly agreed.

"How much is this going to set me back?"

"One-fifty."

"What? You kidding?"

"There's no time limit. You can take as long as you want. Let's call it my grand opening special."

The man laughed, slapped Steve on the shoulder. "Is she up to it, or am I going to walk away disappointed?"

"I think you'll have your way with her. She's feeling pretty good."

"I'll pay you after."

"No," Steve responded quickly. "Up front."

The man shook his head, took out his wallet. "You leave this on the table," he said, "just in case." He peeled one hundred and fifty dollars off a wad and smacked it down. Steve pointed to the bedroom.

Tov was back at the moment when he'd had his weapon planted on the boy's chest, regret making his hands tingle. Steve's customer walked through him into the bedroom.

"It's dark in here," the man said. "Don't you have any lights?"

"Not in there. Sorry." Steve put the money in his pocket. Addiction was mute, staring at Tov.

"I should have done it," Tov muttered. The man fumbled in the dark, found the bed on the floor, felt his way across the empty side to where Kelly lay.

"What kind of sick joke is this?" the man barked. He backed away from the mattress into the lit pathway. "You idiot!" he yelled. "She's dead!" He went for his jacket. "Where's my money?"

Steve turned to the bedroom, his face dissolving.

"Where's my money?" the man yelled, pushing Steve.

Tov flew slowly into the bedroom and heard the scuffle in the kitchen, a body hitting the wall.

"Give it back or I'll break your neck, you little puke!" Their bodies slammed the table, jolted the fridge at impact, fell over chairs.

"Here's your money!" Steve threw the bills. "If you say anything about this I'll kill you too."

Tov stood over Kelly.

"Do I look scared?" the man panted, scrambling after the money. "How are you going to do that from jail?"

"I'm warning you..." Steve spoke through his teeth. A chair hit the wall. There was the sound of ripping fabric. "I said not to tell anyone!" It went quiet. "How are you going to explain what *you* were doing here?"

"It's your word against mine," the man shot back. The front door banged the wall and footsteps faded down the stairs.

Tov knelt.

Life in her was faint. She was not dead, but not far from it. Steve came to look, Addiction leaning into her face. Satisfied, he snuggled into his perch.

"You... stupid..." Steve began to rant a river of curses, kicking the mattress, his foot landing on Kelly's thigh, making her body jiggle.

Tov hovered at the ceiling, wings beating. Steve's shoe connected with Kelly, over and over, but the angel was fixed on the other corner of the room. He felt it before he saw it, a force of debilitating gravity. He had never felt anything like it. Never. And it wasn't even in the room yet.

Lines of blood ran down Kelly's face, but Steve was not done. Tov didn't move. He would leave no access to Kelly. If Steve was determined to finish her off, her only chance was in his ability to hold the perimeter around her and fight. A harrowing noise filled the room, a crackling so low Tov could not discern from which direction it was coming. It grew louder, shriller, arresting his ability to think and stay alert. The scene below disintegrated.

He saw it. The shadow of Death.

It was enormous, heavy, and Tov had the feeling he was only seeing a part of it.

The mass alone would ensure a steady course for Kelly, a ball of living shadows, faces and body parts mashed together, faces with eyes affixed on him, hands and arms reaching. The presence stopped and changed direction to the floor.

"You're going to have to go through me first," the angel hissed.

Addiction was pounding Steve's head, eyes glued to the ceiling. The room was growing cold, Steve frozen with realization at what he had done. The demon struck the boy, pulling him from his tantrum, pounding to get him out of the way. A petrified Steve took his cue and bolted. The last thing Tov saw was Addiction's eyes over Steve's shoulder, bulging in terror.

Death moved.

Tov pulled his sword, embedding it in the wall of flesh. He braced one hand against it for the force needed to pull his weapon free and pain exploded in his arm. Amid the noise addling his brain he plunged again, aware the attacker was now coming for him. Misshapen fingers grabbed his wrist, and the heavenly blade sliced them cleanly. They fell away, bursting into a thousand pieces. Death swivelled, arms reaching. Tov swung his sword, noise detonating fresh with each wound inflicted. Fuzzy with injury, he quickly glanced down to locate Kelly. His vision exploded into white dots, numb with a pressure that squeezed the sides of his head together. He drove his sword upward, punctured the giant arm holding him and it burst into splinters. Tov stared blindly, waiting for vision to return. When it did, he realized they were over the mattress. He grabbed both ends of his sword, one hand on the handle, the other on the blade, cutting his fingers as he gripped. He flew full force and hit the mass broadside, skin burning at contact. Ignoring the arms grappling for him, he kept thrusting. There was no thought of conceding, nothing but the force in his body pushing him forward. He bulldozed ahead, slamming against Death, retreating then striking again, all light and power concentrated in his arms. His fingers, almost severed, wrapped the blade of the sword. Still he pushed, pulled back, rammed again and again.

Until he could do it no more. His body went limp, crumpling, barely able to register the fridge and table below his feet. Sobbing, his chin bounced on his chest. Talons encircled him, squeezing consciousness. He smelled his own charred flesh. The last thing he saw before his sight faded was Ellen on her garden bench.

Chapter Fourteen

It was a relief to slip into the talons of Death. Tov faded as he gave in and embraced the noise, his body sinking into the comfort of wounds withering as brilliant colour took his eyes. A rainbow swirled, dripped from his mind's eye as it funnelled to grey, his body jerking as functions clamoured to restart.

The horrible drone reawakened him, and the thought that he'd been dropped worked sluggishly to find him. He opened his eyes, realized he was floating along the ceiling, and summoned every muscle to turn his body toward the commotion below. He could make out a silhouette of angel wings, a sword glinting like a waving flashlight. He kept turning away and floating against his will as he struggled to maintain position. Strength. He needed strength. Minutes chipped splinters and slivers from his fortitude as his body bobbed feebly along, unresponsive to commands, moving through a wall that would take him outside. He strained to hear the exertion of the angel over the drone of Death in the battle that was his, being fought without him. Determined, he worked each of his limbs, connecting them to his mind, pushing past the end of his endurance to move back into the scene below.

A comrade was giving his life for Kelly. He would do no less.

Chaver looked up in one surprised instant and caught Tov's eyes, marks of conflict scarring every part of his body, a mirror of his own condition.

Tov slid his fingers off the blade to ready his weapon, freeing the embedded sword from the flesh of his hands. He strained to manoeuvre his body into position behind Chaver's shoulder, gaining his balance, letting loose his pain that tore through his throat in shouts as he fell back into the torture of forcing spent muscles into action. Body parts flew from the ball of flesh as they were severed, disintegrating in the air around them as the angels joined strength, moving neither forward nor back, drawing on a power completely outside of themselves to stay fighting. Their bodies absorbed the brunt of conflict from feet planted firm in supplication, that would not give way and move as Death persisted. The apartment moved by them unnoticed, the scene around them changing as Death lethargically relented, its mass coerced backward by a mysterious power it could not overcome. The angels pushed on, picking up imperceptible momentum. Tov became aware that they were in the stairwell moving out into the street seconds before his body snapped forward suddenly, folding nose to knee. The resistance vanished. Death was pivoting its tremendous weight tediously, its momentum rolling and shifting away beyond their reach. Tov could see it in its entirety now, the sheer mass of it making the breath catch in his throat as he held the ball in his sights through blurry eyes, the receding noise welcome evidence of retreat. He listened until it was gone and put his arms around his dear friend, his heart fluttering at the lack of response. They were floating up into the night, suspended, depleted, heads dangling at the mercy of weightlessness, two bubbles released into the sky. He tightened his grip on Chaver, looped his fingers into the belt of his friend's robe before his mind went black.

Light played on his face. Noise crawled into his ears. Tov's insides beat a rhythm of pain, sharp then dull, and he cringed at the intensity. He gave in, opened his eyes to see that he was floating high above a busy street, his neck cracking as he turned to face Chaver directly in front of him. His hand was twined gently around his friend's belt as they drifted as one body far over the heads of unsuspecting people.

"Chaver," he whispered, squeezing his shoulder. His body pounded, his arms and legs ached. He rested his head on the forehead of his friend and tried again, shaking lightly. "Chaver…" He looked a mess. Marks and gashes covered his body through the tatters of his once beautiful robe. His own body looked much the same.

Realization came to him. Kelly.

He could see that they were not anywhere near the apartment, and he gripped Chaver tighter. He surveyed their surroundings, dumbfounded that he recognized where they were. Steve had hauled him here on his deliveries. One side of the street was a parking lot of abandoned cars, and the other had a building with a struggling garden on its roof. Fitting the bleak environment, the dim oasis of planters and boxes was covered with wilting flowers and leaves. He knew exactly which direction to go, groaning at the distance that lay between him and his charge.

Tov let go of Chaver's belt and took his arm, envying his friend the condition of being yet unaware. He started off, tugging and pulling, identifying landmarks, feeling no thread or magnet. And it worried him. He knew that Kelly was still alive, thanks to Chaver, but Chaver's condition was frightening him too. He had no idea how long they had been floating. It looked to be morning, but how many mornings later?

Fear fed his muscles, kept him moving with the angel in tow. He strengthened his grip on Chaver as he saw the apartment in the distance, and with great agony tried to increase their speed. At the second story of the building he was quick to pull Chaver into the living room through the wide-open front door. In the middle of the floor a blanket was pulled into a nest that still held the imprint of a body. Wrappers were scattered everywhere and the bathroom light was on. He tugged Chaver into the bedroom. The mattress had been moved, the sheets stuffed into the space left between the bed and the wall. The empty room was a final blow to his already fragile mind. He let go of Chaver and cradled his face in his hands.

If he had failed Kelly, then an act of mercy would release him now, one he would not turn down. Chaver bumped him. The desire to be with his own kind overwhelmed him, and Tov beheld the face that he loved so much, touched the bruises and cuts, smoothed the beautiful strands of hair. He put his arms around his friend, held the lifeless body tight, and prayed.

A spark of light emanated from them, sailing from between their shredded robes to bounce off the ceiling and walls at incredible speed. Many more launched and soared until the room was an orb of dancing light, grazing their ripped and tattered clothes, mending and whitening, landing on their bodies to leave healthy flesh wherever it touched. Tov clung to his friend, swore he could hear heavenly voices, quiet words and whispers of encouragement that came unhurriedly and delicately, a serene drizzle of sounds and images, faces and gestures that released him from heartbreak and damaged muscles until Tov was no longer aware that he was on earth.

There was movement in his arms. Chaver's eyes opened in a moment of questioning, a look of wonder washing his features until his lids fell. He sighed deeply, mistakenly believing he was home. Delicate threads of colour and light encircled them, healing, strengthening. The steady rain of comfort had no end, no boundaries, gathering them into its depths, bathing wounds, easing sorrows, washing them clean until Tov, too, believed he was home.

Chapter Fifteen

The second he was awake he knew he didn't want to be. He was in the bedroom of the apartment, understanding instantly why he was drifting in and out of soothing music and the comfort of friends in dreams. He was longing for home. Looking at the corner of the room, he saw the empty mattress. Kelly was gone. He held up his arms. Strong hands stuck out from his shining robe. He had no pain. He bent, looking at his perfect body. And Chaver had been with him, he remembered, but wasn't anywhere to be seen now. He was alone, still on earth, and knew his assignment was not yet complete.

In the living room, puzzle pieces needled him. The front door was open. He could see the stairwell outside. The blanket nest on the floor retained the outline of a body where someone had slept. Food wrappers littered the carpet. The biggest mystery was time. How much had passed since he and Chaver had drifted off? He could not imagine Kelly leaving on her own strength. If Steve came back for her, the only place he guessed she could be would be Reese's. It was the only place Tov knew where to look.

He didn't leave through the wall but the door, hungry for clues. Down the steps to the street, he fell in with the pedestrians, scanning faces left and right. He flew at walking speed, crossing with the crowds at the light, checking in front, behind, barely catching a flicker of clothing as it disappeared into Steve's stairwell behind him half a block away. In a flash he was back, catching the same glimpse from the bottom of the stairs as it vanished into the apartment. He hit the top step as it entered the bedroom.

Tov darted in front of a small old woman, walking rather quickly for the hobble in her step. Her lips fell into her mouth and her hair was gray and thin, pulled into a messy bun. Her pants were small and her sweater big, both incredibly dirty. She walked the bedroom, sliding a large canvas bag from her shoulder and settled gingerly on the far end of the mattress, took out a bottle of water and pulled back the sheets.

Tov's mouth sprung open. Kelly was wedged between the bed and the wall.

The old woman turned Kelly's head and poured water into her mouth, using a grimy sleeve to wipe the spill. Peeling back the sheets, she checked cuts and bruises, pouring water on a hanky, dabbing dry blood.

Tov was stunned. He flew to the woman, held the old head in his hands and blessed her overflowing heart. She stopped, sat back on her haunches, folded her hands around the dirty hanky and received. Without reservation, she accepted the peace he gave, her head shaking with tremors, making funny noises in her throat. Tov put his hands on Kelly and the old woman patted the girl and pulled the sheets back up over her head. Tov was moved at the heart that was exactly in the right place when he could see that her mind was not. No knowledge of a diminished brain could rob the angel of the affection he was feeling. She put her belongings back in the bag, muttering the agony in her knees as she rose and left the bedroom.

Kelly was breathing steady. Fresh blood grew in circles on the cloth covering her, overtaking dried purple stains. However well-meaning the old lady was, she had ripped scabs adhered to the sheet, leaving Kelly with open wounds. He could put if off no longer—he had to find help. The thought of leaving her again made him sick.

The bigger picture. He had to remember the bigger picture. Ellen's daughter would not be forsaken. He believed that, especially after what he had just seen. He wished he could pull back the cloth, but whatever reason the addle-brained woman had for covering her as if she were dead, it had kept Kelly safe from view. The simple prayers of a saint, of Ellen, suddenly loomed larger than heaven. He was seeing it… Chaver, this old lady, even Reese… for what it was: something far greater than he could imagine when his Lord spoke this place and these beings into existence. A door opened in his mind, revealing a staggering truth, and as he pondered this his Lord took on dimensions he could not measure. The angels had always been the pinnacles of creation to his mind, but his Lord had eternity past, present, and future in a granule of faith that fit inside a human heart. He rested his hand on Kelly, filled completely with the knowledge of the value of her soul. It was all in place for her. Tov included. The bloodstains spread, growing morbid petals on the sheet. Rising in unbelief that she was not lost, a soft flutter of wings took him to the living room.

Curled up on the floor like a hibernating squirrel was the old woman, knees tucked into her chin, arms wrapped around her legs, making funny noises as her lips sucked in and out of her toothless mouth. Tov smiled at her comely attire, her crazy ranting, her heart of gold that would one day pass through the fire when everything else would be burned away. He touched her in blessing, acknowledging the value that she, too, entirely possessed.

"It is such a privilege to meet you," he whispered to her face. "You have more than earned your rest." He held her head, fingertips tingling as she received. Yes. What a privilege it was.

◊

His heart was beating a fast, pleasant rhythm. He knew where Kelly was. Thoughts of the old woman warmed him. The face of the dog took his mind. He was on his way to Jen and Carl's, excited to see the animal. Silly, he thought. Four legs, a body covered in fur, no language to speak of, and a brain beyond comprehension of angel or human. He caught himself people watching, humming, enjoying the bustle, looking with profound concern into every face, discerning the price-less worth hidden in every heart, each one a prospect to open up a world that spoke to him of his new revelation. How infinitely vast this dimension suddenly seemed.

The house came into view around a corner, sitting defiantly among the larger buildings. He had come before at night, distracted by the dog. Now, in daylight, the house seemed even more out of place, looking as lost on this street as he was in this dimension. It was entirely too hard not to love. He paused on the porch.

"Wonderful," he mused. "I'm looking forward to an animal, and I have feelings for a house." He shook his head, put up his guard. Emotions had done nothing but stymie any of his purposes. Bent on perspective, he entered the door. Between the living room and kitchen he listened, disappointed at the absence of a tail-wagging welcome. There was a hill of dirty dishes in the sink, and a scattering more on the table, and on the floor in the corner were two large ceramic bowls, one full of water, the other polished and empty. Both had the name "Stewart" imprinted on pictures of bones in bold, black script.

"Stewart?" Tov said aloud. "Stewart." He tried it a few times, deciding that Dog would have sufficed for him. Yet he had to admit the name gave the goliath eyes and dangling tongue a tang of personality. Yes. The animal could definitely be a Stewart. And Stewart had his own dishes. This, too, like everything else today, warmed his heart.

Footsteps thumped on the ceiling overhead. They walked the second story hall, then took the stairs. A girl hustled past him to the fridge to stuff an already bulging knapsack with food. She was young, with blond hair, her body the toothpick look of youth. She slammed the fridge door and began searching the house. In the living room she unplugged a clock radio, and ripped the zipper on her bag as she stuffed it in. With a flip of her hair she was out the door, pulling Tov to the window. She walked laboriously, head down, shifting her cargo. She was Kelly, coming and going before his eyes, and somewhere out there, he thought, was a mother like Ellen, twisted with grief, wondering what calamity was attending her. What if he got Kelly here and *she* didn't want to stay?

"Quiet," he scolded troubling thoughts. "We are doing this one worry at a time." He wished the dog would show. Wandering the house, he snooped in the basement to find a washer and dryer, freezer, and pantry. On the second floor he found a cozy room with an old wood desk and well-used chair. The walls were lined with shelves and stuffed with books. Pictures of kids covered all the space that was left. He settled into the chair, imagining the hours of peace and solitude ingested here, away from the noise and workings of the house. Morning plodded into afternoon, yet he waited. He visited every window, eventually settling to watch a cat working the alley buffet when he heard the front door bang. Through the floor he raced, arriving as the boys came in.

A middle-aged man, whom Tov assumed to be Carl, hurried to the counter with a load of groceries. Three boys followed, dumping more bags on the table. The last boy kicked the door shut. Tov's shoulders dropped. No Stewart.

"Oh gross..." one said, peeling paper off the table. "Who was supposed to clean?"

"The girls. They got away late." Carl turned, smiling. "Hey guys, Jen's cooking dinner. Let's clean... for her..."

He got the expected lack of response.

"Now!" he said to the wall. He had the air of authority, and if you didn't buy it from his appearance, his voice commanded it. All three did an about-face back to the kitchen and fell into routine. The kitchen slowly came to order, and Tov was easily pulled into the comfortable atmosphere, putting names to faces. The shortest was Gary, who didn't say much but kept his eyes glued to Carl. He had fine features, too pretty for a boy, and beautiful straight hair, shinier than the glaze on Stewart's bowl. Rob had the mouth. As tall as Carl, his hair was as black as it would come out of a bottle and as curly as chemicals could make it. His clothes were so large Tov could not discern a body beneath. And Rob, he didn't walk. He shuffled, a science conveying a very distinct dance of presence. Rob was in character. Carlos was content to be behind Rob, laughing with him, agreeing with everything Rob said. Carlos' skin was dark, a trace of Spanish in his tongue. In one moment of work they were lined up at the counter from biggest to smallest, the picture of them together absorbed in their task absolutely perfect.

"I forgot they were taking Stewart today," Gary said.

Tov's ears perked.

"I offered to," said Carl. "I should have told Jen I would and saved myself the worry."

Rob spoke from behind the cupboard door. "They'll be fine. I don't think Stewart has a mean bone in his body."

"How do they do it?" Gary asked.

"You never had a dog?" Carl asked. "The vet pulls a bunch of skin on his back and shoves the needle in."

"I… hate… needles." Rob pushed words through his teeth.

"Glad to hear it." Carl punched his arm, the soap on his hand leaving a ring.

"Funny." Rob regarded his shirt.

Tov pictured Kelly at the sink, Carl teasing her. He would give anything for it to have been Kelly leaving jam on the table. He needed Stewart. He needed Stewart now.

The kitchen done, they meandered to the living room to their regular spots on the furniture. Carlos picked up the remote. "Hey… where's the clock?"

"The girl took it," Tov said.

"It *was* right here…" Carlos complained.

"That's not the only thing missing," Tov added.

"I'm sick of stuff disappearing." Carlos went searching.

"Forget it," Rob said. He took the remote from Carlos and turned on the TV.

Tov paced, from living room to kitchen, an automaton on a Swiss clock, circling time. A car pulled into the driveway and he panicked. He hadn't thought this through, exactly how this was going to take place.

A girl came in before the car door slammed. Stewart's nails were clicking up the sidewalk. "Think…" he said. "Think…"

Jen was dragged onto the porch. The instant she unclipped the leash, the dog barked, jumping into the air at the sight of the angel.

"I don't think there's a graceful way to do this," Tov said, ignoring the welcome he'd been waiting for. His mind was sprinting. "I wish you could pass through these walls," he whispered to the dog.

Jen was at the door, knob in hand.

"What did you do to him?" Rob yelled over the barking.

"Nothing! He was fine on the way home."

Tov knelt at the furry face. "We're going to have to go for it. I think it has to be now or not at all…" He made a dash for the door and passed through Jen before coming to a stop. "Come on dog!" he yelled.

Stewart turned to follow.

"What, boy?" the girl asked. She took a hold of his collar.

"Oh great…" Tov backed out onto the porch. "Come… *now!*" he called desperately. "Stewart! Come!"

The girls were gathered around the dog, soothing him, obstructing his view of the angel.

Rob came to take the leash from Jen.

Tov bolted down the sidewalk, afraid to look back. He kept moving, didn't stop until he heard yelling. At the corner he stopped to see Jen clinging to the handle of the door as it banged against the house. Stewart flew past her, throwing her into the wall. Rob and Carlos were galloping down the sidewalk, calling. The curtains parted on the second floor. Carl's face flashed between them. This was not the time to stop.

"Come on boy!" Tov cried. Stewart's tongue bounced out the side of his mouth, his feet clipping a furious pace on the cement. He needed to keep the dog running as fast as he was able. Screams died as they made ground, the dog sidestepping late-afternoon pedestrians without breaking stride. Tov was exhilarated… it was happening. It was actually happening. Gratefully, he flew back to encourage the dog who was panting, eager to follow.

"Good boy!" Tov was breathing as hard. "Oh, you're such a good boy!" He gazed into the determined brown eyes, then started off again at a good clip, the jingling dog tags better than any music he'd ever heard. Conversation bubbled from his mouth. "There is someone you need to meet… you two will get along famously, I know you will. Her name is Kelly, and she is in *dire* need of our help…"

Chapter Sixteen

The late afternoon crowds were thinning, bent for home. Some on the sidewalk merely glanced at Stewart while others stared. It was odd, a dog on his own, walking as if he had someplace to go. This amused Tov, for it was his mission they were wondering at. As much as he wanted to experience the physical, he wouldn't know what to do if the humans could actually see him. He watched Stewart, who couldn't have cared less and kept his gait steady, loping behind in blind faith. Tov had done nothing to warrant such trust that the dog would follow him anywhere.

"Why would you do this?" Tov asked.

Stewart lifted his head, acknowledging him, but never broke stride. Each time Tov turned to check, Stewart's tongue hung lower. As long as the dog was willing, Tov would push, declining his eagerness to cover distance as he could fly it. Guilt slowed his pace. At the final corner, he could no longer contain himself and was flying in circles, his heart soaring.

"This is it, Stewart!" The dog's endurance ebbed as low as its tongue and tail. Tov rushed into the entrance and up the stairs, waiting until Stewart's face peered into the doorway. Tov had stopped, so Stewart stopped too, planting his bottom on the sidewalk.

"No, we're here, just through this door..." Tov pointed, then dropped his arm. The door was closed. There was no padlock, but for all the help Stewart would be, it might as well have been nailed shut. "There's no rush. Take your time with the stairs."

And he did, scaling the steps on sore pads, succumbing to fatigue. In minutes, the dog was lying down.

Tov had to try. He reached for the knob, but his fingers passed through it. He swiped from the side, tried to smash with his palm from the front, and uttered his favourite prayer: "Now Lord... now would be a good time..."

He wished and worked at it for a few minutes, and then eventually sat with his elbows on his knees and head in his hands, to watch the elongated shadows pass below. The dog panted beside him. He hadn't thought the door would be closed. The old lady had left it open before. Had Kelly left? The thought shot through him, jerking him upright.

"Stay here," he ordered Stewart. The dog lifted its head. "Just stay, okay? Please?" He held up open palms. "Don't go anywhere." He pushed his hands toward the dog, then disappeared.

The old lady was asleep in her nest.

"You idiot," he mumbled to himself.

He flew to the bedroom and checked the space between the mattress and wall, finding it empty. The sheets were spread on the bed, and Kelly was underneath.

"Time to get up!" he yelled at the old woman.

He burst back outside where Stewart was sitting, tail thumping.

"Come," he coaxed the dog.

Tov flew back through the door so the dog could not see him. He waited a minute, then stuck his head out again. The dog was sitting. "Come!" Tov said sharply, disappearing to the other side. Nothing.

Back out on the landing, he found Stewart waiting for him to reappear.

"Last time. Come."

He vanished inside and stood his ground until Stewart's nails raked the door from top to bottom. Then silence.

The dog began to call to his friend in earnest. When Tov couldn't hear the scratching over the whining, the old lady stirred.

"Yes!" cried Tov.

She lifted her head, cursing through folded lips. "Hold ye still!" She hobbled to the door.

"Who is it?" she asked, her lips against the wood. Stewart answered.

Opening the door, she beheld the perfect gentleman, politely waiting for an invitation to enter.

"How do you do?" she asked. His tongue hung low. "That's what I figured, with all the noise ye be makin'." She bent and whispered into his ear. "It's not mine to invite ye in. It's not my place."

She looked behind him to see if he was alone.

"But if I don't belong here, then ye might as well be here too." She stepped aside and let him pass, not noticing his attention was elsewhere.

She limped to the kitchen and hunted out a metal pie plate.

"I can only offer ye some water. The cupboards are bereft of food."

Stewart was beside her instantly, drinking faster than she could fill and refill. Cup in hand, she decided when he had had enough.

"I would think that you'd be feelin' better after that," she announced. "Now we sing."

"What?" Tov said.

She clasped her hands to her chest, closed her eyes, and turned her face toward the ceiling, her sunken mouth warbling in a language that was at home on her tongue. Her shrill, thin voice played like the highest string of a violin rubbed ferociously with a bow. Stewart had no choice, given the pitch assaulting his ears, and he threw his head back and joined in. She waltzed the apartment, lost in the strains of song that spared her reality.

Tov returned Stewart's sorrowful gaze as she passed him by. Who in this place would know and understand her when she couldn't even understand herself? Love and sorrow for her met in his heart, but didn't spare his ears. He motioned for the dog to come, stopping briefly at the bedroom door.

"Stewart," Tov said, "I am so very, *very* pleased to introduce you to Kelly Whitcomb."

The dog approached Kelly and nudged her body, stopping at her elbow as it fell limp onto the sheets. He curled up, fit onto the mattress beside her, and closed his eyes, dismissing the angel.

"You have no idea how good this is," Tov whispered to the pair. He backed into the corner where he could see Stewart, Kelly, and the old woman as she wandered the living room in circles. This had been a good day.

◊

The angel woke to silence. Kelly and Stewart were asleep. The naked bulb in the kitchen was on. Tov flew to the living room where the old lady was on her knees, her blanket laid out. She was rolling it, tying it tight with a piece of string before she pushed it through the handles of her bag. It took her a while to straighten, her body protesting. Stepping over the garbage on the floor, she made her way to the other bedroom and smiled at the pile of clothes.

"Time to shop?" Tov asked.

She held up various articles for inspection, choosing a large sweatshirt, struggling to get it over her head and onto her arms. It fit her like a big dress, settling at her knees.

"Yes, a very practical choice," Tov acknowledged.

She smoothed it along her body, then picked up her bag, her smile all gums, her face brighter than the kitchen bulb hanging from the cord. Tov threw his head back and laughed. She walked through him on her way to the door.

"Where are you going, at this time of morning?"

Backing out, she pulled the door closed behind her. Tov followed as she navigated the stairs, tottering her way to the bottom. Out on the street, she walked in and out of shadows, her legs shuffling beneath the sweatshirt. The angel watched until she was but a speck.

"Where are you being called to?" he whispered. He held up his hand, covering her form in the distance, uttering blessings for her journey. "I will see you when your work is done." He smiled at their next possible meeting. He would look forward to that.

Morning nudged night from the room. Stewart stirred first, lifting his head, checking for the angel before snuggling in closer to Kelly, planting his nose on her cheek. Kelly rolled to her back, groaning, purple bruises on her face taking shape in the growing light.

"We have to wake her," Tov told the dog. He touched her arm, over and over, motioning for Stewart to do the same. Stewart scratched gently, and Kelly cried out at his nails across her hand. She took hold of his fur, squeezing weakly, fighting the wakefulness that gave her a pair of brown eyes staring directly into hers. She seemed more pleased than surprised. Thick fur moved under the motion of her massage, fingers kneading to the warmth of skin beneath.

Tov longed to impart the blessing of his touch to her as Stewart was doing. He hovered, contemplating, and put his hands on her. Warmth took his arms, moved into his fingertips and out of his body. Light and tranquility eddied to a whirlpool of conditioned response as he cradled her face between his hands, touching tears that ran down the sides of her head. Kelly sucked it from him like a hole at the end of a downhill river, the gravity of her need pulling at it with force. Heaven emptied into her darkest moment, began cleaning her of every excuse and reason that had kept her bound. She was letting go, her pain now bigger than her past, seeing it from the bottom of a pit and looking up to a hand that offered to pull her out.

Tov threw his head back and cried out, filled and emptied, filled and emptied in a cadence beating to his purpose. He fought emotion, pushing it away, desiring to leave them both open to the heady celebration of surrender. He marvelled at the soul coming alive in her, at putting Ellen's prayers in the places carved so carefully by her faith, at the light of heaven completing her, meeting the desire of her heart until it was filled with unearthly peace. Eventually they fell into harmony, still, quiet, and complete.

Stewart had moved to watch from the doorway.

"Come here," Tov told Stewart, waving him over. Kelly opened her eyes at a whimpering so quiet it was merely air passing the dog's throat.

"Hello there," she said to the dog. "I know what you want, but I don't know if I can move." She rolled, closed her eyes to muster strength. With a sharp intake of breath, she forced weight onto her good elbow and sat, giving voice to the explosion in her head. Stewart watched, puzzled, as she squeezed her temples, explored the bruises, reached her limp arm and found the broken bones. The dog brushed her with his nose.

"Just a minute. I'm dizzy." She put her arm around his neck, the dog bracing to take the weight. Tov chuckled as Stewart's tongue, like a frog catching flies, took a swipe at her face.

"Thanks," Kelly muttered. She shifted, making it to her knees. Hand on Stewart's back, she pushed in one quick motion, shaking, unable to see through the haze of white dots, but she managed to stand. "I'm in Steve's apartment..." she whispered, focusing, straining, listening. It was a long while before she knew they were alone.

"What are you doing here?" she asked the dog.

Stewart walked over to the door in reply.

"Right behind you," she said. It was an effort to make it to the door, testing her legs, grabbing the frame for support. She limped to peek in the bathroom mirror. "Oh... my..." She traced her cuts and bruises, took in her blood-spattered shirt. The smell in the room was coming from her. "I've got to get out of here," she said, not taking her eyes off the horror in the mirror.

She moved past the angel and struggled into the living room, slowing as she approached the door. Hand on the knob, she waited only a second before turning it, and found herself looking at the cement wall of the stairwell. "Thank you," she sobbed. "*Thank you.*" She peered into the hazy light down the steps. "Just one more thing," she told the dog. In the bathroom she took the towel from the tub and wet it under the tap, washing her face and hands, cracking the mirror as she threw the cabinet door open. She applied a thick coat of base to the bruising and painfully jerked the brush through her hair, sacrificing it for knots. "Okay. Time to go."

Tov could not stand to be at the rear. He flew to the bottom of the stairs. She was breathing hard, and very pale. Hand on the wall, swaying, her knees buckled on the first stair before Stewart wedged himself in front of her. Together they inched their way to the bottom where she collapsed, hugging herself.

"We've got to get out of here," Tov urged. "Anywhere but here. Come on, Kelly. A little farther…"

She moaned, clutching at the dog, pushing her head into his neck. A breeze blew by her and she lifted her face to catch it.

"We'll find a place to rest. I promise," Tov told her. The angel fit his body into hers, sitting on the step with her as one. Her mind screamed resistance, but her heart now prodded her on. She grabbed the fur on Stewart's back and he pulled her to the sidewalk where they stood, people dodging to avoid her. Tov turned and aimed his entourage down the street, Kelly's feet moving only because her hand was hanging tightly to the dog's collar. Stewart was walking ahead, wresting movement from her body, every step an effort to be pulled from her legs as she fell into an anguished rhythm. Tov flew backwards, his eye on them, encouraging the duo on, the first blocks introducing him to reality. Her legs couldn't possibly keep going, and he was expecting her to trek the city. He shot Stewart a look that warned him to keep moving.

From down the street, intent eyes watched the dog pull Kelly down the sidewalk. The bench in front of the coffee shop was suddenly empty as they turned the corner out of sight.

Chapter Seventeen

Their progress was the slow motion of a bad dream, Stewart sensing the impatience of one and the agony of the other. The angel knew their destination, but for Kelly it was a marathon without end. And they were getting a lot of attention, strangers staring then averting their eyes. Kelly was a case for tolerance, a stain on the normal, daily routine of others. Tov kept telling himself he was imagining it. With her bruised skin and dangling arm, she looked like she needed help. But there wasn't one person who stopped to make the effort. It was disgusting, an invisible angel and a dog the only beings looking after the needs of one of their own. To be in need meant to be alone, he surmised. Tov was invisible, but Kelly was deemed that way by those who chose not to see her.

Shuffling by a store window, the transparent Kelly took one look at the ledge and decided she'd had enough, giving in to the cry of her legs. She sat down without letting go of Stewart, who followed suit on the sidewalk, pushing against her while pedestrians balanced on along the rim of the sidewalk to cut a wide swath around them. Tov hovered close by. They'd been going for the better part of the day, not covering any great distance. Tov looked into the window where a balding man was taking cash from a line of customers, his attention stolen by the girl who had taken up residence at the front of his store. He was giving her every glance he could spare, leading his customers to do the same. Tov looked at Kelly, her eyes closed, head resting on the glass, and saw what they were seeing. Clothes bloody and wrinkled, the make-up on her face not as forgiving as she thought. He saw what Kelly in her condition could not, and waited for the inevitable.

The line at the till dwindled, then disappeared, and the man closed the register. Eyes ahead of his feet, he made his way through the aisles, smiling reassuringly to all those who were watching. Tov turned away before the bells jingled on the door.

"Hey you!" the man yelled. Kelly did not respond. "I'm talking to you, kid," he growled. The curious on the sidewalk slowed. "If you don't want trouble, move on." He poked his thumb down the street.

Stewart's tail went down, his ears flattened. The man took in the size and stance of the dog as a crowd gathered.

"It's okay," Tov whispered, "let's go…" He flew away, but the dog wasn't having any of it.

"Take your dog and get out of here!"

Kelly rolled her head, turned her face. She opened her mouth to speak.

"I said get out of here!" The man took a step and stopped when the dog did the same. Kelly grabbed a fistful of his fur and clung tight as Stewart tried to pull her from the window.

"Please help me," she begged.

Lip curled, he lowered his voice. "Take your dog and go away before I call the police." Seconds passed, Stewart frozen to the challenge. The bells cracked against the door glass as the man bolted back into the store.

"Okay, now will you come?" Tov asked. Stewart didn't take his eyes off the man as he made his way into the back of the store. "Will you come now?" Tov asked again.

The dog's ears lifted.

"All right then." Tov flew backward so the dog would follow, pulling Kelly. The crowd parted before them like the Red Sea as the bald man watched from inside, phone to his ear.

Tov searched doorways and openings, needing to find a place where Kelly could be safe and unseen. They walked a surprising distance before it happened again.

Stewart whimpered when Kelly arrived at another standstill, tears weaving down her face. The only option was an opening between two buildings. Tov flew into the fading light at an alley and stopped at two dumpsters overflowing with cardboard boxes, some flattened and open on the ground.

"Come here, boy," Tov called. The dog pulled his charge into the alley, bringing Kelly into a corner behind the bin and against the brick wall. She dropped onto the bed of disassembled boxes, her broken arm on the ground beside her. Stewart waited intently for instructions.

"We have to change our plans," Tov said. Kelly was crying softly, making him wonder at the wisdom of what he'd just done. "We're going to have to find a way to bring Jen to Kelly."

There was only one way to accomplish that. How was he going to get Stewart to understand what he needed? Tov surveyed the alley. They were back far enough from the street so Kelly was hidden, but he could not even think about leaving her here, alone behind a garbage can.

"What am I supposed to do?" He closed his eyes, the only option playing over and over in his mind. He clenched his teeth and bit into the idea against his will, not comfortable with it at all.

Her crying stopped and she curled up on the cardboard. In his mind, Tov saw the crazy old woman snuggled up in her blanket nest. Somewhere in the city, that shining heart wrapped in a dilapidated body was bunking down for the night, resting at the mercy of the streets the same as Kelly. The bigger picture. He had to remember the bigger picture. Was Kelly covered in Ellen's prayers or not? Stewart was studying him, eyes bursting with trust.

"I can't think of anything else," Tov confided, running his hands through his hair. "I have this odd feeling…" He looked around, searched the growing darkness to put his nerves to rest, and saw nothing. She was well on her way to sleep. If they left now, they might make it back before she awoke. "We have to make good time," he warned Stewart. "I don't want her to know you're gone." He procrastinated, mulled over the apprehension playing tag in his gut, just in case he changed his mind. Heaven was silent.

"Come on boy, you know how it works." Stewart vanished from his sight as Tov flew around the corner. "Stewart," he called. No dog. If Stewart wouldn't follow, he couldn't think of a reason to go. Back at the bin he knelt, hands on the animal's head. "Now..." he prayed, "now would be a good time..." They moved through Stewart as if he were not there. "I do admire your fierce loyalty, and I feel the same as you do leaving her here, but I need you to come." Tov looked both ways into the black tunnel of the alley. "I know I am asking you to choose, but we don't have time to waste." He rose, knowing there was only one tactic. He turned his back on the dog and left. Rounding the corner, he continued, fighting the urge to look. He kept pace to show his intent not to return. Full forward he went two blocks, realizing he'd gone as far as he could before taking the next corner. And he took it without slowing.

Out of eyesight, he stopped, his great hope and idea fizzling. He might have to consider the possibility of going alone. Kelly would be protected, but how would the great invisible Tov get anyone to follow? A trip alone could be done at a speed that would defy the dog, but it would be without a guarantee that he could get anyone to come. As he debated he realized he had nothing to lose. Kelly could not make the journey. The dog could be stubborn. The streetlights blinked on. He hated the night, its long shadows and even longer hours, hated conceding failure to its gloom. He rose above the poles and wires, propelled above the spheres of light and looked back. A set of brown eyes was watching him.

Tov melted, a rush of relief warming him. "I know it's hard to leave," he told the dog. "But we have to get back before Kelly knows you're gone." He extended his wings, beat them in short quick bursts. "Come on then," he yelled heading down the street. Stewart leapt into the air. "Yeah!" Tov punched his fist, soared above the lights, coaxing the dog. Stewart's nails began to click, the sound making Tov giddy. Excitement rained from above and drenched the dog running below. Wind whistled past, and Tov was aware of it on his face. His fingertips tingled and his pace slowed, by no wish or thought on his part. Gravity was teasing him, playing with his body, pulling at him from the ground. He looked at Stewart racing to keep up, and his insides surged, trembling with the thought of what lay ahead. But his flying felt funny. There was a downward pull on his body and it was slowing him. A picture of Kelly curled in a ball and sleeping in the alley flashed in front of him, and was gone. He thought of stopping, but Stewart was galloping the sidewalk at a good pace, eager to follow. No, he would keep going until they got to Jen's. Or something stopped him.

Odd sensations were taking his body. For a brief second he turned into the wind, arms spread, his insides chilling as he felt the arms of his robe flap against his skin. His hair was tugging the roots of his scalp. Blinking hard, and harder, the draft on his face was sucking moisture from his eyes. The ground *was* pulling him, and his muscles were burning to keep his wings in motion.

"Oh Master," he whispered. "Oh Lord…"

He was starting to feel.

◊

It was disgusting how easy Kelly was to follow, her pace so slow it was annoying. Steve had put in some time in on the bench in front of the coffee shop watching the doorway to the apartment, waiting for someone to discover the body. The vigil had been so hard to keep that he thought about going back himself. But he had seen someone go in and out, and he'd thought the time had come. No police cars had showed. No one else came or went. Nothing happened.

Bewilderment catapulted into shock when he saw Kelly walk out by herself, guarded by a big dog. He'd risen from the bench, moving closer to make sure of what he was seeing, astonished that she was alive and on the street. His miniscule guilt disappeared completely as the surprise of seeing her wore off.

Dead, she was silent. Alive, she was dangerous.

He chewed on growing rage, had the urge to feel her flesh give beneath his fists, to grind her bones under the soles of his feet. But the dog. It was a puzzle to him as the day unfolded. He'd watched Kelly give in and crash on the ledge of the store window, and it was clear the monster dog was not going to let anyone close. How odd, that the animal would lead and protect her. It had to be her dog. How it'd found her he had no way of knowing, and the annoyance of that just pissed him off more.

He'd seen little but a microscopic circle of the back of her head most of the day, and to pass time he'd conceded to sombre thoughts skittering in his mind. One kept coming that he was completely drawn to. There was strength in it. She should be dead. However scared he'd been that he'd thought he had killed her, the thought of doing it now consumed him. Fate had given him a chance, but he'd screwed up. She was in agony, a broken arm dangling. It wouldn't take much. And she was out of his apartment. There would be nothing to link the two of them. Morbid excitement played in his mind, but he had to figure out what to do with the dog.

The day had been a test of patience as he settled intensely into the idea that he held her fate. He would trail behind for as long as it took. Each place she slowed or stopped, he worked out scenarios in his mind. His arm out like a rifle, the sight of her at the end of the barrel, he shot her, over and over. Then he could feel her delicate neck in his hands as he squeezed, wondering what sound her crushing windpipe would make. Her beautiful head tight in his hands as he smashed it into the concrete until it was flat. It was euphoric, intoxicating, made him feel ten feet tall.

The sun fell behind the buildings and he shortened the distance. Foot traffic was thinning, making it harder to blend in. He was sure Kelly wouldn't notice him, but was wary of the dog picking up on his presence. Where was the stupid animal taking her? It looked like it knew exactly where to go, impatient when Kelly stopped, spurring her on. He tried to convince himself he was imagining it, that it was just a large, ordinary dog. But the incident at the store made him wonder if the shop owner had felt it too. And the people who'd stopped to watch. No one would go near the animal. The dog never showed aggression to warrant the response it got, but like the old man, Steve was feeling warned.

Night pulled in tight around him and he saw Kelly give up one last time. She stopped, and the dog strangely did not pull her on. Steve ducked into a doorway, not believing she was being led into an alley. Sticking to the wall, he slunk to where they disappeared, approaching hesitantly, straining to see into the limbo between day and night. It was too risky. He backtracked, took refuge between the buildings across the street to the entrance of another alley lit with the beams of a streetlamp that reached across the opening. He found a stairway leading down to a basement that was as black as blindness, but he could poke his head over the opening and the alley across the street lay open for his inspection. He could see the outline of two dumpsters and no light beyond that. It was a dead end.

"Dead end," he said, chuckling at his wit. He didn't see Kelly, but the dog was moving, giving away its position at the second bin. Steve stared until the lack of light played with his eyes and he settled against the steps. Now he had to think, to keep his eye on the dog, take advantage to move and follow at quick notice if they moved on. His hands tingled with a spray of pinpricks, thinking of what they could do. He squeezed them to ease the sensation, circulation fading as his bones mashed together turning his knuckles waxen. No one in the world knew he was here. He loved the dark, its forgiving shadows giving him all the safe places to hide in life. The dark didn't tolerate cowards, or weakness, and he could come and go as he pleased, for he was anything but weak. He was in charge, remembering the first time he'd felt that power, when he had run away from home, then losing some of it when he hooked up with Reese. He could learn it again. How stupid to trust anyone, to give people a piece of yourself. It took something from you, made you less than what you were.

It started small. Steve shook his head, swearing. Why did it have to be like this, screwing him up when everything was going so good? His head pounded, stirring familiar sensations and starting up the routine. He banged it quietly on the wall as needles hopped on his scalp. They jumped high, piercing hard as they settled into their dance, penetrating with vengeance, asking. In his shock at seeing Kelly, he'd walked away from his knapsack on the bench. His face clenched at the pain as it snaked into his body. This was the only part he hated. It was impossible to fight, like being held underwater against your will, holding your breath so your lungs didn't fill until it felt like you were going to explode. Tortured, he looked up to the surface and beyond, out of reach. Drenched in sweat, the needles crawled.

He could shut down. When it got like this, he could slip into "zombie" mode, like he'd discovered he could do when he was just little, when his dad was beating him. He could slip out of his body, forget where he was, take off without going anywhere. He could go numb, turn inside himself. A memory came. He was a little zombie. On a chair in the kitchen, his mother kneeling in front of him. She was holding his face, crying. He asked what was wrong, upset at her tears because he always knew when to come back. He often thought about that, if he would have stayed away, floating in his head, if his mother hadn't pulled him away…

He dug in against the storm in his body until the pinpricks rolled to the ends of his extremities. When he was younger, the only time he'd ever seen the ocean, he sat quiet on a huge boulder, biding his time until the tide receded after it had chased and surrounded him. He knew how to sit quiet. How to wait.

When he felt the cold concrete seat puncturing a chill into his legs, he knew it was time to come back. Craning his neck, he squinted across the street into the alley. The dog was gone. He held onto the wall in front of him, half standing. He hadn't been unaware long enough for the dog to move Kelly. It could still be there beside her. He hadn't seen what had happened.

He climbed out slowly, not relishing the thought of startling the dog in the dark. If they weren't there anymore, he had to make tracks to find them. He crept out. One car passed, illuminating then discarding him. He stared down the alley, taking his time, inching ahead, eyes darting, listening, watching, adrenaline pumping. He stood for long periods, feet planted, back to the wall, cautious, not taking his gaze from the spot where he'd last seen the dog. His heart was running miles ahead of him before he made it to the bin and stopped. Holding his breath, he leaned around the corner. There was no dog, but a full view of the dumpster and the wall behind it. Someone was lying on the ground, a body curled so he could see only feet and legs. He didn't have to check the face. He could not believe his luck, much less his eyes. It as Kelly.

"Meant to be," he whispered.

◊

Tov's body was slowing, faltering, allowing Stewart to take the lead. It was no longer a race. The farther Stewart pushed, the slower Tov flew, dealing with the drag of the wind, the pull of gravity.

It was happening. It was finally happening. When he'd dreamed of this moment, he had never anticipated feeling terror. He was still able to fly as he contended with the transformation, with the cataclysmic changes happening to him. His hands went solid, giving him the ability to touch and monitor his body. He explored, feeling flesh firming beneath his fingers. He wasn't sure what to do with a body of weight and blood. It frightened him that he would be suddenly limited. He had no idea how long it would be before he would be joining the dog on the ground. Stewart was racing away from him, his course set.

"I hope he knows where we're headed," Tov muttered. They'd made excellent time. Overtop the blocks of rooftops he could see their destination, and Stewart was right on course. He watched the dog, then looked ahead at the distance, realizing he wasn't going to be able to make the trip in the air. Before he lost flight, he gathered all the steam he could to lift his body, but as he beat his wings furiously he continued to slip from the sky. He had to stick with Stewart to make sure Jen would follow. Maybe that was the purpose of being given the physical—that he *had* guessed right for once. He calmed himself with the thought that he would eventually make it to Jen's even if it was long after Stewart.

Still high above the buildings, Tov stayed a course along the street, his muscles burning. An invisible thread attached itself to his stomach. In mid-air he twirled, facing the direction he'd just come.

"No," he silently pleaded, "no..." Had he chosen wrong?

His middle jerked. It was not a slight string, but a thick rope, seizing all movement. "Please," he gasped, putting all his effort into changing direction, clinging to everything left in his body that would keep him in the air. It felt like he was being poured out onto the ground. His arms and legs flailed. He gulped lungfulls of wind that had only iced his cheeks until now. His chest was thumping; he could feel it in every part of him. The tops of buildings loomed below, growing larger.

"I don't know what to do!" he cried out. Afraid of the ground, he couldn't anticipate landing. He had to keep level, line himself up with the road, stop flapping and think. It was hard to be still, not fight it, but when he did, he could hear the whir of his wings, praying as he tried to steer down the middle of the road. The urgency of the call could only mean one thing.

Kelly was in trouble.

He had to fly, cover as much ground as possible, having no idea how long it would take him to reach her after he was fully physical. The wind assaulted, clothes flapped as he pushed with every muscle that was coming alive. The ground was getting closer. To strain against gravity was useless, yet he could not give in. Level with the streetlights, each one he passed flashed in his eyes, blinding him to shadows as if the darkness was painted on the inside of his eyes. Windows and signs blurred. His only thought was hitting the ground. He fought to stay upright as the final parts of his body jolted into reality, every inch of him detonating in small explosions of feeling as the rope kept pulling.

His feet bumped and dragged, and he feverishly flapped his wings but felt them fading. He knew he had to get his legs into the rhythm of a run to gain balance, to pump his arms in time with his feet. Many times he had seen the motions he needed to mimic. His wings fluttered one last time, then disappeared. All that was left was the fight for breath as he attempted to run. His feet were cramping. His sides hurt, and he was swallowing air too fast trying to coordinate his arms and legs, to get them working together to slow down. When all his movements were finally working in sync he was able to come to a complete stop. Doubled over, hands on his knees, straining for breath, it was a relief not to be moving.

It was nothing like he could have imagined. Everything was pushing him down. He looked to see a pair of running shoes on his feet. "Thank you," he said, laughing. Noise filled his ears, inside his head and not just in his thoughts. Tov looked to his hands, needing to think of them before he could lift them. The clothes covering him made it difficult to move. He had on real blue jeans and a T-shirt. His robe seemed to have disappeared with his wings. He pulled at the material, pinching it, feeling it against his fingers, aware that his sword was still in its sheath tight against his body. It was odd to be limited to one sensation at a time, to concentrate to make everything work. He had to think about his feet to shuffle a full circle and see all around him. He was standing next to a brick wall, like the miles and miles of brick he'd flown by since his arrival. He touched it, amazed at how different it was from his clothes. It didn't move under his fingers. It was not at all like the skin on his body.

Then he had the oddest sensation. He *felt* someone looking at him. He glanced down the street and saw someone coming. Goose-flesh crawled up his arms as the footsteps approached, hearing them as clearly as he could his own breath. The man was watching him, Tov the invisible, Tov in the flesh. Hypnotized, he stared back.

"What do you want?" the guy mumbled.

He was not going to waste his first conversation, thinking carefully before settling on a reply. "I want to make it to my destination before it's too late."

The man slowed, made a face, kept moving.

"Really. I'm afraid that my body will be too slow," Tov shouted to his back.

"Nutcase," he said to the angel and walked on.

Tov waved. How wonderful was this?

"I will make it!" Tov yelled. "I will!" He was absolutely giddy. The rope in his gut twisted. His feet firmly on the ground, he pushed his legs to make them walk, having the faintest perception that he was still flying. His step was like a hover, too long in the air. He smiled at the advantage of retaining even some miniscule angelic quality for whatever lay ahead. A few people gawked at him, whom he acknowledged with nods, finding it difficult to watch and walk at the same time. Someone walked by very close as the angel approached, and Tov turned his head after they passed. He could not resist the sensation of their proximity, wanted to smell their smell, feel the breeze on his face as they passed.

Pain shot suddenly into his skull, cut to the centre of his eyeballs. Stumbling backward, he fell, scraping his elbows. The metal gong clanging in his head reverberated slowly, then faded. He refocused, found himself staring foolishly at a lamp post.

"What a stupid place for one of those," he muttered. Laughter erupted behind him.

The rope tugged, calling him to stand and stumble ahead obediently. Walking hurt even more now. His body was pain. By the tightness of the thread, Tov knew Kelly couldn't be far. He prayed for endurance, asking that his heart alone would carry him even if his body could not. One footstep followed another, over and over, until he was at the corner where he'd waited for Stewart. Forgetting about clearance he turned too soon, his shoulder clipping the wall, causing him to stumble again. Involuntarily, his newfound voice shouted pain as he hit the pavement. From the ground he could see the alley entrance just ahead. He scrambled, tried to run. The last corner he took wide, slowing as he approached the dumpster. Someone turned, stood abruptly in surprise.

The thread dropped. Tov's light burned hot, rushing through him like a door had been opened for it to escape. Through the corner of his eye he saw Kelly being dropped, heard the thud as she hit the pile of cardboard. The boy was startled, coiled with the instinct to fight. The demon on his shoulder screamed curses in a language that made the angel's blood cold, grabbing at Steve and embedding its curved claws to send them both crashing on top of Kelly.

There was no mercy to be had. "It's time," Tov said quietly. His eyes blazed. "It's time…"

Chapter Eighteen

Steve's back was against Kelly, maniacal thoughts jumping in his mind, water beads in a heated frying pan. If only he had a knife. He pictured himself running the man through, plunging deep, then deeper. He could still feel the warmth in his hands from Kelly's neck, the sensation of wringing life from her before this stranger interrupted. The power, the excitement undulating in him wasn't wilting. He was pumped for action, but this man was big. Steve was trying to read body language, preparing his muscles to spring, but apprehension held him, a premonition telling him that this was not going to be a fair fight. Far down in a place Steve wasn't used to visiting, he cowered, hating the fright in his gut. Something *inside* of him was being threatened, and he had no idea how to defend himself against that.

The man lunged, grabbing Steve by the neck, pushing him sideways across the wall and away from Kelly. His neck locked in a giant set of hands, Steve gurgled for air, clutching at fingers to pry them loose. He was no match for the strength of this man. Steve pulled his knee up and planted it in the man's stomach.

"Leave us alone!" Addiction shrieked, flinging at Tov, its screams shrill against the angel's newly sensitive eardrums. "What do you want? Leave us alone!" Caught in the grip of the angel's hand on Steve's neck, a torrent of obscenities flew from its mouth as fire seared skin to the roots of every hair follicle on its legs.

Steve twisted, planting his foot beside the angel's, and flung him into the side of the dumpster. All the air was instantly sucked from Tov's lungs. He buckled, gasping, and struggled to his elbows, acquainted now with a pain he didn't even know existed. Steve came at him again and a boot connected with the side of the angel's face, his cheek grating raw as it slammed and slid against pavement. The weight of Steve's body stood on his cheekbone, mashing it into the asphalt. Tov was on his stomach fighting for air. There was only one part of his body he could move. With all his might he kicked backward, connecting with Steve's leg, causing the boy to lose balance and fall heavy on top of him. The pressure on his face released, Tov rolled the boy on his stomach to pin him, forcing the boy's wrists over his head, and Steve could no longer fight. Panting, Tov adjusted his position and clamped down. Addiction was curled into a tiny ball in the crook of Steve's neck, muttering threats, one thin arm hugging Steve's shoulder.

Steve's voice was ice. "Who are you?"

"Leave us alone!" Addiction whimpered.

"Leave us alone," Steve echoed.

Tov looked at the worm cradled into Steve's neck and focused his light onto the demon. Addiction clung, contorting in pain as surreal light burned pathways across its skin. "What do you want? What do you want?" it hissed. Smoking bumps of skin popped and crackled as they incinerated and Addiction raised it head and screamed, making a move to defend itself. It flew at Tov, claws flexed to tear flesh, impulsively abandoning its grip.

Dazed, dizzy, Addiction was suddenly on the ground far down the alley, fluid oozing from a deep wound on its side. It pushed itself off the ground, raising a wobbly head, and turned in circles to focus on the silhouette of the angel standing over the boy. The angel's eyes, two points of light in the dark, stared back. A blade glimmered in the angel's hand, moving up and down with Tov's heaving chest. Only the heavenly messenger and the demon knew the implication of the angel between itself and the human. Addiction lifted its head and howled, a sorry mess writhing in slime trickling from its side onto the ground.

Tov turned to Steve.

◊

Every hair on Steve's body was standing. The man had wielded a blade that came out of thin air, then suddenly released him and jumped away. Now he towered over him, having complete advantage. But the stranger stood staring down the alley into the dark. The power Steve felt surging through him moments ago was gone. He felt empty... completely empty. He knew, somehow, that what he'd been fighting for was gone, and he wasn't even sure what it was. He tried to conjure up the gall that so dutifully kept his heart beating, but it was vague and distant, elusive to him now.

Steve stared into the funny eyes. Something was moving in the void he was feeling, and he searched the man's expression for any understanding. His dad's face appeared, an obscenity forming over the stranger's countenance as if he were seven years old again, the shadows of his father's arms gyrating, connecting, thick around him, reducing him to a snivelling pulp. Then he remembered the first time he'd risen out of the ashes to stand calmly on top of the anger, searching his dad's face for some clue of what he'd done that his father couldn't love him. The face dissolved and his mom's appeared. He was little when that sorrowful expression of hers was burned into his memory, letting him know she stood far outside of any hope or help he needed. Steve had begged, pleaded with that pitiful expression that surrendered responsibility, which announced that the weight of the world was too heavy for her gaunt shoulders. Her face peeled away and Reese's took its place. This was the face that had saved him, for a season at least, that had fostered a tiny trust that earned the title of friend, one Steve had never given away too easily. He studied Reese, hoping to see his confidence had not been wasted, but Reese's features dissolved, fell into the pile of rejects and discards. Faces came and went, flipping through his memory like a thumb releasing the pages of a book.

Then the intense eyes of the stranger were back, looming over him. He felt like he was losing something. In the absence of the force and power that had always protected him, the hate that had helped him survive, was something he had never felt. The only thing familiar was that he didn't ask for it to happen. It was someone else's choice, someone else doing it to him. The face with the funny lights in its sockets took its place in Steve's Polaroid memory of times he wasn't in control.

◊

Tov was looking past the eyes into the parts of him Steve didn't know existed, to the soul resting in a place shut down so effectively that the boy was not even aware of its existence. The angel probed, touching as only the light of heaven could, and found this human called Steve to be empty. Addiction was howling, its lament as hollow to the angel's ears as the soul before him. Sadness found the angel, and tears chilled a path down his face. He could not fathom the absence of spirit, to be so utterly without hope, or love, or purpose. The suffering that had been born into this life completely arrested him. All he could do was stare.

"Who are you?" Steve asked.

Tov struggled with words, with the affliction of pity. He pulled hard for air, wiping his face with the back of his hand, leaving smears of dirt. He blinked, clearing his sight.

"I am your chance."

Steve raised himself up on an elbow. "My chance for what?" he spat.

Tov refused the possibility that this was a situation with no hope, that he should actually save his breath. "Your chance to start again."

"No such thing."

Tov was being dismantled, emotion by emotion. "How do you know?"

"Where have *you* been?"

A chuckle tumbled through the angel's tears, surprising them both. He wondered at the wisdom of what he wanted to say, how many times he had dreamed of standing on the street shouting, "I am an angel from heaven! I am real! I am here!" It was, well, unbelievable.

"I've been around," he said.

160

"I've been around too. There's no starting again." Steve's mind was clicking, working the opportunities. "You offering me a job or something?"

"No, not offering anything like that."

Steve looked him over. "Drugs?"

Tov laughed, arching his eyebrows. It was his turn to look at the human over the tops of his eyes. "How ironic is this?" he thought, but heard the words coming from his mouth.

"What?"

Tov shook his head. "Wide corners and audible thoughts."

"What are you saying? What's wrong with your eyes?"

"I'm not what you think I am. I can see inside of you."

"So, you're superman. That makes you a fruitcake."

"I can help you, Steve. If there is ever a time in your life you can be helped, it's now."

Tov glanced down the alley toward the beady eyes honed on them with absurd ferocity. "Believe me, it's now."

Steve pulled back. "How do you know my name?"

"I know a lot about you."

"How?"

Tov didn't answer.

"Have you been following me?" Steve's words came slowly. "What do you know about me?" He looked at Kelly.

Ellen's daughter lay quiet and still as the angel looked at her, too.

"Yes," Tov said, "I know."

"Are you a cop?"

For the first time, Tov sensed a soft skin of fear on Steve's insolence. He hadn't thought of that, being mistaken for law enforcement. That would be one way of handling it, even though there was a system in place here to deal with Steve. But it would leave the boy as he was, accomplishing nothing. Tov looked up to the heavens, to the end of all things, barely able to discern the stars, marvelling at his presence here in this moment, at this exact time.

"No. I am not a cop."

Steve relaxed, rose to sit.

161

"You'll never do it by yourself," Tov said.

"Do what?"

"Change."

"Who says I want to change? You're assuming a lot."

"So are you," Tov answered quickly.

"And you're going to help me?" The confidence was back. "I don't trust anyone. I have myself. That's all I need."

"You're wrong about that."

"If you believe that, then you're just a stupid prick." Steve spit at the angel's feet.

Tov pulled back, incensed. A rustling came from down the alley. Addiction was creeping slowly, eyes pinned to the angel, dragging its body and leaving a trail of ooze. Tov turned back to Steve. Nothing inside this human was responding, nothing that would give him an inroad into the empty space Steve was guarding with his life.

"What do you want from me?" Steve asked, agitated.

Addiction gurgled phlegm, called to the boy.

"I want to help you."

"You still haven't told me how."

"I want to give you your soul."

Steve swore under his breath. "You looked like a religious freak. I should have guessed that right off the bat."

Tov held Steve's eyes until they looked back with the same intensity. He let loose his light, pushing at doubt and ignorance, plummeting into the void where Steve's soul lay dead. Tov's breathing accelerated as he worked to find a crack, and he heard Malheev. *"Keep your eyes open while you are here. What you will learn is more than the perfection of heaven."* He saw the face of the angel of inspiration, reached out to touch it.

◊

Steve was being swallowed, eaten by the man's countenance. He could not look away, a moth drawn to a hot bulb. His insides quavered as he gripped his stomach with one hand and found balance on his knees with the other. Control was evaporating, consumed in those burning irises. His body came to life as the man with the funny eyes reached out to his cheek. He propelled himself backward, crab-walking to where he could not be touched, fighting for what he knew was true. He needed no one. The man's eyes dimmed. Steve blinked as they turned from orange, to yellow, to white, then to a sliver that only hinted they had been on fire before they went completely dark.

These silent conversations between them were starting to wear thin. He looked at the man, at the weakness of a guy who had cried in front of him, for Pete's sake. What a bloody waste of skin.

◊

Addiction was whispering, reaching, feet away from the boy. "It hurts… it hurts…"

"You are worth far more than you know," Tov said. "There is one who loves you…"

"Like I'm going to trust you!" Steve yelled. His voice cracked.

"It hurts…" the demon chanted, closer. "You are hurting us…"

"This is your chance," Tov whispered. "Take it!"

"No!" Steve screamed. He stood, defiant, ready to fight.

The second he was on his feet Addiction scrambled, jumping up the boy's leg, swinging to its perch. Suddenly quiet, afraid to look at the angel, it held tight, staring into space, eyes wide in unbelief. Though wounded, it was the backbone the boy needed to stiffen and rise taller.

"Why?" Tov asked. "Why won't you take my help?"

"You're like everyone else. You can't control me." The snarl was in his lip, the cockiness in his demeanour. "I don't know what it is you want, but you ain't getting nothin' from me."

"It can be different, Steve. I'm here to tell you."

"Yeah, well you told me."

A lump took Tov's throat, the wonder of grace so lost on this boy, thrown back in his face like mud. He had failed. The sorrow he had for this human lay trampled between them. They stood so far apart, as if the spiritual and the physical could never meet. There was one hope left, one thing Tov could plant in this boy's mind, if not his heart.

"You will remember me," Tov told him. "You will always remember me. One day you will realize who I am."

"You're the one who needs help." Steve glanced at Kelly. Backing up, he kept his eyes on Tov all the way to the alley entrance. Attitude thick, the strut overdone, Tov could not resist. He made a step for him and Steve's boots tore up the dirt and rocks beneath them as he whipped around the corner in a flurry of dust that wafted in the streetlight long after he was gone.

$\Diamond$

Tov picked Kelly up and laid her down on the cardboard. Blood oozed from her hands. She had tried to fight. He smoothed her hair and saw the marks where Steve had taken her by the throat, wounds scratched into her flesh.

"It's okay," he whispered. She struggled against him. "It's okay," he told her, soothing her, holding her loosely. He persisted until she responded, going still, her body resting against him, rising and falling with agitated breath. "You don't have to be afraid anymore."

He could barely hear his own voice, quiet with concern. He held her in awe, gently, with a painful awareness of what he was being granted. He could say nothing else. The angel squeezed Ellen's little girl to his chest, hugging her as hard as he dared, face buried in her hair. He wasn't aware he was crying until he felt her head wet beneath his chin. Tov rocked her, as Ellen had done when she had received his comfort, whispered promises to her that were the very echoes of her mother's voice. He kissed the top of her head, lavishing the love upon her that had been entrusted to him.

"It's okay," Tov told her.

Kelly opened her eyes.

"Your Momma sent me to find you."

Kelly stared. "She did? How did you find me?"

Tov held the word a moment, clasping a treasure so valuable he had to take his time to give it away. The girl he had found on the park bench was looking directly into his eyes, asking it of him. Bigger than anything was the truth he could speak into her.

He put his finger on her lips. "Prayer."

"You heard my prayers?"

"Yours, and your mothers."

She narrowed her eyes.

"I am not God," Tov said quickly.

"Who are you?"

He left it unanswered. She would know what this meeting was as her life unfolded. It was hers to discover, the window of heaven that had opened here for her. He could not waste this precious time. He tightened his arms, lost himself in the pleasure of human embrace. It wasn't the same as the hugs he and Chaver had shared. It was the weight of their bodies, the warmth of skin touching, the sharing of space that was made to keep all physical things separate. It was more powerful than he could ever have imagined.

There were footsteps. He turned to see a head as it appeared around the dumpster. He cried out, laughing. "It's you!" Stewart stepped up gingerly. "It's you..." Tov said quietly, reaching. Refusing to take his arm from Kelly's shoulder, he put his other hand on the dog and held it there, taking in the first feel of fur as Stewart's tail banged pleasure on the bin.

Understanding blossomed on Kelly. "This is your dog?"

Tov smiled through the dog breath thick on his face. "No."

"He knows you."

"Yes." Short on words, intent on his chance to experience the dog, he ran his hand from Stewart's head down the side of his face. The hair covered his fingers and he scratched beneath to the skin, feeling the heat. The dog pushed, determined to get the full benefit of the rub. It was utterly incredible. Tov took his arm from Kelly's shoulder, leaning her against the wall. He took hold of Stewart's ears, one in each hand, and played, holding them out, feeling their undersides. Sliding his thumbs down the bridge of the dog's nose, he explored, feeling the bone, eventually stopping on the cold, wet end. Stewart pulled back, repositioned for a head massage. His tongue hung from fatigue, and Tov grabbed the slobbery surface before if disappeared back into Stewart's mouth like elastic, smiling at the gob of spit in his hand. He wanted it all.

"You're amazing." He put his face on top of Stewart's head, the hair tickling his cheeks. The smell of dog filled his nose as he rubbed his face over the hair from side to side. "Amazing," he whispered.

Stewart leapt away, shattering the moment. The dog was being called, but Stewart did not run farther than the opening of the street. He barked response, feet jumping off the ground each time he answered.

Tov heard the vehicle stop. A door open. He did not move, realizing his moment was passing. It was time to hand Kelly over. This was what he had worked for, and it would soon be wrapped up in one neat package, tied with the finishing piece of string that was his foray into the physical. It was done. And he didn't want to be delivered into the next moment. He pushed the hair away from Kelly's upturned eyes, and in his heart heard the celebration beginning in heaven. The ecstasy of angelic existence, the party that began over and over, never ceasing, as names were constantly added to the heavenly books. He looked at the battered face of the girl in front of him. One of those names.

A second door opened, followed by muted conversation. Footsteps. The knowledge of celebration could not assuage the melancholy adding more weight to his already heavy body. These moments were not enough, and they would soon to be gone. Sensation in his hands started to fade. He hugged Kelly, pushing his head against hers, not letting go as the jogging beam of a flashlight skirted the bin.

"Oh Lord…" Jen exclaimed. Carl stepped towards Tov, but he saw Stewart beside the angel, calm and relaxed, and he stopped. Tov took his arms away and stood. Carl and Jen moved in, talking to Kelly, reassuring her, feeling her legs and arms, checking her over with the presence of blood. The scene pulled into the distance. Tov was behind it, aware of the metamorphosis happening. There were no hands reaching for him, no eyes on him. The heaviness was departing, the pull of the earth falling away. His body was leaving, but emotionally he was still here. The wind died on his face, the cold hard alley crumbled under his feet. He could still feel Kelly in his arms, his voice vibrating as he comforted. It was over, and he was crazy with misery, grabbing at the last twinges of flesh and feeling.

Carl turned. "Where did he go?" Jen searched the shadows. They were alone with the girl. Carl walked the corner of the dumpster but found no one. "Why wouldn't he stay? He seemed upset, didn't he? I swear I saw tears in his eyes."

"Yes," Jen agreed absently, intent on Kelly.

"What was he scared of?" Carl asked. "Questions?"

"I don't think he was responsible, Carl," Jen said. "Stewart and the girl were both okay with him."

"I thought so too." He lifted Kelly off the cardboard. "I thought maybe Stewart was his."

Carl looked around one more time. "But the guy just left."

"Are you okay to move, honey?" Jen asked. Kelly nodded.

"How did Stewart know she was here?" Carl spoke as he collected Kelly's broken arm firmly in his hands, Jen stabilizing her from the other side. "That was one heck of a distance to come for us." Carl looked at the dog, at sudden revelation. "Stewart must be hers," he declared, nodding at Kelly.

They took Kelly to the street, Carl helping the girls into the van. Jen sat on the floor beside Kelly, holding her, reassuring her. They fussed, covered her with a blanket from the back seat, made a pillow from a jacket on the floor before Carl opened the driver's door to let Stewart ride shotgun. He put the van in gear and drove away.

The alley was dark and upsettingly quiet. Tov listened to the motor die away, stared at the pile of cardboard where Kelly had been, but it was not the same as his human ears and eyes. He had been a part of it. It was going to inhabit his thoughts for a long, long time. Remembering would forever change his feelings about this place. His Master had come to earth and experienced what he had just done, and He alone would understand if Tov ever tried to describe it. Full of longing to feel it again, he held out his arms, the folds of soft white material hanging from his garment.

"Yes," he sighed, no longer fooling himself that he was talking out loud. "Back to angelic duties." He tried to walk with the stride that had carried his physical body, pushing his feet against the cement, hoping no heavenly eyes were watching. He reached for the brick, passed his hand through the wall, and dropped it to his side. Would he ever be the same?

He came out of the alley and saw the van at the corner and without effort or pain flew high above the buildings. Chuckling, he caught up and settled himself on the van roof and crossed his legs, chin in hand. The smile on his face consumed his features, and he uttered his thanks to Carl for driving. There was now nothing sweeter than his experience than the time to contemplate it.

Chapter Nineteen

They approached a fully lit building, bustling as the city dozed, a beacon in the dormant hours of early morning. Carl pulled the van to the doors and parked while Tov looked through the windows. Uniformed people moved about inside, one or two noticing them as they got out. It was not as big as Ellen's hospital, but the building looked and felt the same. Carl lifted Kelly in his arms and up the sidewalk, painfully aware of Stewart barking displeasure at being left behind. The big black nose was pushed against the rear window through a ring of slobber and fog growing on the glass.

They approached the front desk, the angel following. A receptionist looked up and smiled. "Hey, you two. Haven't seen you for a while." She eyed Kelly. "What's up?"

"We just took her from the street. We don't know her, no idea what her condition is," Carl said.

The receptionist looked past Carl into the hallway. "Take that gurney." She pointed. "I'll get someone." She left through a set of double doors.

"It's okay," Carl reassured Kelly, laying her down. "You're in an emergency room at the clinic. A doctor is going to take a look at you."

"What's your name, dear?" Jen asked. Kelly didn't answer. "I'm Jen. This is my husband, Carl. Do you remember being in the alley?"

"Yes."

"Do you remember what happened to you?" Carl asked.

Tov watched Kelly's face from the end of the gurney, a horrible feeling gnawing at him as he deciphered the look. He had seen it the first time he submerged himself deep into her green eyes. She was shut, locked up tight, a safe withholding valuable information. Jen and Carl waited, but the only answer they got was involuntary on Kelly's part. She started to shake.

"Could we have a blanket, please?" Jen called. In a minute she was tucking Kelly into an oven-warmed blanket, running the backs of her fingers over the girl's cheek, speaking softly.

"I'll take the van and go back," Carl said quietly. "You don't need me. Call as soon as you know anything,"

Jen gave him a peck on the cheek. "I'm going to assume she'll be with us," her voice so tiny that Tov had to strain to hear, "unless she's breaking probation. As soon as I get a name I'll let you know so you can check."

Carl left, and Tov had no compulsion to follow. He was not leaving Kelly now. The three of them took up residence in the hallway and waited, Jen rubbing Kelly's back and face, letting her know she was not alone.

The doctor came with two attendants, pointed them to a room split with curtains. Jen and the doctor knew each other, talking easily, trading information, wading through a well-practiced routine. Tov was relieved, but confused. No amount of stretching his brain could allow him to understand the girl. They asked her name, and she told them "Kelly" and nothing more. Tov followed through the gamut of her of X-rays, splints on her fingers, a partial cast on her arm, and the stitching of her wounds. She lay quiet, restraining herself through the ordeal.

Had he imagined it? Had it been wishful thinking that she'd had a change of heart? He went over the events that led them here, coming to the same conclusion. For the life of him, he could not figure out what was going through her head that she would not give them what they asked. He endured the hours, as frustrated and perplexed as Jen.

The doctor summed up Kelly's injuries, writing them down as they talked. Her left side had a broken arm, two broken fingers, some cracked ribs, and large gashes on her temple, shoulder, and hip that required stitching. Tov had lost count of cuts the doctor had pulled together with butterfly tape. There were not many places on her you could touch without attending the pain of a bruise. The doctor was unflustered, a professional doing his job. Jen was gentle and patient. Tov listened absently to the noises of the clinic, lost in the green of Kelly's eyes that had winced and scrunched as many times as the doctor had poked.

The angel had stood with Ellen inside her dissolving existence, knowing the shred of will that kept her here. He was suddenly afraid that Ellen's resolve would not stand against Kelly's inability to deal with what was happening to her. Was it pride? Would it make her that fickle? The knowledge he had of her mother would crush this girl. Why didn't he speak it to her in the alley rather than lose himself in selfish indulgence? He wanted to be with Ellen now, not knowing if he had the patience to wade through the mire of Kelly's ego.

"Take these." The doctor handed pills to Kelly. "Every four hours if you need them." He raised his eyebrows as she swallowed them without water and gave the container to Jen. "Good luck." He took a last look at Kelly's closed face and touched her knee before leaving the two of them alone.

"Is there someone I can call?" Jen asked. She was choosing words carefully, knowing the wall between them would take time to scale. No answer. "Okay, you'll have to come with me then. This is a clinic. You can't stay here overnight. Once they're done with you, they kick you out."

"Why?" Kelly didn't look up.

"Why what?" Jen assumed the question went deeper than clinical regulations. "Why would I help you?" Kelly's nod was small. "Carl and I have a home for kids in trouble, kids with no place to go. You definitely seem to be in some kind of trouble. And you're welcome to stay as long as you need, to get it sorted out."

Kelly wouldn't look at her. "I'm not a street kid."

Finally, thought Tov, a small but important offering.

"I know."

"How do you know?"

"You don't fight hard enough. Look at you."

Kelly's lips thinned. The acknowledgment was important.

"I'll phone Carl."

Kelly retrieved her clothes from the back of a chair as Jen left. At least Kelly was willing to go peacefully, Tov thought.

"Make up the bed," Jen said into the phone. "Nope. Nothing." She looked down the hall to where Kelly was changing. "See you soon." A second of repose was all she gave herself before heading back.

Tov remained by the front desk, Ellen's face tugging him, honing a desperate desire to go. Ellen would give her last hours of breath to be where he was now, with Kelly. And Tov would give anything to impart the knowledge he had to Ellen. Torn yet again, he conceded that this never-ending ride of emotional turmoil was part of his new job description. Jen was in charge now. Kelly was under the benefit of her experience and love. He could think of no reason to stay, other than the fact that this is exactly where Ellen would choose to be. If he was the extension of Ellen's heart in answer to her dying prayers, then he had to ignore his desire, like he should have done in the alley. He would do for her what she could no longer do.

Out the front window, the sun was elbowing clouds, jockeying for position on the horizon. Another day was taking its place in history, and people on the street began their routines without even a thought of it.

Arms hanging loose, hands folded, Tov extolled the wonderful virtue of his newfound patience and went outside to wait for the van.

Chapter Twenty

The ride to Carl and Jen's was quiet. Tov sat in the back seat beside Kelly, staring at Carl's head, initially disappointed when Stewart didn't arrive with the van, but now that he had silence he found he was in need of it. The dawn was a most fitting display for heavenly eyes, the night turning wispy around the appearing sun. Melting oranges and reds reached for him, taking hold of his troubled heart. In this dimension it was a splendid show, making the complicated things of earth seem almost intelligible against the simplicity of its purpose, but no one else in the car seemed to notice.

As they pulled into the yard, Kelly did a once-over of the house, her face a blank. Altogether let down that the oasis he'd provided for her in the middle of her personal hell was nothing to even warrant a reaction, Tov abandoned her for more amiable company, smiling the minute Carl's key was in the lock. Toenails clicked across the upstairs floor and raced the stairs. Stewart hit the steps and was at the front door in a handful of leaps.

"That's more like it," Tov said, glaring in Kelly's direction as she came in, though she was obviously as pleased as the angel to see the animal.

"That's quite a dog you have," Carl said.

For the first time, Kelly registered expression. "You're giving him to me?"

Jen and Carl looked at each other, a theory crumbling. "Isn't he yours?" Jen asked. Kelly shook her head. "That's how we found you. He came here and literally dragged us to you." She stalled mid-thought, eyeing the dog.

"How does he know you?" Carl asked.

Kelly shrugged. "He found me."

"In the alley?"

Kelly looked away, buried her face. "I was in trouble, and he kind of found me."

"Well, he just showed up here one day," Jen said, "scratching my door. He hadn't eaten for a while and had no collar. So we adopted him."

"He hasn't been here long. Not even a week," Carl said.

"I would be upset if someone came to claim him now." Jen gave Stewart a calculated stare. "He's way too smart for his own good. I get the feeling he knows things we don't."

"You and me both," mumbled Tov.

Kelly did look around now, indifferently inspecting her surroundings. "Can I sleep?"

Jen exchanged glances with Carl, then motioned Kelly down the hall. "We happen to have a spare bed that was vacated a few days ago." She turned, talking as she walked. "You have the luck of the world following you, don't you?"

"Nope," Tov said. "Just me."

The bed was ready for her. After Jen pulled the curtains, she turned, intending to ask Kelly if she needed anything, but Kelly's shoes were on the floor, her head sticking out from beneath the comforter. Stewart strolled in to claim his share of the bed, taking Jen in through the corner of his eye. Everything was under control.

"You bet. I know the drill." She ruffled his ears. "What I wouldn't give to know what's going inside there. Sleep tight..." She hesitated at the door before leaving, taking in the sight that was pure enchantment for the angel.

Tov couldn't believe his eyes. He could do nothing but stare from the end of the bed. Ellen's daughter was here, in Jen's house.

"You did it."

Tov spun to the voice. He was just thinking that only one thing could make this moment better. Chaver reached for him and they hugged.

"Can you believe it?" Tov asked. He pointed to the bed. "Can you *believe* it?"

"I am so glad for you, Tov. Words are so small in the face of the victory for her life." For time immeasurable, they watched Tov's sleeping charge.

"I have you to thank for that, my friend," Tov said. "If it weren't for you, I doubt she would be here at all." They released hands, remembering the battle that had brought them together. "You left before I awoke. I was worried when you weren't there."

"It seems we are both missing some time," Chaver answered. "I have no recollection past the fleeing of Death."

"We were drifting far from where we fought. I was in such pain, I did not want to waken you to yours. Oh, we were in bad shape. It was no easy task to get us back, but gratitude to you was my sole strength. If you had not come, I cannot think what end Kelly would have met. How can I thank you?"

Chaver didn't answer but held Tov's gaze. "It seems to me that I should ask the same of you. How on earth…?" Chaver chuckled at his joke and began again. "How on earth did you manage to get us home?"

Tov remembered, smiling. "I was sorely tempted to go there and take you with me, because when we returned to the apartment, Kelly wasn't there. I prayed to be released from this mission. My prayer was, and wasn't, answered. I can still see your eyes… when you thought we were in heaven."

Chaver's look questioned.

"I didn't have the heart to tell you otherwise. It has been so long since you have been home."

"We were *here*?" Chaver asked.

"The host came to us." He saw Chaver's face colour with homesickness at the memory of healing light, of angelic voices, the feeling of being held once again in the arms of unwavering love. "When did you awake?" Tov asked.

"I was surprised to be on earth when I did." His voice withered. "It was a mystery to me, until now. We were complete and whole, and I had to convince myself that our battle was not in my imaginings. I didn't want to wake you from your heavenly dreams for the same reason, I guess, that you did not want to awaken me to my pain."

"I thought as much." He reached to touch Chaver's face. What they had accomplished bound them tight, knitting a kinship stronger than either could have foreseen.

"Are you released now? To leave?" Chaver asked.

Tov suddenly understood the sadness that had slipped into the moment. He was, for the first time since leaving the alley, happy at the answer. "No." Tov's heart jumped. The alley! Chaver did not know about the alley. Emotions rushed him, caught him off guard once again. "Oh…" He was breathing quickly, not sure where to begin.

"What?" Chaver moved closer, interpreting his friend's excitement for agitation. "What is it?"

"It happened," Tov blurted. "To me!"

"It did?" Chaver's eyebrows jumped.

"I was here!"

"You were?"

"Yes!"

Chaver was staring.

"I had a body. I could feel!"

Chaver's chin fell. His eyes rounded. "You were given the privilege? You were *here*?"

"Yes!"

"Touching?"

"No. *All* of me."

Chaver's voice was so small. "Tell me."

"I couldn't believe it when I realized what was happening. I was flying, and my body started to change, pulling me to the ground. How can I describe heavy? I know it, but how do I say it?"

"Heavy?"

"My thoughts were separate from my body. My body was power, not thought. The freedom to *be* was gone, but I had the freedom to *do*. I was bound to things, but free." Tov thought again. "Heavy."

Chaver concentrated, trying to imagine. "What did you touch?"

"Everything! The wind pulled my hair, and my thoughts would go there. My fingers went cold, and my thoughts would go there. I pushed my legs to run, giving me such pain... oh, the pain..." he remembered, cringing. "Touch *was* everything. My thoughts went to what I touched..." He was watching Chaver closely. "Am I making sense?" Tov dropped his hands, his voice. "I met Steve." Tov nodded, adding the weight of truth to his words. "I looked him in the eye. He saw me."

Chaver could barely breathe. "You stood before him?"

"Yes."

"Did you fight?"

"Yes. There is so much power in a body, power like we have never known, but it is to be had at the price of pain." Tov shook his head to one side, wanting so badly for Chaver to know. "We did fight, and it was not like anything we felt facing Death. It was slow, tedious. I was uncertain what I could do. Emotion was power." Tov knew it in the telling. "Anger." The alley became clear in his head. "There was power in matching my anger to his."

Chaver's mouth was open. "How did he fare?"

Steve's look still haunted him, the one after Tov had knocked the demon off the boy with his blade. "I had my chance to rid him of Addiction... I gave it grievous injury, dismantling it from his shoulder. But it was his to choose. Steve saw my light, but his anger was far greater. I was done fighting when the ultimate purpose of the Master to bring the boy to himself came stronger to me than my wrath." Tov's lips curled. "We can never be fully human, Chaver. I was feeling what a body could feel, but I was still heaven on the inside." He looked away. "He detested me for my knowledge of his affliction. I could see it in him, closer than his heart. It *was* his heart."

"He knew you could see inside of him?"

"I'm sure of it. That's when I thought I would surely overcome, but it only seemed to make him angrier."

"How did you leave him?" Chaver asked, captivated.

"As he was." Tov's voice quieted. "Just as he was. When I would no longer fight, he took to hating me. My hostility was gone and he could not face what was in its place."

"The Master's love," Chaver filled in. "He spurned our Master's love?"

"He did."

Chaver shook his head.

"It was Kelly I was sent for," Tov said. "My privilege was that. But I left something embedded in Steve that the years will unfold. He saw my eyes, looked in me for a brief second. He has to answer to what he saw, for his own peace of mind. I spoke it to him, put it into his future." Tov crossed his arms. "I am content that he has a seed."

"What of Addiction?"

"They are back together. Wounded, but they are still together."

"Then what happened?"

"I held her." Tov's eyes misted. He looked at Kelly. "I embraced her in my arms. It was not as we know it, Chaver. It was as the walking, and the seeing, and the being seen... the feeling of it takes all the thought and truth in you so that there is nothing else. It was not an encompassing of everything, as it is for us, but the embrace only. There is only the embrace and nothing else, and when there is only that, it is very, *very* strong."

"It seems almost... contradictory."

"That's it!" Tov bounced the palms of his hands together. "Peaceful, but consuming. It took something from me, and filled me." Tov stopped. "I am saying it wrong, but there doesn't seem to be the words."

"No, you have done well. These are thoughts I have not had before," Chaver encouraged. "I have touched briefly, felt with my fingers, but it was not mine to have an experience like yours."

Tov smiled.

"What?" Chaver asked.

"The dog," he said simply. "I touched the dog."

"Oh, now..." There was a hint of jealousy in the smile.

"He is as amazing to touch as he is to know." Tov put his hands out, as if to rub the fur. "It was so soft, not cold or hard like brick. And he loved it, pulling the caress out of my hands. It was the most satisfying pleasure."

"And...?"

"And, it was there and gone. The chance came and was gone. Just like that." He went quiet watching the dog on the bed. "I cannot look at him now without the desire to feel him. It took the heaviness from my hands as heavenly song takes one's thoughts. They definitely have pleasures made for them as we have ours."

Chaver looked at Stewart with longing, the dog's head on Kelly's knees, snoring. "*That* is one experience I would like," he whispered. Noises rose and fell from the mountain of fur as the angels listened, entertained.

A thought flew into Tov's head. "Where were you? When I moved into the physical, did you feel it?"

Chaver looked sheepish, gave a small nod.

"Why didn't you come?" Tov cried. "Oh!" Tov did a half-circle where he stood. "Oh, if you would have been there!"

Chaver raised his eyebrows apologetically.

"I can't believe you didn't come!"

"I did feel it, Tov. I knew something was happening." He shook his head. "I just couldn't."

Tov raised his hands, inviting his friend to fill him in.

"I was at the preacher' house."

"The preacher?"

"Reese's father."

Tov deflated, went silent. "You followed him home?"

"You bet. Did you think I was going to miss that chance if it ever came?"

"Not likely." He backed away from his own story to give Chaver the attention due such a long-awaited victory. "That... is... wonderful," Tov told him, giving each word weight. He hugged his friend. "That is absolutely wonderful."

"What they live is hard, Tov. I watched them try to come together, and it was such a struggle."

"It did not go well?"

"As well as can be expected, I guess. Reese's mother was a mess. She cried. Made it hard to hear, actually."

"Perfectly understandable."

"Oh, yes. But her reaction was easier to fathom than that of the two grown men. They hugged a lot, cried a little, but there was something between them, such distance. They tried to talk, and I swear Tov, I could have taken my sword and split the air." Chaver took a long breath and sighed. "For all the prayers that the preacher prayed, I thought his heart would be soft, but there was a pride in him. He was pushing Reese, forcing him to go places in conversation that Reese didn't want to go."

Tov looked at the bed. "Pride," he whispered. "At least you had a reunion in spite of it. I fear I will not get one because of it."

"She is not willing to go home? After all she has been through?"

Tov shook his head.

"Why is it so hard for them? I listened to Reese and his father, learning more about humans than I have in all the years I have been here. I know it will work out, or I think it will. The Spirit is strong in one and growing in the other. But just think of all the time wasted. Why is forgiveness withheld, and apologizing so hard?" He looked at Tov. "Don't you think it's funny, that we are spared that in our existence?"

"There is something I have learned in my few short weeks here that I would never have learned in an eternity of heaven."

"What is that?"

"Our Master has a relationship with these beings that we will never have. It is in the worth of their souls." Tov swept the room with his hand. "Everything was put in place for them. All of it." He paused. "Even us."

Chaver looked at his friend, then away. "I suspect I know that, as difficult as it is to give up the notion that we are the centre of it all."

"We are," Tov said, "for now. We get to work both sides of the fence, at this point in history anyway. All I know is that my love and respect for our Creator has grown, if that is possible. There are depths to Him that we could only see and learn of here."

"As frustrating as it is sometimes..."

"Perplexing as it is," Tov agreed. "But it is also exciting, is it not?" He gave Chaver's shoulder a squeeze. "Just look, Chaver. Kelly is in Carl and Jen's house."

"What of her now, do you think? All should work out well."

Tov pursed his lips.

"No?" Chaver asked.

"It seems that she knows her heart only as well as I can guess at it. I may have delivered her from one trap into another."

"It takes them a lot of years, doesn't it, to figure it out. She is so young yet..." Chaver said in her defence. "Waiting is hard, but hopefully it will be a lot harder than her pride. If you are ever in need, as always my offer stands."

"Always?"

"Come on, you don't need me. You seem to be conquering this world all on your own. I am your cheering section. Your very loud cheering section."

"It sounds like you're preparing to leave."

"Reese is moving to a clinic today that will help him get rid of Addiction. Those things are so blasted ugly... I can't wait to see the end of it. Reese will need me in the days to come, more than he ever has in the past eight years."

"You love that more than anything, don't you, the ministering part?"

"Yes, that is the best, putting the power of prayer where it belongs, filling the empty physical spaces with heavenly stuff."

Tov laughed. "Stuff?"

"What about you, my philosopher friend? You will not quit thinking until you have it all figured out, will you?"

"It's mine to figure stuff out, and yours to put stuff where it belongs."

They traded looks. "I wouldn't give up what I do for anything in this world, or the next," Chaver said.

"Me neither."

Chaver raised his hand, unfurled his wings, flew backward from Tov, and waved his way out of the room.

Tov could not get enough of Kelly sleeping in Jen's bed, at Stewart snoring loud enough to wake the heavens, and, as some would undertake the counting of sheep, the angel was content to celebrate his victory and fall comfortably into the counting of answered prayers.

Chapter Twenty-One

Kelly had slept so serenely, an escape from life awake. Things will be different, Tov thought, his mind slipping into scenarios that Kelly's pride could pursue. "Well, she's safe," he would say in consolation. Ellen and Kelly, reunited in his musings, led him down the bumpy road of false expectation. Shutting that down put Tov back at the beginning. "Things will be different," he said. Thus was his vigil, a pendulum ride across hope and reality that left him drained. She was facing the window, awake now and still, resting for a time, staring into the soft light of the curtains, remembering or forgetting while the angel waited across the room.

The door opened and Carl peeked in, listening for noise. Kelly's eyes widened.

"You'd better come in," Tov told him. "The first move is going to have to be yours, trust me." He drew back, surprised as Carl walked in.

"Morning," Carl said quietly.

The absence of response was his test.

Carl moved closer to the bed, his movements restrained.

"Try food," Tov said. "She'll do anything for food."

"We can cook you some breakfast, even though it's afternoon," Carl said. "Are you up to it?"

"Oh... my... gosh..." Tov's mouth hung open when he realized that his suggestions were finding Carl's voice, not in the least surprised as Kelly turned at the mention of food. "She is telling you yes," Tov explained.

"I'll tell Jen to cook something." Carl didn't wait for an answer, but left.

Skin on the angel's body was charged. He had nothing to lose. If his words were being absorbed into their thoughts, he was not going to waste opportunity. "You can trust him," he said to her. "Don't be afraid, Kelly. You are supposed to be here."

Kelly bit her lip, squeezed the comforter in her fists.

"How hard do I push?" he asked, hoping, praying without ceasing, hovering over the bed until the smell of bacon snuck under the door. "Trust them, Kelly. They can help you."

Kelly ran her fingers through her hair, ridding it of snags, then threw the blankets and sat up.

"I knew it!" Tov shouted. "I knew it!" He clapped his hands, danced his joy dance. "Do you know what this means?" he said smack into the middle of her face, then smiled at the ceiling. "Do you know what this means?" he laughed to heaven.

She straightened her clothes and the covers on the bed and left for the kitchen, where Carl and Jen sat having coffee. Stewart, lying on the floor, jumped to offer his official Stewart greeting, letting Kelly bury her face in him as she waited for an invite to the table.

"You'll never guess what!" Tov told the dog. "You can guess, but you'll never guess…"

The dog bounded, barked. They watched him making a fool of himself in the doorway. "What the heck is he doing now?" Jen asked.

Tov bent, aching to touch. "They can hear me!" Tov said. "Well, they don't *hear* me, but I know I am suggesting thoughts."

"Stewart!" Carl called. The dog barked.

"Maybe he's not all there," Jen lamented. "He seems so smart…" she winced at the dog doing circles, talking to the ceiling. "So we have to put up with a few foibles…" Their silence was the unspoken agreement that this was a part of Stewart they had no choice but to accept.

"Is he like this with you?" Carl asked Kelly.

"I don't know him." She wasn't prepared to offer more. She had come for food, not talk.

In the business of picking up cues from disgruntled teens, Jen took a plate from the counter and piled up the bacon and eggs, motioning to a chair as she buttered toast. "Coffee?" she asked, amused, almost losing a hand as she set the plate down. Tov chuckled from the doorway, witnessing again the transformation of Kelly in the presence of food.

"Yes, please," Kelly said politely.

The angel alone knew the excitement suffocating inside her, memories of the diner on one of their first mornings together when she'd inhaled much the same meal. "Don't expect conversation," Tov warned.

A look passed between husband and wife as Carl joined Jen at the sink, working to look busy. He poured coffee and set it down on the table, an excuse to watch. "Hungry?" he asked, shrugging off the warning look from Jen.

Kelly dove in and completed the ritual, eventually pushing the plate aside, immediately uncomfortable in the triangle with Jen and Carl as they sat.

"There are procedures we have to follow when we take kids in, Kelly. I want you to know that Carl and I will do anything to help you, whatever your problems are. You just have to be up front with us."

Kelly was watching steam curl from her mug and disappear—no doubt wishing she could do the same, Tov thought.

Jen waited, then tried again. "Are you from around here?"

Tov moved between Jen and Kelly into the centre of the table, looking at the mess of Kelly's face, a rainbow of black, blue and red, an uncomfortable feeling in his gut. Was she afraid? Embarrassed? Her eyes were downcast, averting attention, closed to intruders.

Tov reached for Jen. "You can get in. I know you can."

The angel's hand grew warm, but nothing in Jen's demeanour acknowledged she was receiving. She was looking at Carl, questioning him with her eyes, deciphering the thoughts of her husband as he shook his head. Jen pleaded with unspoken words, resisting the urge to touch the child, waiting for permission. There was an urgency in Jen to enter the space that she had to earn the right to enter.

Tov prodded her on. "She knows love, she will understand it."

Jen's eyes implored, but Carl still shook his head ever so slightly. "Trust your feelings, Jennis," Tov told her.

Jen contemplated, then put her hand on the bruised cheek. Kelly's face was stone, not a muscle flicker or twitch, attention honed on the coffee mug. Her eyes filled and Jen rose, her arms wrapping Kelly, holding her in the circle of her body, and Kelly's head fell to her, emotion stored behind her eyelids for far too long. Jen's mother heart, the one that was so by default, claimed yet one more of her children. The angel embraced Jen and Kelly, the language of heaven so natural it turned him fluid.

Carl slipped from the kitchen, footsteps quiet as their tears.

Kelly's hand did not leave the table, gripping the mug, unable to return the hug. She soaked in the acknowledgment of someone standing in her space, someone not afraid of her suffering. The angel felt the part of Kelly that resisted, that wanted to push Jen away, but the love offered was a relief fast outgrowing her afflictions. There was no end to Jen. They locked, soul and shadow, slipping into cracks past language, grasping at a peace that pulled them together in their need. Jen embraced until she felt the time for parting, pulling back to take Kelly's face in her hands, mirroring anguish into the green eyes.

"I know it's hard," Jen told her. "There's nothing you can tell me that will shock me, or make me not like you." Her thumbs caressed softly.

Kelly heard the voice in her head. "Let it go," Tov said. "You can make it right. Now is the time to make it right."

Jen sat back, her hand on Kelly's arm, not willing to lose the connection she had forged.

Tov had no idea if he could do anything more. It was up to the will of the one given her free choice. Could he influence her to choose what was best, or wise, or right? The thought stopped him. What *was* right? Didn't he know by now that the will to choose gave Kelly the best of what she had to learn? It was not only Kelly's privilege, but his, too. He could wait, as Jen did. Questions and worries blew through him, then away, and he stood at last in the peace that his spirit craved.

"I'm scared," Kelly said.

Jen was quick to respond. "Of who?"

"I'm scared to go home."

Tov's head moved with their dialogue, Jen taking her time, choosing carefully. "Did this happen to you at home?"

Kelly huffed. "No."

"Then who did this to you?"

"A guy I met."

"Who?"

Kelly didn't answer, so Jen regrouped. "Where is your home?"

"Here."

"Do you live at home?"

Kelly nodded.

"Are you in trouble with the police?"

Kelly was startled. Tov realized that this had never occurred to her, her mouth curling as she considered the possibility. "I don't think so."

"Have you done anything wrong?"

"I ran away."

"That doesn't get you into trouble. They are probably looking for you, though." She removed her hand from Kelly's arm, content the ball was rolling, gently handling the tentative offerings she was being given. "Who is at home with you?"

Tov cringed, the three of them quiet as Jen was left to formulate an answer.

"I assume then… that things were so bad at home you had to leave."

Kelly's face was clear.

"No?" Jen asked.

Kelly ran her tongue across the back of her teeth, Tov figuring how she was going to play this game. Jen was going to have to come up with all the right questions. He waited in unbelief as Jen went quiet, refusing to think that she had given up. He pulled back, surprised, when Kelly spoke.

"There's just me and Momma at home. Daddy died when I was nine."

"I'm so sorry, Kelly. How long ago?"

Kelly spoke distinctly. "Eight years."

Jen did the math quickly, did her mental filing. "You miss him?"

"Of course." Kelly cocked her head. "It hasn't screwed up my life, if that's where you're headed."

"Maybe not, but I'll bet its hiding somewhere in your problems."

Kelly gave her an exaggerated blink. Not going there, it said. Not now. Not ever.

Tov was learning that Jen had a second language at which she was very adept and fluent. She was reading Kelly's body. "How about your mom?"

"What about her?"

"How's she dealing with it?"

"Fine."

Jen took a breath. "So, he died, you are both fine, and there are no problems that would cause you to run away." She gave Kelly a nod in the same language as Kelly's blink. "*Now* I get it."

Sarcasm, Tov thought. A third language.

"If I'm missing anything, just butt in and correct me," Jen added.

Kelly didn't resist. "Okay."

However rude Tov thought it was, Jen laughed, loud and genuine, apparently appreciating Kelly's wit and tenacity to give it back. The faintest smile started on Kelly's mouth. It was perfect. Jen was perfect. He never understood more than now how right it was that Kelly was here. Tov looked at the dog, causing his tail to thump. "How lucky can you be, to call this home?"

Distracted, Kelly slapped her leg, inviting Stewart to put his head in her lap.

"Now, there is one question I would like answered," Jen said. "How did the two of you hook up?"

"He came where I was staying."

"Where was that?"

"Somebody's apartment."

"Do you know the person?"

"Not really."

"Was that person responsible for hurting you?"

Kelly nodded.

"But you won't tell me who?"

"I only know his first name."

"Could you take me back to his apartment?"

"I'm not going back there."

Jen conceded. "Why did he hurt you?"

Kelly was going to answer, but stopped. "I'm not sure. I don't remember." She pulled up her sleeve and rubbed a purple vein. "He was making me take drugs."

"Making you?"

Kelly was shutting down.

"Not now," Tov begged her. "She doesn't understand. Let her know."

Kelly took in Jen from the corner of her eye. "He slipped them in a drink. I got mad, and he apologized, said it was an accident." The knowledge of stupidity was evident in her tone. "I believed him."

"Why?"

"Because I needed to. He was going to help me."

"Help you with what?"

"Get on my feet and get a place of my own."

"But you said you barely knew him."

"I had just met him, and he seemed nice. I needed a place to stay."

Jen sat back, fighting feelings Kelly was evoking, Tov eavesdropping on her thoughts. She could paint the rest of the picture Kelly was drawing without another word. How many kids were going to come to her and tell her the same story? She let the silence ride, letting Kelly feel the need to clarify. *Even in this you are perfect*, Tov thought. He knew Kelly was going to tell her what she needed to hear, that the girl was going over the story in her head, needing to fill it in for herself. All of this Jen knew, completely unaware of the precious knowledge that her experience was. It came as naturally to Jen as it did to Tov. He folded his arms, ready for the story, mildly curious how accurate it was going to be.

"I spent some nights sleeping on a park bench. One morning this guy offered me breakfast." Aware of how lame it sounded, she added, "I was hungry, and he took me to a coffee shop. He offered me his place until I could find one of my own."

"And you never thought that this wasn't a good idea?"

"I didn't have a whole lot of choice. I wasn't going to sleep outside anymore. There was nothing that made me think I couldn't trust him."

"And then?"

"I didn't know he locked the door from the outside when he left."

Jen put her elbow on the table, her face on her hand, her anger in check, afraid Kelly would think it was directed at her.

"I was cleaning up his place and he came back with food. We talked a bit, and I had a drink that had something in it." Tov heard the emotion dragging at her words. "I've never done drugs before. It made me so sick. I didn't even know what happened."

"When did you figure it out?"

"When I woke up, it dawned on me. I tried to leave and that's when I found out the door was locked from the outside."

"He wasn't there?"

"No."

Jen took a long breath.

"Ask her, Jen," Tov prodded. He entered the table and knelt, looking between them. Something was happening. He could feel an old wound opening, and Jen was steeling herself as the scar tissue was ripping away from memory. There was a reason Jen was sitting here at this table with Kelly as she had done with so many before her, a reason Jen slept in this house with them, giving her protection and love when they needed it the most. Understanding welled inside the angel, the path of Jen's life becoming as clear as the path Kelly was describing now. Moved, the ache of mercy reduced him to a ministering spirit, and he took hold of Jen, the woman who still needed the touch of heaven to soothe her damaged past and shredded heart. Healing ran like water, purging his veins and out his fingers, inching into Jen's mental and physical scars that lay quiet, camouflaged into the fabric of her life. Tov cried out as he touched the damage done to her body that had closed her womb, light projecting devastating memories into his head. Jennis Croft, the healer, needed healing. Jen, like Ellen, took it greedily, feasting on the light that probed and touched. Recall stabbed her brain. She took deep breaths, welcoming the familiar peace that she had come to expect in these moments as horrid pictures abated and emotional bleeding subsided.

"Ask her now," Tov said, keeping his hands on her until she visibly relaxed.

Jen rested her eyes on the table. "Then what happened?"

Kelly was puzzled, riding out the break, stealing quick glances. The question was a relief when it came, the immaturity of her years taking blame for the silence. "I waited until he got back so I could leave."

"Is that when he beat you?"

Kelly shook her head. "No, but I couldn't get away," she whimpered. "I couldn't leave."

"Why?"

"There were men outside that started coming after me, and I had to go back inside." Her voice grew. "I hated going back. I hated him because I had to go back."

Jen was functioning between the lines.

"She is telling you the truth," Tov assured her, desperate to help.

"Did he take advantage of you?"

"No." Kelly looked surprised, then unsure. "I don't know," she said feebly.

"He never raped you?"

"I don't think so." Kelly started to shake.

"You don't know?" She leaned in.

"I don't think so," Kelly repeated. "After that night he drugged me again, and I'm not sure what happened after that." Her chin quivered. "I think that was when he beat me."

"We should have had the doctor check," Jen said.

Kelly put her head back. "I don't think he did. Wouldn't I know?"

"Would you go back to the doctor and let him check?"

Kelly turned white. "Would you go with me?"

"Yes."

Kelly sunk into her track of thought. "I was mad at him for keeping me there, but I was never afraid. He did get angry, but I was never scared. Just confused. After the first time he drugged me, he came back to the apartment with breakfast, soap, shampoo... told me to get ready to go job hunting. He was fixing up the door so I could come and go as I wanted. I tried to stay mad at him, but he was helping me." She paused. "If I had thought he would hurt me, I would have fought harder to leave."

"You don't remember how you got out of his place?"

Kelly ruffled the hair on the dog's head. "Stewart came."

"The guy who had the apartment, is it his dog?"

Tov saw Kelly putting it together as she spoke. "No. I've never seen him before." She screwed up her face. "That's funny. His name is Steve."

"Why is that funny?"

"He never told me his last name. I never thought to ask." Her brain was starting to flip from telling the story to deciphering it. "He wasn't there when I woke up. I haven't seen him since that last night at dinner." She checked her cuts, her cast. "He must have hurt me after he drugged me again." She focused on the fur in her fingers, the weight of the head in her lap. "I am a mess, aren't I?"

Jen smiled weakly. "Yeah. But you clean up real good."

"She needs to see her mother," Tov whispered to Jen.

Jen wrestled with that one.

Tov tried again. "Her mother needs her."

The mother-heart in Jen broke. "Your mom is probably worried sick. Why won't you let her know you're okay?"

Kelly shook her head. "No. I won't let her see me like this."

"Don't see her, then. Phone her."

Kelly shook her head.

"Can I phone her?"

"No."

Tov bent to Kelly's ear. "She's dying, Kelly." He waited for an indication that she'd heard, but the great wall of Kelly was falling firmly into place.

"No," she said again.

"Okay," Jen said. A little quieter, "Okay."

Tov backed away. Leaving the kitchen, he stopped at the doorway and turned to Kelly, staring down her pride, her stubbornness, dealing with the situation he prayed would not happen. His disdain for Kelly's vanity made him consider, again, the option of going, as Ellen would eventually have no choice but to leave. She deserved more. The struggle in his heart was torture.

Jen was talking. "What do you need more? A cup of coffee or a hot bath?"

"Her mother is dying," Tov said.

"Both, please," Kelly answered. "Could I have my coffee in the tub?"

Tov was listening, but it was suddenly distant. "Why?" he said, apparently to himself. Stewart nudged, his ears perked. "Why now?" he asked the dog. "Why can't they hear me now?"

Tov fixed his eyes on the scene outside the picture window in the living room, idly watching, daring to ask. "Can I go to her now?" he whispered. Stewart whimpered, finely tuned to the concern of his friend.

"Can I go?" he pleaded. He heard nothing, felt nothing, terribly afraid he was on his own because he had considered taking matters into his own hands. He had stood by her hospital bed, not wanting to leave. But he had, for all the right reasons. He looked at Stewart, acknowledging the answer to the only living soul who could hear him now.

"This is where Ellen would have me be," he murmured. He heard Kelly and Jen at the sink, but kept his gaze pasted on the window.

◊

The nurse checked her watch. On her next pass, she ducked in Ellen's door and went to the bed to turn her body and smooth the sheets, clicking the radio on and turning down the volume before she left. The song was hushed and quiet, moving into every space, defying stupor, goading the silence to embrace its melody.

Ellen was standing in a room, curtains closed to the sun as they flapped on a breeze that blew in through the open window, their shadows playing on the wall behind the crib. She stood above the cherub, saw little hands folded together in deep sleep. Ellen hummed the song that suddenly came into her head, the one that clung to the air long after it had soothed her. She touched the soft face, caressed the fine silky hair. The little person filled her so completely that she continued to stroke and touch, resting her head on the crib rail. The notes of the song lingered, spinning a cocoon, connecting them in dreams and whispers. She was safe. Her little one was back, safe.

Chapter Twenty-Two

Jen and Kelly left the kitchen, leaving the angel a statue in front of the window. No amount of Jen's coaxing could get Stewart away from Tov's side, so she left him there staring calmly into space. Bathwater ran in the tub down the hall. Doors opened and closed. Conversations sifted in and out of life in the house. Tov was not aware of time, focused on the distant sky and all that lay beyond. Jen and Kelly took up sweaters and shoes and left the house, but he stood unhearing and unmoving. Carl left later, Stewart merely glancing when he was called to come. The dog was giving Tov his unswerving attention, leaving a perplexed Carl to venture out on his own.

They were as furniture, fixed and inanimate, Stewart the first to grow weary and settle at Tov's feet. Snoring eventually broke through the angel's contemplations, and he looked at the house around him, not thinking of the other kids until now, looking at the empty mat by the door where there was normally a pile of shoes. It was an agreeable arrangement for him that everyone had left. The vacant house was compatible with his mood. He hadn't even considered leaving with Jen and Kelly. Triviality had taken their talk, given him permission to tune out while the weight of the situation that Jen and Kelly knew nothing about vexed him, kept him anchored to the floor. The moment of Ellen's leaving was closer at the passing of every earthly hour. He had always entered at the last breath to take the newly born with him almost as quickly as he had appeared, never thinking about the network of lives surrounding the person, nor to the ends that did or did not tie up neatly at the moment of death. He was elated for Ellen, underneath, somewhere. But it was concealed in torment new and foreign to his experience of escorting. He could not accept the inevitability of the situation, nor could he change it.

Tov heard movement and turned to Chaver entering the kitchen. His heart grew still as he lay down thoughts to welcome his friend. They didn't speak but embraced, a gentle motion, slow and deliberate like the soothing presence they were to one another. They hugged, thoughts mingling and melting, solidifying into an understanding that they were both seeking solace. They rested hands comfortably on each other's shoulders, Tov profoundly moved that his breaking heart was the only summons his dear friend needed. He could see it in Chaver's eyes.

"How did you know?" Tov asked.

"Know what?"

"To come."

"I came for me." Chaver's voice was thin, an afterthought almost. "I am weary of prodding and motivating opposites to merge for a common purpose when it seems to be last on a long list of misplaced priorities."

"Reese and his father?" It had been a while since Tov had thought of them. His expression softened. "Then we share a common agony. You are to bear the pain of a father and son as I am to bear it for a mother and daughter. Their love is so imperfect, it seems doomed to fail, doesn't it?" He added quickly, "Except for Jen. Her love is unimpaired because of her pain. I know now that she is part of your mission here, her past being such a tremendous burden."

"I never feel so completely at peace as when I take her affliction and imbue healing." Chaver went quiet. "Is it only their deepest pain that responds to the love we are sent with?"

"It seems that way, doesn't it?"

"I can't figure the two of mine out. It should be easy to put the past down and come together if it is what they both want, but they hold things so tightly... I stand back watching them wound each other."

"Pride." Tov tightened his lips, the word changing sounds. "Pride," he said, sharply. "What is its purpose? Don't all things have purpose? I am determined to ask about it when I return home."

"Is it all pride?"

"I think so, or I imagine it is with Kelly."

Chaver was thinking. "If that is so, then I think Reese holds the fuller measure. He seems to want to come to his father, but keeps himself at such a distance."

"It's hard for the humans to let go of feelings once they are a part of them. I see the same in Kelly." Something flashed in his head. "It may be the time factor."

"What?"

"Ellen, Kelly's mother, has the knowledge of eternity. Like us, she knows she can let go of a lot in her life here because of that knowledge. Reese's father, too. Kelly and Reese do not have a sense of that yet. They don't see themselves in the bigger picture."

Chaver narrowed his eyes. "But they *are* in it..."

"But they don't know it. They live their lives measured against the knowledge that time is limited. They will hold tightly to that until they realize time does not rob them of anything." Tov dropped his arm from Chaver's shoulder. "If you believed that you didn't have eternity before you, if you had to measure all of your time, would you be here now?"

Chaver's answered quickly. "No. I would not leave home. I would stay in the presence of my Lord, not to waste a moment away from him." The thought stopped him. "That would be hard, wouldn't it, if my Master would ask me to sacrifice what I wanted to do for what He had in mind with my given time?"

"Lack of respect for time makes one selfish, I think. That is the case when people think time is more precious than the one who gave it to them."

"But time is non-existent, really."

"You and I know that."

Chaver clasped his hands inside his robe. "I admire your wisdom, how you can make sense of it. I comfort, heal, desire to pour myself out for the Creator's cause, letting perplexing thoughts fly in and out of my head. You, I believe, will make sense of it all."

"Just how much different is our world from theirs? All the angelic beings are as varied in their creation as the humans." He took a breath and held it. "I don't know why it is so important for me to figure it out, but I know that my Lord grows bigger and more glorious to me every second that I spend on this side of creation."

"You mean we get smaller and smaller."

He looked at Chaver, deliberating. "Yes. That's it exactly." He had one more thought that claimed his face before his voice found it.

"Yes?" Chaver asked.

"They are higher beings than we are," Tov blurted.

Chaver's face pinched, his mind stretched.

"We should learn all we can from them. The day is coming when their knowledge of our Lord will surpass ours, and their experience of Him will be more complete than what we will ever have. I know it. Maybe that is my struggle, accepting the truth unfolding before me."

Chaver's eyebrows furrowed, dumbfounded.

"It is that thought alone that gives me the slightest measure of peace when I think of Kelly, and Ellen, and Reese, and his dad… what they battle. Heaven only knows that their conflicts are much more monumental than what I can ever make mine out to be because I visit here." Tov took in the look on his friend's face. "Am I upsetting you?"

"No… no…" Chaver jumped in to reassure him. "I concede that your mind is far above mine in thought, as far maybe as the humans are above us, as you say. See, I do understand a bit of what you are saying, and I do agree that we are to learn every aspect that shows the diversity of our God."

"I cannot stop thinking any more than I could have stopped myself from being created," Tov lamented.

"That in itself is a very deep thought. You have not troubled me. Our hearts are both heavy with the same matters. I am just deathly curious as to the outcome of all this when it is finally finished."

Tov heard him speak of endings and he knew, for some reason, that this would be the last time they would speak here in this place. The knowledge came suddenly and painfully, numbing him. Not once did he think about being without his friend, but there was a surety in him that this was their final meeting. Chaver's mission was a long and difficult one, and he would be left to endure it alone. All his philosophical words now cowered against the reality of sudden endings. He was leaving Chaver. He had no choice but to abandon Steve. Maybe he would be told to walk away from Kelly. Her resistance made this a powerful possibility. He felt instantly sick

"I have upset you," Chaver said.

Tov shook his head.

"More thoughts to share?"

Tov could not speak.

"I am thinking it is a curse now, to think so deeply. You seem far more troubled than I."

Tov was holding Chaver's hands a little too tight, the face of his sweet ministering friend distressed in wrongly acknowledging that he was the source of Tov's disheartening. When a tear found Tov's cheek, it was more than Chaver could bear.

"Okay now, I refuse to bother you further," Chaver stated. "Let us anticipate our next encounter to be for the purpose and celebration of good." His smile was impotent as he leaned in to touch his cheeks to Tov's wet face.

Tov was coming apart, anguished to remain silent, knowing this was the only way to do it, sparing Chaver the knowledge that he would be on his own again in this place very soon.

Chaver pumped his friend's hand. "Okay then," he said, "back to battle. Let me know if strategies change."

"Okay." Tov was barely audible.

"Okay." Chaver pulled his hand out of Tov's, flashed him a puzzled look, and left quickly.

Tov's heart was gone, carried away with his friend. He was left looking at the wall, at the bothered face of Chaver that would remorsefully be etched in his mind, and he fell to his knees.

Chapter Twenty-Three

Jen set the tray on the table as Kelly put the shopping bags down on the seat, choosing the side of the booth that faced her to the wall. Jen had watched her do it all day, ignoring uninvited stares, convincing herself she was invisible. The shopping trip had been a success, Kelly gushing pleasure in having new clothes. The sales clerk had to cut the tags in the store so Kelly could wear her purchases out the door. Shopping had been a salve that temporarily soothed wounds, and Jen had spoiled her. She probably shouldn't have, but Kelly's enthusiasm was infectious. Conversation flowed easily, smiles popped up when Kelly forgot to be sullen and withdrawn. Then, catching herself in a mirror or window, Kelly would flip personalities.

Jen moved their lunches off the tray, grabbed like a deer in Kelly's headlights. The girl was bowing to pray. Their eyes met, Jen's stomach churning. Somewhere was a distraught mother who had taught this little girl to pray. By her look she let Kelly know she had seen, then bowed her own head to give thanks for more than the food.

The fact that they were strangers came back in their silence as they ate. Without clothing racks, the chatter of overly friendly sales people, or banal comparisons of ghastly and lavish garments, they were left in a space that required Jen's efforts again. She was well aware of looks coming from the other side of the table.

"Do you miss your mom?"

Kelly finished her forkful. "Sometimes."

"What's she like?"

"Persistent, like you."

Jen smiled, having dealt with an armload of comeback queens within their rights of puberty. Shutdowns were not obstacles, but invitations. She feigned surprise, loving the challenge. "Just like me?"

"No."

"Is she older?"

Kelly fiddled with her food. "I don't know."

"I'm thirty-nine."

"Then, yes."

This was euphoric for Jen, burrowing under Kelly's skin where the real person was hiding. There were a few ways and means of getting there. "Is she prettier than me?"

"Are you pretty?" Kelly asked, pretending distaste, her fork resting forgotten on her plate.

"Yup."

"Isn't that kind of conceited?"

"I don't think so. Carl tells me that all the time. If it's not true, then you'd better tell him."

Kelly ducked her head, not before Jen saw the amusement in her eyes.

"So," Jen persisted, "is your mom pretty?"

"Yeah, I guess."

"Do you look like her?"

Kelly shrugged. "Probably."

"Does she love you?"

"What kind of a question is that?

"Does she love you?"

"Why would you ask?"

"Has she ever told you that she loves you?" Jen asked again. Kelly fidgeted, gave her plate attention as Jen slid beneath the first layer of skin.

"It's not wrong to believe it, you know. I can argue with Carl, but I won't ever change his mind. He thinks I'm pretty." Jen cast words, let them settle to the bottom of deep waters. "He thinks I am pretty, and I think that you are loved."

"How do you know that?"

"Because I think your mom has told you that. It's hard to believe when someone thinks good things about us, but it doesn't make it any less true."

Kelly formed the daggers, the warning look. "Why are you doing this?"

"I was beaten and raped when I was young, and the damage he did left me unable to have children." Her voice wavered. "I didn't feel pretty anymore. I never thought I could be pretty again."

Kelly was caught completely by surprise.

"I have never had kids, but I have a lot of them. And I love each one as if they were my own. Some love me back. Some break my heart. But I love them all." Jen stared her down. "My heart is broken for you, Kelly... *mine*. And somewhere your real mother is living in torment for you, and she loves you even more."

Kelly was very quiet.

"Kelly, these kids I love aren't even my children." She stopped, worried she might be pushing too hard, but kept going. "Do you know that somewhere your mother is trying to put the pieces of her life back together without you?" She was tuned into her intuition, hoping she had read the situation right, trusting the inner voice that would not relent.

"I'm sorry." Kelly fumbled words, wiping her nose. "I'm sorry it happened. How old were you?"

Jen had found a few of them over the years, the rare treasure of a tender heart encased in an emotional vault. Carl teased her that God knew a few softies thrown into the mix would keep her bent on a mission to save them all. "Sixteen. My childhood stopped when I was sixteen. If there's anything you want to ask, go ahead."

Kelly bit her lip. "Did you now the guy who did it?"

"A little. We were acquaintances. He was a friend of a friend."

"Where were you when it happened?"

"In the back seat of a car. We'd been to a dance, then left to go drinking. Six of us, three guys and three girls. We finished all the beer and decided to drive around and wreak a little havoc. The guy who had the car was the one who did it. He told me he was going to drive everyone home, but everybody else got dropped off first. He had some story about somewhere else we had to go before he took me home. I was so drunk I believed him." Jen rubbed her face. "There was no one around for miles and not a thing I could do. I have never been so terrified in my life. He thought he had killed me—dumped me into the ditch when he was done. I had passed out, partly from the booze, partly from terror. What a blessing I did. What I do remember keeps me in nightmares."

"Who found you?"

"A farmer, the next day, driving by in his tractor. That part I don't remember."

"What happened to the guy?"

"My parents and I went to court and charged him with rape. He served six years, then got out and did it again."

"Incredible." Kelly pushed words through unbelief. "What toilet bowl do these guys crawl out of? You have to be the lowest form of life to do something like that to someone..." Her voice petered, acknowledging the same side of life had crept into her beautifully controlled, untouched life.

"What happened to you was just as awful."

"Not as bad," Kelly said defensively.

"I think it is."

Kelly opened her mouth. Shut it. "Did you hate yourself?"

"Afterwards? Yes."

"Do you still? I mean, now?"

Jen shook her head slowly. "No."

"How long did it take?"

"A long time. Someone else had to love me before I thought I was worth anything." Jen gave Kelly a few seconds. "I know what you're feeling."

"How mad I am... how I look back and wonder how I could have been so stupid? All I wanted was a place of my own, to be in control of my life."

"Because you and your mom weren't getting along? Is that what it was?"

"She drives me crazy. I can't stand her."

The Attitude was etched on the girl, Jen's honed theory that each child had a mask at birth buried beneath an innocent face until adolescence pulled out the rolled eyes and permanent sneer. "The 'Tude." She'd seen it a thousand times, the tip of the nose raised, the curl of the lips.

"You're going to be sitting on this side of the table one day, realizing how it feels to want the best for someone who is on self-destruct." Jen made the face back at Kelly, changed her voice and gave it right back. "You're just like my mother... you sound just like her."

Unaware of how conditioned her response was, Kelly rolled her eyes.

"As mad as you are, everything you've been through has taught you some hard lessons that will help you become the independent person you want to be. All this tough stuff we have to wade through, the mistakes we make... it takes us to better places if we learn from it. If I hadn't gone through what I did, I wouldn't be here with you now. Where would *you* be if it wasn't for my mistake?"

Kelly was looking around, hearing but pretending not to. The soft hearts didn't need a whole bunch of words. Just reminding.

"Was it Carl?" Kelly asked.

"Who loved me?"

Kelly nodded.

"Uh huh. It was a long time before I trusted any man. He was older, a lot more patient than guys my age. He stuck around until I fell in love with him. I was twenty-five then, he was twenty-nine. We bought our big old house eleven years ago, the year after we were married. Carl knew how much I wanted kids..." Jen's head dropped. "I like to pretend that you're mine, for a while anyways." She tried to coax a smile from Kelly. "Does it bug you that I pretend I'm your mom?"

The soft heart, even buried so deep, was dissolving like sugar in warm water, turning the corners of Kelly's mouth. "It's okay having a mom I can actually talk to."

"Why can't you talk to your mom?"

"She's a religious freak. Everything in her life is about that. I hate it." She stopped. "It hurts her when I talk like that."

"I'm one of those freaks," Jen said, peeling away another layer.

"As if…" Kelly looked at Jen as if they'd never met. Caught off guard, she picked up her fork, signalling the end of that conversation.

Jen leaned in, elbows on the table.

"Don't even start," Kelly warned.

"Start what?"

"Preaching."

"Not going there," Jen assured her.

Kelly narrowed her eyes.

"Honestly, not going there. But there are some things I need to know."

"No."

"No what?"

"No God stuff."

"I want you to explain to me the presence of Carl, and me, and Stewart in your life. I want to know how you think you got out of that apartment. I want to know your theory on how you happen to be sitting in front of me right now, in this place."

"Could it be because you're a mom wanna-be?"

Jen pulled back, the wall slamming down in front of her. She turned away, wondering if she had read her wrong, that she wasn't one of the tender ones. It wouldn't be the first time.

"How can you buy into all that crap? How can you not be mad at God for what he did to you?"

Jen faced Kelly at the line she had drawn, toe to toe. "What did he do to me, Kelly?"

"You know, what happened to you. You can't have kids, and you wanted them so bad."

"You think God did this to me?"

"Who else?"

"I was drinking. I was where I shouldn't have been with people I shouldn't have been with. We hate ourselves afterwards because we can't take the responsibility for the consequences."

"God allowed it."

"God let me choose."

"I don't see much difference." Kelly's eyes challenged, her pupils dilating to pinpoints. "What is the difference? Parents end up without children. Children end up without parents…"

Confirmation, what a wonderful thing, Jen thought. She *had* hit the nail on the head.

"What?" Kelly fired at her.

I have plenty of strength to keep us both afloat, Jen told herself. Already, in her soul and mind, she was pulling Kelly away from the sidelines into the water. It was her calling, her life's work. Her mind calm, her feet and arms settling into a powerful rhythm against the fervent undertow, she dove.

"If I would've had four children of my own, where would the hundreds be that have passed through my door?" No holding back. She was after the truth, she had to give it. "I honestly don't know if I have loved every single one as if they were my own. I've never had a child to know what it feels like. But I have loved as fully as I know how." The little voice within was daring her, prompting her. "I don't hate God for giving me more than I ever dared to dream. When I was little, I always said I wanted a hundred kids. And God knew when he made you and me that one day we would be sitting here, at this table, talking, because he has bigger plans for the both of us than we can ever dream." There, out and done. "And I'm sorry."

Kelly pulled her head back. "For what?"

"For preaching."

"Is that what you're doing?"

No, Jen mused. She hadn't made a mistake. She knew the softies. "Kind of."

"I've never heard preaching like that before. I've only heard stuff that makes me feel bad."

"You are not bad, Kelly. You are *not.*"

Jen's world was slipping wonderfully into place again. She could almost see the hand of the Almighty resting on Kelly, hear the voice of a mother who had learned to trust her precious child to God. The two of them sitting at this table was all the evidence she needed.

"How long have you been gone from home?"

"I don't know." Kelly was genuinely puzzled. "What's the date?"

"August nineteen."

"Are you kidding? I've only been gone for like, eighteen days. Seems like a lifetime…"

We can work with that, Jen thought. She checked her watch. Carl would be home shortly. He could take what little they had and start the process.

"The others are coming home from work and summer school. We should go."

Kelly's lack of enthusiasm was not lost on Jen as she stood to gather bags and clear their dishes. "You don't want to meet the other kids…"

The tone of voice answered adequately. "No."

"I appreciate your honesty, but you're not the first. So we have a house rule. You are allowed one full day of privacy in your room to settle in, if you want." She decoded the look. "No, we don't have a lot of rules, but you can have one day. Take it or leave it."

"Take it, thanks."

"Your choice." Jen scooped up the garbage and dumped it into the receptacle. "We have to stop and pick up something for supper." The promise of privacy, the thought of getting away from her probing, she knew it was all the motivation Kelly needed. She picked up the bags Kelly had left for her to carry, thinking how much she loved her life.

Chapter Twenty-Four

Pat Ramer sat on the hospital bed holding Ellen's hand, stroking it in long, gentle motions. She was waiting for Ellen's eyes to open, but hours passed, trampling her hopes into the darkness that hung over Ellen's bed. Her visits were quiet and draining, but as long as Ellen drew breath, Pat came to offer herself as the last link to this world. It was hard, always thinking that her smile would sneak into their time together, or her mouth would move with a silent message to say she was just resting.

A hand squeezed her shoulder. It was usually James stopping on his rounds. She rested her own on top of it. "So?"

"Nothing new," James said.

She figured as much. "You've made a decision?"

"Yes."

He paused, one more chance to think it over, to change his mind, she thought. "We think it best if it plays out naturally," he said. "She isn't in pain, not that we can see anyway. There isn't much we can do. Do you want the diagnosis?"

Pat shrugged, nodded.

"The specialist narrowed it down to glioblastoma, a malignant brain tumor that's very hard to treat, common for our age group." He drew breath. "It grows rapidly, and is very invasive. She waited far too long."

"There's no treatment?"

"That would be surgery, to debulk the mass, followed by radiation, but Ellen is far too advanced. Putting her through that now would not save her life, just make what she has left very miserable. Do you want to see the scans?"

Pat shook her head. They meant as much to her as the medical jargon.

"I don't see any point in prolonging it," he said.

Pat had to agree, for his sake. She looked to the bed, imagining how it was for James to make the decision, then into his eyes, to apologetically and passively consent. He would have made the decision as Ellen's friend, not her doctor. There was no one to ask. Ellen had no family, being an only child, with both parents and her husband gone. Now Kelly was, too. That left James Ramer, Ellen's friend and doctor, to make all the decisions with a specialist.

"What would be the difference?" Pat asked.

"In time, you mean, if she would have treatment?"

"Yes."

"Pat, you know it's always a guess."

She checked him out through the tops of her eyes.

"I would say days, maybe a week or more without IV or medication. If we intervene, she might have a week or two more than that." Pat was listening. "I said *might*, and it's only a guess. I can't justify it."

Pat shifted her body, reality a different colour than it had been minutes ago. She had been in touch with Ellen's lawyer, already making it seem like Ellen was gone, and she was not the least surprised to find Ellen's estate in perfect order, down to the provision of her funeral. When Ben died she had made many difficult decisions in shock and mind-numbing grief, and vowed no one would ever go through that on her behalf. As the executor of Ellen's will, it was a matter of Pat letting the lawyer know Ellen's situation, to check the arrangements made for Kelly.

"I've been thinking," Pat said. "I'm going to the police station to let them know the situation, in case Kelly shows up."

"I'm praying too," he said softly. They had not really spoken of it until now. He kissed the back of her head. "What a test of faith this is…"

Pat swallowed, but the lump in her throat remained. "I can't believe it's going to end this way," she whispered. "If you would take an

X-ray of her, you would find her heart completely broken. What kind of a reward is it to die like that?" She took a second, gaining control. Her next question was for the doctor. "If Kelly were to come now, would Ellen know?"

"Yes." It was not the doctor she heard, but her husband, Ellen's friend, believer in miracles.

"Okay then." Pat stood abruptly and reached for her purse, giving him a hug that left wet on his cheek. "I'll be at the police station. What time are you done your rounds?"

"Early evening."

"Dinner will be waiting."

"No."

She stopped and turned. "No?"

"Nope. I've a little Italian place in mind." He clasped his hands behind his back as the idea registered. "We got a date?"

Through tears, she smiled and walked back to give him a kiss, then left before he could see the batch of new ones coming.

He waited for her walk down the hall before he took the chart, holding it for a second before he scribbled, keeping professional, ignoring the stab of grief as he looked at her body tucked into the blankets. He stayed for a while, watching her as Pat had done, before he left for rounds.

◊

The kids came home in groups, noisily reclaiming the house, Tov watching the parade from the living room. Stewart abandoned his post, desperately needing to greet them all before Carl came in to bring order to chaos by assigning chores. Carl himself donned work clothes, had stopped for a drink of water when Jen and Kelly walked in. He watched them closely for signs of the day as Jen dropped her bags and stood tip-toe for a kiss.

"Help me cook dinner?" she asked Kelly.

"What happened to my day of privacy?"

"Just thought I'd give you an out."

"I'll take the alone time," Kelly said.

"Okay then. We'll bring you a plate." She smiled to let Kelly know it really was her prerogative.

Kelly looked back and forth between them. "I appreciate what you guys are doing for me." Feeling left out, Tov pulled up roots and went to the kitchen, hearing something in Kelly's voice, wanting to see it in her face. She was looking down at the bags on the chair. "I don't deserve it."

"You're wrong." It was Carl who spoke, waiting for Kelly to look up. "You are deserving, and it's our pleasure."

Kelly gathered her bags and left. Carl questioned Jen with his eyebrows. Tov had no qualms standing in their faces to listen.

"She's a good kid," Jen said. "She needs help sorting out some stuff, but she's a good kid."

"You found a soft one?"

"I did."

Carl put his arm on Jen's shoulder. "My news first. They've picked up my contract for another six months. Once more, and I'll be permanent staff. How's that for sticking it to the school board?"

"That'll be the day they phase out counsellors. There isn't a teacher alive that would stand for a heavier workload." She squeezed his muscles. "My hero," she sighed.

"I jump tall buildings in a single bound…" Carl flexed, "…and take on school boards out of sheer stupidity. If I would have known what a head-banger it was going to be, I'd have spared myself."

"Did you get to the government building today?" Jen asked.

"You want more good news? One piece isn't enough?" He stared at her as if she hadn't asked. "What?"

"We got it, didn't we?"

He looked absurd, fighting a smile.

"You are such a bad bluffer." She punched him. "We got it, didn't we?"

"We are now operating our home on a double grant, approved for a life devoid of begging and roped line-ups." He danced her in a circle. "What do you have for me?"

"Not quite as earth-shattering. You probably won't even call it news." Jen looked apologetic. "She's as soft as jelly and tough as nails."

"What do you have?"

"I have a feeling so strong I can't ignore it. It won't go away. We have to find her mom. In every conversation we have, that's all I can think about."

Tov looked through Jen, past her face, into her eyes, uttered a blessing he intended her to feel to the bottoms of her feet.

"Any leads?" Carl asked.

"One."

His face brightened.

"It's *so* small," she said. "I have the date she left."

"That's it?"

"She won't give me her last name. She won't tell me where she lives. I don't understand. I think she's ashamed of what's happened to her. She doesn't want her mom to know." Jen's lips flattened. "Sounds like her home life is fine. Her mom goes to church, maybe pushes a little too hard. Kelly does have a wide rebellious streak."

"If that's the whole story..." Carl shook his head. "If it is, it's one I hate to hear. So, that's all we have to go on..."

"August the first. That's when she left." She ran into her next words. "Can you go tonight?"

"Tonight?"

"If for no other reason, go for me. The urgency is driving me crazy." She flashed him a look that had taken their entire marriage to perfect.

"Oh, now, Jen... that's not fair." He groaned. "Don't give me the... Jen, that's not fair..."

Tov started to dance, across the kitchen, around the table, hands over his head. Laughing, he thought of the crazy old woman announcing that it was time to sing. Well, he thought, now it was time to dance. He worked out his glee before putting a hand on each of their shoulders.

"Tonight?" Carl asked again.

"I wouldn't be able to resist it either," Tov said, looking into Jen's face.

Carl sighed, wrapped his arms around her.

"Yes!" Tov pumped his arm.

"I'll have supper ready in a jiff," Jen told him, turning to the bags.

"I was going to cut the lawn."

"You have time." She unpacked, throwing him a kiss to keep him on board.

"Who's supposed to be helping you tonight?"

"Tina, I think"

Carl went to the hallway. "Tina!"

A door opened. "What!"

"Your turn to help with supper!"

The door slammed and a skinny girl walked into the kitchen, orange hair cut so short it stood up. A trail of earrings ran up her ears onto her eyebrows and into her nose that Tov hadn't been in the mood to look at when she'd come home. But he was noticing now. Curious, he went to gawk.

"Hi you," Jen said. "Have a good day?"

"Okay. How about yours?" She leaned into Jen, inches from her face.

"You're the nosy one, aren't you?"

"Where is she?" Tina asked.

"In her bedroom, exercising her right to privacy."

"She better than us?"

"Yup." Jen squeezed Tina's cheeks. "You've got to stop walking into those," Jen warned.

Tov flew to Kelly's bedroom, found her sitting on the floor, back against the bed, the curtains open. Other than the chatter in the kitchen and the bang of pots, the room was peaceful in the coming dusk. She was crying, but not really—crying without noise. Tears dribbled, held her chin, dropped onto her new shirt. Tov watched the stains spread on the fabric. He sat beside her and turned his head to the window, listening to the sounds of dinner being prepared in the calm before her storm.

◊

The angel grew antsy, waiting through the meal and the cleanup, following Carl the way Stewart usually followed after him. Even Stewart had grown tired and had long since found a corner in the living room to lie with one eye open, sensing Tov's growing tension. Eventually Carl left, saying goodbye to Jen, Stewart visibly upset at being left behind again. He stood on his hind legs and watched them through the window on the porch door.

It was hard for Tov to follow Carl at his human pace, fiddling with keys, buckling his seatbelt, playing with the mirrors.

"Okay…" Tov sang, his voice rising and falling.

It was almost dark by the time they pulled into the police station and walked through the front doors where Carl took a chair to wait. The angel paced, keeping an eye on the organized anarchy until someone got off the phone and waved him over.

"Hi Carl, how's it going?" the officer asked. The man was as tall as Carl, younger, wider around the belt. They shook hands.

"Jerry," Carl said heartily. "Where the heck have you been?"

"Took some time at another precinct. Needed a break. This downtown one gets a little hairy."

"Where did you go?"

Tov paced, talking to himself, drowning out the senseless conversation.

"Yeah, the wife likes it better when I'm closer to home…" Jerry was explaining. He asked about Jen, the house, how many kids they had.

"This is your cue, Carl," Tov said. "You're here because…" He drew out the last word long before he spoke right into Carl's face.

"We have a new one I need to check out."

"A runaway file?" Jerry asked.

"Yeah, a runner. Jen is adamant we find her mom, has this feeling in her gut." Carl shrugged. "Don't have much, just a first name and date of her disappearance."

"No surname?"

"She won't give it."

"Okay." Jerry rolled his chair to the computer. "Give me the date." Carl told him and he punched it in. "It wouldn't be entered for twenty-four hours after she left, so we look at the next day." Carl and Tov leaned to peer at the screen. Jerry wasn't typing fast, lacking a little needed concern. "We have eleven. Female?"

Carl nodded. Jerry typed. "Eight female. First name?"

"Kelly," Tov said.

"Kelly," Carl told him.

Jerry punched it out with one finger. "We have Arliss…" Reading under his breath he was scrolling files "…Cheryl…Kerri…" he said louder. "Nope. No Kelly."

"Check a later date then," Carl said. "Maybe it wasn't called in right away."

Jerry fiddled, changed dates and screens, took them through a week's worth of files. "I do have a Kelly. Kelly Whitcomb." He leaned closer. "Kelly Whitcomb," he verified.

Tov and Carl bent over him. "Do you have a picture?" Carl asked.

Jerry poked the keyboard and a picture of Kelly popped up. "That her?"

"Yes."

Jerry shrugged, typed more. "You of all people know I'm not supposed to do this, but here's the address and phone number. Her mom called in the report." Jerry turned. "How did you end up with her?"

"We found her in pretty bad shape in an alley. Funny thing, a dog showed up and led us to her."

"She took her dog with her when she ran?"

"It's not her dog. We can't figure out who it belongs to."

Jerry wasn't buying. "Some stray led you to her?"

Carl nodded. "We're hoping no one shows to claim him. He's kind of found his place in our house. Big dog. *Huge* dog. He decided we were his home, and we didn't argue."

"The word is out that you'll take in anyone, hey?" Jerry laughed, snorting.

"Guess so. How do you want to handle this?" Carl asked. "I get the feeling Jen would like to be first contact."

"We would still make the initial phone call to…"—Jerry stopped and squinted at the screen—"… Ellen Whitcomb, to let her know we found her daughter. Just a minute. There's a note here at the bottom…" He kept reading. "You won't get her at home, though. It says here that Ellen is in the hospital. If Kelly is found, it's urgent that we contact a Pat Ramer at this number." He took a pad and wrote it out. "Tell you what. You give this Pat a call and let her know that you have Kelly."

"Does it say what the problem is?"

"Just says urgent." Jerry checked again.

"Jen was right," Carl muttered. "Amazing instincts, that one."

Tov stepped back, words in his heart too tender to utter, feeling the release of tremendous weight as Jerry and Carl talked. All he had to do now was watch it unfold. He had come full circle, feeling so insignificantly small as Kelly's story played out to the only ending he could ever envision. Tov hovered behind Carl as they left the station, jumped into the van beside him, debated rushing back to be with Kelly before her world came apart. But once he was inside the van he was at ease, content to sit beside this man who was being carried along by heavenly events, a link in the chain of Ellen's prayers. It was surreal, to be moving on this path fashioned by her petitions, to be here after remembering the day he came to find her on her knees.

Carl drove, oblivious to the dominoes he would set tumbling when he delivered the news, his face yet blissfully unaware. "Two totally separate worlds," Tov muttered. He put his arm across the back of Carl's seat, resting his hand on the man's shoulder.

Carl looked beside him, right through Tov for as long as he dared keep his eyes from the road, searching the emptiness for the presence he swore he could feel.

"Yes," Tov said, "I am here. We are in this together." He patted Carl, put his attention to the scenery that would soon exist only in memory.

Chapter Twenty-Five

Carl turned off the engine and lights but sat, leaning on the steering wheel, observing the house.

"What?" Tov asked, his head through the window. "What is it?" He lined up with Carl, taking the vantage point of the driver's seat. A glow radiated from inside the home, filtering through the curtains. "It's heaven on earth, isn't it?" Tov asked, feeling the pull of it. He was not surprised to see Carl searching the space beside him again, trying to alleviate the feeling that he was not alone. "I'm still here," Tov told him. The angel's senses were soaring. Nothing in him was as still and peaceful as the man beside him.

Carl jingled keys up the walk and peered into the window before opening the door. Tov had been in and out twice already, alerting the dog.

"Now I know why they need doggie psychiatrists," Carl mumbled, ruffling the dog's fur on his way to the kitchen, not bothering to look at the ceiling that held Stewart's focus. The dog paid no attention to him when he came in.

"I'm so sorry." Tov knelt in front of his friend. "They think you're nuts because of me." He reached, hopeful, but his hand passed through the hairy head Carl had absently patted. "If it's any consolation, I don't think you're nuts. You're remarkable."

Carl was in the kitchen, looking out a dark window above the sink, arms stretched along the counter.

"How am I going to find the words to explain you when I get home?" Tov asked the dog. "I don't know if this is goodbye."

A door opened quietly down the hall. The situation didn't seem real. He had played it out so many times, like a book already read, but the humans were in the process of slowly turning pages.

Jen appeared and walked by him to the counter. "I thought I heard you come in," she whispered.

"Did Stewart, the living doorbell, give me away?" Carl pulled her close.

"So?"

"You were right. Something's wrong."

"What is it?"

"I talked to Jerry and got the information."

"What's the problem? What kind of trouble is she in?"

"Kelly's not in trouble. Her mom is in the hospital. Jerry gave me the number of a family friend who said the situation was urgent."

Jen stood back. "We don't know what it is?"

"No. I'm thinking we should call this family friend and get the story before we talk to Kelly."

Carl pulled the paper from his pocket and Jen read it aloud. "Kelly Whitcomb..." She looked at Carl. "Whitcomb. The secret of the century is Whitcomb?" She folded it in half. "Do you want me to call?"

"I think so. Pat Ramer sounds like a woman."

Tov was numb.

Jen checked her watch. "Do you think it's too late to call?"

"Probably. But urgent means it doesn't matter, right?"

"If it were my daughter, or the daughter of a close friend, I'd hope someone would call me out of bed."

Sadness penetrated the angel, drowned the warmth of the house in the inevitable.

"I think we should call tonight," Carl said. "You've been right so far."

Jen studied the name again. "We should phone from your study."

They walked through Tov, down the hall and up the stairs to the study, the sound of the door closing gently clicking against the ceiling. Tov looked at Stewart.

"This is it." He sighed. "This is it." He didn't fly directly upward, but walked as Carl and Jen had done, memorizing the tapestry runner on the old wood floor, the curve of the banister. Tov put his hand out, pretending to rest it on the dog as they climbed. Walking into the final chapter and pages of his mission, he had no means of measuring the comfort he had gained from the dog. The loyal steps beside him kept him moving. The provision of heaven that this animal had been was going to be hard to leave behind. They reached the study door and Tov stopped on the other side.

Stewart knew the drill. If he wanted in, he would have to knock.

"All right... all right..." Jen got up from the desk as the scratching started. "You can't stand to be left out of anything, can you?"

The dog checked the room before curling up at Tov's feet.

This was the moment. It was here. Every prayer Tov held flowed serene. He released them, one final offering on Ellen's behalf. "Your will be done," he said.

Jen dialled and sat back, counting rings, prepared to give up if the call was too late.

"Hello." It was a man.

Jen looked at the paper. "Is Pat Ramer there?"

"Yes, she is. Who's calling?"

"My name is Jennis Croft."

"What is it regarding?"

"Kelly Whitcomb."

The phone went quiet. "Just a minute..." She heard him put the phone down. She looked at Carl, who left his place by the bookshelf to lean on the desk.

Someone picked up the phone, breathing quickly. "This is Pat Ramer."

"My name is Jennis Croft. My husband Carl and I run a group home for street kids. We got your name and number from a constable at our precinct." Jen paused. "We have Kelly here with us."

There was a sharp intake of breath. The man and woman were talking in the background. "Is she okay?" Pat asked.

"She's not in good shape, but she'll recover."

219

Pat was quiet. "What happened?"

"She met up with the wrong people. As far as we can see, it's nothing serious. We had her checked at the clinic."

"How long has she been with you?"

"Two days."

Pat relayed the information, crying, and handed the phone off.

"I'm James Ramer, Pat's husband. This is a little hard. We're good friends with Ellen and Kelly. You have no idea what it means to hear from you."

"I think I do, believe me. I'm sorry it took us a while to get in touch with you. Kelly didn't want us to make contact with her mom. She's shaken up. Ellen, that's her mom's name, isn't it?"

"Yes."

"You have news of her mom?"

"I'm their family doctor."

"The message said urgent."

James was struggling. "Yes. And no. It may be too late."

"I don't understand."

"Ellen is in a coma. She's alive, but non-responsive."

Jen's face paled.

"What is it?" Carl asked.

"She's in a coma, Carl. She won't even know." Jen remembered the phone, put it back to her ear. "What happened?"

"A tumor in her brain, malignant, very invasive and fast-growing. It would have been difficult to treat even if we had caught it earlier. We didn't even have time to do tests before she slipped away. She ignored the symptoms until the pain was too much. The stress of Kelly leaving probably accelerated the process somewhat."

Jen closed her eyes, hand to her face, her mind emptying. She tried to think. "Are they close, Kelly and her mom?"

"In spite of the difficulties they've been through, I would say yes. Ellen's been single parenting. She lost her husband nine years ago in a car accident."

"Yes, I know."

"Kelly mentioned that?" James asked, surprised.

"Not voluntarily."

"It was hard for them. Ellen had her faith to get her through." He paused and added, "Kelly had her anger."

"Yes, I know that too." There was a lull. Jen took a breath, which amplified into the receiver.

"I know there's no easy way to do this," James reassured. "I would recommend we don't wait. Ellen is holding her own day to day." There was the tiniest break in his voice. "Pat thinks she is holding on for Kelly."

"Would you believe me if I told you I have never had such a strong compulsion to contact a parent before?"

"Well," James said, "I don't know where you stand on the issue of prayer, but Kelly is covered under a mountain of them."

"That's obvious. You should hear her story."

"Can you bring her to the hospital? Pat and I will meet you there."

"We have to tell her first." Jen rubbed her forehead. "We have to tell her."

"Of course. I'm sorry you have to do that." Pat was talking to him in the background. "Phone us when you leave."

"Which hospital?" She picked up a pen.

To Tov, Jen was speaking from a great distance as she hung up and repeated the news to Carl. The angel was observing Stewart, curled at his feet. He closed his eyes, blinking hard. Stewart was studying him. The dog was an extension of his psyche, a sponge for his emotions.

Jen and Carl hugged. "Okay," she said, pushing him away, wiping her cheeks with the back of her hand. They stood in the open doorway, coaxing Stewart to follow, waiting patiently as the dog gazed at the ceiling for orders.

"Come on then," Tov said. "You should be there for her."

With merely a thought, Tov disappeared through the floor and he was in Kelly's room. She was lying on top of the comforter in the dark, fully dressed. He flew to the bed to find her eyes open, the moon throwing its silver light across her face through the window. Kelly was serene, her face reflecting the moonbeams that had traveled the sky to find her. Her hands were wrapped around her shoulders, her knees pulled up to her chest.

Tov heard footsteps on the stairs. He put his hand on her cheek and felt it warm instantly. Peace washed over her, the extra measure he knew she would need. Her world was going to crumble, and his world was going to fall perfectly into place. The presence of the Spirit spanned the precipice that had divided them, and they were united, finally, giving the room where they waited the same aura of holiness that had filled Ellen's living room a memory ago. Tov took every prayer, every blessing and wish of faith he had for her and bound Kelly tight, the business of the heavenly messenger concluding in the dimmest moment of his existence. And he thought of home, so close, pulling at him. A thread took hold of his insides.

The footsteps stopped outside. Lifting his hand from Kelly, he backed away from the bed, floated to the ceiling to hover in the corner.

Kelly turned her face from the window at the knock. "Come in."

Stewart was first, searching for Tov, stopping below the ceiling where the angel waited. "Go," Tov said, pointing to the bed. "She needs you." He motioned with his hand until Kelly patted the comforter, and the dog didn't need more invitation than that. He hopped up almost on top of her and snuggled against her stomach. Tov stayed for as long as it took his memory to snap a picture of the two of them together on the bed, the moon covering them just as he had done with prayer. This was the picture he wanted when he would remember.

"Goodbye," he whispered. He saw Stewart through blurry eyes, furry face upturned, eyes imploring. Tov tried to fly straight and steady, but his heart would not allow it. He stopped at the long, mournful howl rising behind him and gave himself permission to expend his own sorrow. In answer to his special friend he cried out, then disappeared along the pull of the thread.

◊

Jen sat down beside Stewart as the dog rose suddenly in distress, howling. It was heart-wrenching, prophetic, invisible fingers tickling the length of her body. She looked at Carl, amazed. He was stroking Stewart from behind, attempting to calm him.

Kelly sat up. "What is it?" She cupped the dog's head in her hands, inches from his nose. "What happened?"

"I…" Jen started… "don't know."

"Are you hurt?" Kelly put her head on the dog and closed her eyes. "It's okay," she soothed. "It's okay, boy."

Kelly consoled while Jen's heart sunk under the news that lingered there. The time was right. Unexplainably, there was expectancy in the air. She felt Carl's hand on her shoulder, her heart slammed inside her, yet she had a peace she could not justify given her mission.

"Kelly, we have news about your mom."

Kelly kept her hands on Stewart. Her eyes hardened. "I told you I didn't want to talk to her."

"I know. I didn't betray your trust," Jen tried to explain.

"Does she know where I am?"

"No. I didn't actually talk to her. I talked to James Ramer, your doctor."

She had Kelly's attention.

"What for?"

"We went to the police station to check if there was a missing person's file on you, and there was an urgent message to get in touch with Pat Ramer," Jen told her.

"What happened?" Kelly let go of the dog.

"Your mom is in the hospital, Kelly. James said that she is in a coma. There isn't much hope that she will come out of it."

Kelly's breath stopped, her body went rigid. "What do you mean?"

"It is a brain tumor that she waited too long to have checked. The pain was finally too much. There wasn't even time for tests." Jen gave Kelly time to absorb.

"She's been having headaches for a long time now." Kelly was speaking through her hand. "She hasn't been herself." Tears flowed. "She's been saying funny things, doing funny things." Every breath was fighting to get out. "I didn't know. How was I supposed to know?"

Tears started for Jen when she felt Carl's hand rubbing her back, encouraging her, making her strong. They stayed that way for a long while. Jen grabbed a handful of tissues, taking some herself and pushing the rest into the hand that stuck out from the end of Kelly's cast while Stewart, quiet now, took the tears that dripped from Kelly's chin onto his head. There was no way to settle the room, to go back to the seconds of normalcy, breathing without grief, thinking without the ache of truth. This was the funeral, the dirge of lament, the moment of the utmost fragility.

Carl spoke. "James said we have no way of determining how much she is aware of."

"You don't understand." Kelly's voice jerked in stops and starts. "I told her I hated her." She spoke again, louder. "I told her I hated her." She started to rock. "I said things just to hurt her. I wanted to hit her."

Stewart sat up.

"I hurt her so bad... I did this to her..."

Jen was trying to hold her, to take her in her arms. Kelly was inconsolable.

"Go away!" she yelled. "Get out! Don't touch me!" She pushed at Jen, who turned to Carl, motioning for them to leave.

"No," Jen whispered, "I can't leave her..." Jen listened to the gut-wrenching sounds, worried about Kelly furiously rocking off the bed. Jen's nose and eyes were gushing when she turned to Carl again. He took her by the arm, pulling her out into the hall.

Tina, Rob, and Carlos were waiting in wrinkled pyjamas, hair at odds. Carl put his finger up while he closed the door. Jen fell against the wall.

"What's going on?" Rob asked.

"We're going to have to take Kelly to the hospital to see her mom." He tried to speak quietly, but had to raise his voice over Kelly's. "Her mom is dying."

The kids were silent, touched through the walls by Kelly's agony. "We'll keep an eye on things here. Don't worry," Rob said.

Carl hugged him. "I know. Thanks guys." They were all at a loss now. "I'll make some coffee. We're going to have to be ready to go when she is."

Jen shook her head, listening to Kelly working out her grief. "I think I'll stay right here," she whispered.

◊

Stewart lay drenched, patiently answering every tear, every cry of her nightmare, touching his nose to her cheek, never letting her forget he was there.

Kelly's face hurt. Her healing cuts stung from the salt. Everything above her neck pounded, one gigantic headache, and she went quiet to ease the pain. But the one in her heart wouldn't stop. She prayed hard, as if praying that way would grant her answers, to trade places with Momma, to die. Reality hit her in bursts.

"Please... please..." Fatigue took her throat and hushed it. Cycles of guilt and remorse ran marathons in her, the finish line unattainable, the running unstoppable. This was her life now, reality and despair, praying in her belief and unbelief. She could do it no more, wearing herself down to the sharpest point where her only need was to see Momma. She tried to call up pictures in her mind, but the only portrait she could conjure was Momma with her hands in front of her face as Kelly poured out her hatred. As hard as she tried, she could not picture her any other way. She stood up, hoping to leave the picture on the pillow, yet out the window the silhouette of the trees was a backdrop for that face lost to her behind hands.

"Oh God..." she pleaded, "...Oh God..."

◊

Jen was startled by the sound of the doorknob. She stood quickly, dazed from semi-sleep. Kelly's face, red and puffy, peeked through the crack. "I want to see her," Kelly said.

Jen stood from her squat, held out her arms and Kelly stepped into them, resting her head on the offered shoulder. Almost too tired to move, they made their way to the kitchen to find Carl sitting in front of a mug of cold coffee.

"Ready?" he asked.

Jen walked Kelly to a chair and sat her down, Stewart glued to her side, while Carl and Jen made quiet preparations, slow-motion gestures of donning coats, finding keys, making phone calls, writing notes, and waking Rob before slipping away into the hushed darkness.

Chapter Twenty-Six

It was impossible to concentrate. Pictures of Ellen flickered on Tov's eyelids every time he blinked, skirting the periphery of the earthly scenes he was so tritely trying to absorb, still frames of her lifeless body lying on the bed imprinted on the street and sides of buildings.

He reverently slowed his pace. He would be home soon, and he would be taking Ellen with him. He was stuck in the cobwebs of their first meeting in his mind, wondering if all his missions now would be as complicated as this one, if his days of simply escorting were over. His job had become much more mysterious and tangled than it had been when he was sent to get Ben Whitcomb out of his car.

Then his thoughts would find Stewart. Again. He didn't have to hazard a guess that the dog would forever show up in his mind at odd moments. He could not come to terms with how affected he was by the animal. He remembered the fur in his fingers, the warm, sloppy tongue. He chuckled at the Stewart he loved most of all—ears at attention, waiting and almost beside himself, intent for instructions. Tov had never, in all his travels, expected to find love like that here. He was upsetting himself now. In what seemed to be his previous life, he would have been enraptured with the privilege of what he was about to do, the thrill of seeing eternity for the first time through another's eyes. Yet emotions plagued him, and he was irked to be feeling anxious when he was finally following his heart and going to be with Ellen.

"How do you do it?" he said aloud, lifting his hands to the few souls braving the night, talking to those hiding behind walls and drawn curtains in sleep. "How do you?" he asked, louder than he intended to the windows that watched him pass like moving eyes on a painting. "How do you find your way through all these feelings?" he shouted.

Fingers of guilt poked him. Kelly was probably on this same route now, on her way to Ellen. He had chosen not to be there when she was told, justifying the inadequacy to deal with his tender heart because she had Jen and Carl, and of course, Stewart. He had left her in a moment of his weakness, not knowing if he could watch her fall apart. There was going to be enough of that ahead of him.

He didn't need the thread to pull him on. Approaching the hospital, he stopped at a distance as it twinkled in the dark, cloaked under the blanket of night, resting from the numbers of people that filled it by day. It felt peaceful, prepared for his coming, winked at him in the shared knowledge of his mission.

He covered the distance quickly and slowed at the electric doors. Through the glass he could see the waiting room deserted for all but a few people and the token front desk staff. He hovered past unseeing eyes, through whispering voices. Floating as if he were the air in the room, he coasted to the ceiling as uniformed bodies walked quietly and nurses congregated at desks, talking in subdues voices. Somewhere a phone was ringing. He moved upward through the hallways before turning right. Unhurried, calm, he made his way to the second-last door.

A light shone behind the drawn curtain. He moved into the illuminated circle and stopped at the end of the bed. Ellen was resting so unnaturally on the pillow he had to catch his breath, unable to match the face he had ministered to in the living room to the one he was looking at now. Yet there was peace. Nothing he could feel within the confines of the room, or even from Ellen herself, suggested distress or pain. He quietly watched the faintest movement of her chest through the wrinkled blanket, visible only because lamp light and shadow played across her body.

"You're still waiting." He put his hand on her and was instantly pulled to where she was, through the dark portal of her impending passing. He could see a faint ray of brightness, the very same light that existed in him. It was keeping her safe, holding her to this bed so she could not yet leave. Not yet. "It won't be long," he reassured her. It started to flicker. Life was fighting to stay, grasping to hold something that no longer existed. Her will to live was waging battle with the beacon of heaven, the last of the physical a shrinking shadow against what was to come.

"Don't be afraid," he told her, over and over, speaking into the stream that kindled her soul. He spoke until the flickering stopped. Tov stood beside the radiance that was now Ellen. "She's coming," he said. "It won't be long now. She's coming."

He closed his eyes and released his own glow into the stream of her brilliance. He penetrated it, letting loose all the energy he had, shimmering alongside Ellen to give her the extra strength she needed. He cleared his mind of everything but holding her to this place. In the presence of the transforming Ellen, he was preparing them both for Kelly's arrival.

◊

James and Pat were standing inside the front doors of the hospital lobby. Every headlight that moved in the parking lot pulled them forward, and with every set that left without dropping off Kelly, James squeezed Pat's arm.

"They're coming from downtown. It will take a little longer," he said. She couldn't believe how calm he sounded. The only way he could stop her from shaking was to touch her, to remind her he was close.

"I can't help it," she apologized. "I have to see her with my own eyes..." She glanced at him and back out the window. "I have to be here for her..." She knew the role they had to play, the buffer they would be for Kelly. As a doctor, many times James had been the portal for people to walk through emotionally before facing death. It was not new to him. For Pat, it was something she'd always prayed she would never have to do. Now she had to be that for two people who owned pieces of her heart.

Heaven and earth passed before a van pulled up. Three people formed out of the night and took shape in the entranceway. The doors slid open, Kelly walking inside the arm of a woman, a man close against her on the other side.

Pat gasped, holding out her arms the second they were in the door. Kelly looked up, eyes flooding, reaching. They came together, awake again to the fresh truth of this awful new existence that was now theirs. Pain lay raw between them and they held each other, trading the strength to stand. Carl and Jen stood apart, no awkwardness with their presence, Jen wiping her eyes with her sleeve. Catching the motion, James looked over and held out his hand.

"I'm so glad to meet you," James said.

They spoke introductions quietly.

Pat lifted her head. "Thank you so much." She made the effort, but could not let the words go, her cheek on Kelly's head. "How can we thank you?"

"Don't think about it," Carl answered. "We're not about to take credit for divine appointments."

Pat pushed Kelly to the length of her arms, ran her finger over the stitches and cuts, then put her hand on the cast. "What happened?"

Awkward, Kelly turned to Jen, the seasoned rescuer.

"It's a long story," Jen offered. "I haven't even heard it all yet."

"Where's Momma?" Kelly asked.

"How much do you know, Kelly?" James, the doctor, was taking over.

"She's in a coma. She might not know I'm here."

"I have to be honest with you. She's not going to come out of it. She will never wake up." James gave her a minute. "She looks different."

Kelly was quick. "How?"

"She's lost weight, her face has changed. Her body is barely functioning." He hesitated. "We think she's waiting."

"For me?" Kelly's chin quivered.

"We think so dear," Pat said.

"When I come, will she die?"

"She's already dying," James said softly. "It's just a matter of time."

Kelly's breath was coming quick and shallow. "Can I see her?"

Pat looked at James, thankful for the strength that emanated from him, the self-appointed protector of all. "I'll take you," he said, giving Pat a look she had no trouble reading.

"We'll wait for you down here." Pat shepherded Jen and Carl to a circle of chairs. "I think a cup of coffee and a talk would be our best medicine." She regarded the bone-weary strangers. "Well, for me anyway."

Pat walked with Jen and Carl, but her head was turned. James had his arm around Kelly, the way he had held Pat inside his safe harbour only moments ago. His mouth was moving. Bent toward Kelly, he was speaking quietly into her ear. The elevator dinged, the door opened, and they stepped out of her sight.

"The least I can do is buy you a cup of coffee," Pat said, and again to herself. "The very least I can do…"

◊

Aware of someone entering the room, Tov flew from the place where he waited with Ellen and skittered back to the bed. He heard sniffling. "Kelly," he whispered. He thought he was prepared, but by the jittery reaction of his body he knew he was not. "She's here," he breathed to Ellen. "She's here…" he said to himself. She's here. He was facing the curtain. Two pairs of feet approached. He saw a man first, and then Kelly barely walking in the crook of his arm. Anguish almost crushed him as Kelly dug her face into the man's chest.

"Do you want to be alone with her?"

Kelly nodded, moving his shirt up and down with her forehead.

"I'll be outside the door. I'll get a chair and sit right outside. If you need me, I will be right here…" They moved apart. He took her to the end of his arms.

She nodded.

The man wiped her cheeks with a Kleenex he picked up from the bed table. Tov heard him kick the stopper from the door and the soft nighttime hallway noises disappeared behind it.

Kelly was limp, trying to focus through eyes rimmed with tears. Grief for this goodbye suffocated any gratitude Tov felt for Ellen's answered prayer. There was nothing in heaven or on earth or in eternity but the three of them in this room facing unalterable reality.

She came to the side of the bed and looked into Ellen's face, touched her cheek so lightly that her momma's skin was but a tickle of air under her fingers. Her chest began to heave.

"I'm sorry, Momma." Her head dropped to Ellen's chest. "I'm so sorry, Momma!" she cried, trembling. Words jumped from her mouth in uneven blasts, jerking her head. "Can you hear me?"

Even as he reached for her, Tov knew consolation would find no footing for Kelly. Regret held Ellen's daughter as tightly as Ellen would have herself. There was no means of easing the girl's agony, yet he moved to stand with Kelly as he had done for Ellen seconds ago. It was as close as he could get, a bystander, given to listen as Kelly plunged the depths of her remorse, endured the bed of blistering coals that were her mistakes. They filled her now as the angel longed to do, so fully that he could not split her contrition and find a way in.

This was the meeting he had prayed for, the one he had dreamed so often in uncountable wary moments. He had longed for it, not once suspecting he was not strong enough for it. Grief and sublime tenderness fractured him. He was balancing atop the blade of a large knife, the sharpest point that could be ground, his feet resting on the tip. Sorrow pressed down on him, caught him between one of the greatest loves that his Master had ever created. One hand on Ellen, the other on Kelly, the intensity of love between mother and child was a force that displaced his mighty power, bigger than anything Tov had ever felt. And on top of that rested a love even greater still. The Creator's love for them both, more compelling than the splendour of heaven, more painful than the angel could conceive. He held tight, joining them, the closest coming together they could ever be now on earth. Heat ran his arms and poured into his hands. It was Ellen. He bent to her face, felt the pull, and could not stay where he was.

Light consumed his eyes. He stood beside her, and for the first time Ellen looked upon him as he appeared, turning the head of her perfect, radiant body. They were connected in the knowledge of their presence, with the ability to communicate now where they waited. Tov took in her smile, the one he remembered that so amazingly fit her face.

"She's here," he told her.

Ellen's face was surprise, and acceptance, even anticipation for the long-awaited show that the curtain was rising on. "She's here?"

"Yes."

She looked almost afraid to speak. "Kelly?"

The angel nodded.

"Is she coming with us?"

"No."

"Is she okay?"

"Yes."

Ellen's smile quivered. "She's okay," she whispered. She held her arm out to Tov.

"No, not yet," he said, clasping his hands together in promise.

She shook her head, raised her brows, her face expectant.

"Can you wait a little while longer?" he asked.

"For Kelly?"

Tov nodded. She now knew. He had moved heaven and earth it seemed to make this come to pass.

"Yes," Ellen said. "Oh…" She covered her cheeks with her hands.

◊

James was pacing. It was hard to sit, harder to listen. He did sneak away once when the room went quiet, but walked no further than the coffee machine down the hallway. From a distance he could see the speck of Pat coming to check on them. Again.

"Should we go in now?" she asked.

James shook his head. "I don't see how we can help her, as much as I want to. She has to do this her own way. She'll carry this time with her for the rest of her life." He examined the floor, then Pat. "We have to be careful how we handle this. I think the wisest is to let her speak to Ellen without an audience, let her get everything out that's on her heart."

Pat's maternal instincts told her otherwise, but in her quiet conscience she knew James was right. Kelly did not need comfort now. She needed to deal with her guilt, the consequences of her actions, the impending death of her mother. She looked at James' eyes. It was all in his eyes. Not just strength, but wisdom. She could not love him more.

"What?" he asked.

She realized she had been staring and merely smiled her private thoughts. "Jen and Carl went home for a bit. They're going to try and get a bit of sleep and come back later." Through the bottom of the door, they could hear Kelly, crying and talking muffled by blankets. They held each other in their own helpless grief.

"You can have the chair. I can't sit anymore." He gave her a quick massage on her shoulders, and by the time she had fished a tissue from her purse and seated herself, James was pacing again in slow, methodical steps.

"What now?" she asked.

"I'm sure we've had the same thoughts."

"We told Ellen we would take Kelly if anything happened," Pat said.

James stopped. "And?"

"Carl and Jen have offered to take her." Pat was looking into her lap. "I hate talking like this, like she's already gone."

"We don't know them at all. Neither does Kelly."

"She knows them better than we do. Wouldn't it be her decision?"

"How can you even think of going back on our promise? Why would you even ask her? I can't see making any decisions like that in the face of what she's dealing with."

Pat shook her head. "I'm sorry. This is not the time." There didn't seem a time for anything anymore.

◊

The sun found its way down the stretch of gleaming hospital floor. James monitored the changing sky at every pass of the window and checked his watch. Six-thirty. He had been up all night. Pat's head was stuck to the wall behind the chair, hands open in her lap. He was thankful she was dozing. There had been no noise from the room for about an hour and he was thinking it was time.

"Pat," he whispered. He ran his hand up and down her arm. "Pat…"

It took her a moment to work the kink from her neck, the grogginess from her mind. She sat to attention, remembering where she was. "What happened?"

"I haven't heard anything for about an hour. Maybe we should go in."

Pat was on her feet, taking his arm after rising so suddenly. James opened the door and they crossed the room, stopping at the curtain.

Kelly was asleep, her breathing steady. Shoes kicked to the floor, she was cuddled into Ellen's side with an arm around her, her red, swollen face sticking out from the pillow. Pat threw a worried look at James. He motioned to be quiet and went to the bed, putting his finger on Ellen's neck, and Pat let go of her breath when he took the spare blanket from the chair and tucked them both in before they left again.

Chapter Twenty-Seven

J ames called his part-time receptionist and asked her to cancel his appointments, then spent some time trying to find someone to take his rounds. He took Pat to the cafeteria and bought them a big breakfast, putting in a good effort to linger over coffee, chatting through a pretend rest, but they eventually gave up the pretence and took their coffee with them.

Kelly was still sleeping when they returned. A lounge at the end of the hallway offered them a view of the floor, allowing them to see anyone at Ellen's door. They sat inside the cluster of chairs and talked, inspired by the sudden appearance of Kelly, confidences and issues finding their way into the open as the precipice their lives balanced on became more precarious. They needed to find their way across it, holding Kelly.

Ellen's estate was in order—handling everything to do with the will would be the easiest hurdle to jump. According to Ellen's wishes, James and Pat had agreed to take Kelly until she turned eighteen, or longer if needed. But Kelly had been a young girl when that decision was made. Much had changed. It was clear that neither of them would even consider going back on their promise, but the situation was more complicated now that Jen and Carl had offered to help. They discussed memories of having a teenager around, not the least bit naïve of how it would alter their empty nest. Kelly was living in rebellion, as one of theirs had done, and they had no way of guessing if Ellen's death would trigger Kelly's anger even further. It was a challenge even when Ellen had sought them for advice and a sympathetic shoulder after she was widowed and Kelly began to find her own defiant feet. For their friend, they needed to come up with a plan to fulfill their promise.

Pat told James as much of Kelly's story as she had heard from Jennis. He sat with his head lowered, clenched his jaw often. "We don't know if she was raped?" he asked calmly.

"Jen says Kelly doesn't know."

"Time won't change the results if she was. I don't think this is an appropriate time for a physical, but it needs to be done."

"For what's she's been through, I don't think she could have ended up at a better place than Carl and Jen's." Pat treaded softly, eyes on her coffee. "Jen shared with me how they came to have their home for street kids. She was beaten and raped herself when she was sixteen. It left her unable to have a family. Her heart belongs to the kids who live with that type of violence all the time." She raised her eyes. "She has a real passion for them. She really does." Pat halted her monologue, watching James wrestling with where she was headed. "They know what they are doing," she said softly. It was so hard to stand up to his confidence.

"We have experience, with our own kids," he said.

Pat read him. There was no job he could not do. Proud, stubborn, up to any challenge. "Bring it on" was his motto. It's what made him a good doctor. "Yes, we do," she agreed, "but they have experience with everybody else's."

He put his cup down. "What are you saying, Pat?"

"I'm saying I don't think Kelly ended up there by accident. I don't have any idea what it would be like to go through the horror of what Kelly has been through. Do you?" She waited on him.

"Are you saying you think Kelly should go with them?"

"Not go with them, but let them help. I feel like you James, that it's somehow letting Ellen down. But things have changed. Kelly is not a little girl anymore. Ben's death devastated her. Even Ellen had difficulty helping her cope with it. Kelly is very sensitive and I think we have to consider that she is going to need all the help she can get to get through this. And I'm not just talking about Ellen's death, but what she's just been through as well.

"Did you see her, James? She's is in as bad a shape inside as she is outside. If she doesn't get some proper help, a lot of her emotional wounds will stay." Pat was aware of how hard she was prodding. She didn't do it often with James, but when she did he took note to listen. "I think she needs more than what we can give her. I know what we promised Ellen. We promised to look after Kelly. We just have to figure out the *best* way to do that."

James unclasped his hands, rubbed his palms together. "They may be able to help her come to terms with what happened to her since she ran away," he said, "but I think we are still the best ones to help her deal with Ellen's death."

"I agree," she said, louder than intended. "I agree with that. It's not like this is a custody fight. Kelly will have the best of both. Carl and Jen, and us. Whatever she needs..." Pat had to stop, tell herself what was happening was real. "I can't even imagine being in Kelly's place right now. I can't get my mind anywhere near there."

James was studying his hands. "Okay... I get it. I have a hard time seeing this from Kelly's perspective."

"You're a doctor, James. You want to fix everyone and everything. Sometimes people just can't be fixed the way you think they should. We might not be enough for Kelly right now. Can you live with the idea that maybe somebody else can help?"

She understood him so well. It was uncomfortable for him when she took him apart this way, understanding where he was coming from far better than he did himself sometimes. She was a perfect balance for the other end of his scale, his perfect complement. After Ben had died, the realization of what she had with James gave her a soft spot for Ellen. He had confided to her that he could never figure how one was expected to go through life without the companion who balanced your scale. He had grown tender toward Ellen since she'd lost her equalizer, watching her on the high wire alone.

"Bulls-eye," he said.

"You'll consider it?"

He nodded. "I will."

The elevator door opened, spilling Carl and Jen into the hall searching in all directions. James waved. These strangers had already put their lives on hold for Kelly and had come back again out of concern. It had to figure into the solution. Pat knew James could be proud, but she also knew he was not one to thwart the provision of the Almighty. If a little humility could be a portion of Kelly's prescription, it was a very small price to pay. She thought of Ellen, all the times she had been hanging on the end of her rope in need of help with her daughter.

They would have to consider it.

◊

Carl and James shook hands.

"It was too hard to stay away," Jen confessed, "and we couldn't sleep. How is Kelly doing?"

"She's sleeping." Pat looked to James. "We found her in bed beside Ellen."

Jen steeled her face, her puffy eyes divulging that she had lost all previous battles with tears.

Pat touched her arm. "I know." Her voice quivered.

James motioned to the chairs, but there was no settling. They perched on the edge of their seats. "Did you get a chance to talk to her?" Jen asked.

"We thought it best to leave her alone," James said. "We hope she will be able to deal with her guilt and grief as long as Ellen is still here. She has all the time in the world to talk to us after." He caught Jen's look. "We could hear her through the door," he clarified.

"We hoped that would happen." It was Carl who spoke.

Conversation stalled. Eyes strayed to the carpet.

"Pat was saying you have offered to help... with Kelly."

Carl and Jen acknowledged.

"I… I hate talking like this… but… Pat and I are in charge of the arrangements. Ellen won't live much longer…" James was uncharacteristically reluctant.

"Don't think we don't understand how our being here might be uncomfortable for you," Jen offered. "The circumstances are unusual. We have never been involved in anything quite like this. But the way it has unfolded has left us wanting to help."

James flashed Pat the warning look that he was going to jump in. "I don't know how this is going to sound, but Pat and I know Ellen very well. There is something we have to talk about before this discussion goes any further."

"Okay," Carl said.

"Ellen has tried her best to raise Kelly to have a faith in the Lord. As much as Kelly has rebelled against that, I know it would be Ellen's dying wish that Kelly would continue to be led in that direction."

A smile started on Carl's mouth, jumped chairs to Jen. "We know it was God and the prayers of a godly mother that brought Kelly to us," Jen said. "We were concerned that her healing take place in the light of faith as well. It was part of our motivation for offering. Recovery needs the spiritual as well as the physical… there isn't one of our kids that we don't introduce to Jesus."

James sat back into his chair.

"I feel I can help," Jen said. "I've talked with her. She has such a tender heart, and I can work with that."

"It's her specialty," Carl interjected.

Jen continued. "She reminds me a lot of me."

"She never really got over the death of her father," Pat said. "We were with them through that. I think we need to be here for Kelly now, too, to help her deal with Ellen's… passing…" The word couldn't find her voice. "We will always be her link to Ellen."

"For sure," Carl agreed. "We just know that it was anything but coincidence that bought Kelly to us, and we want to offer what we can do."

"How exactly did you find her?" James asked.

Carl chuckled. "You won't believe it."

"Pat didn't fill me in on this part of the story," James said.

"We didn't get around to it." Jen's head bobbed, wondering how to start.

"This big dog showed up at our house," Carl started.

"Big, *weird* dog," Jen corrected. "Not normal."

"Jen, being Jen, took him in... she never refuses a wayward soul. He stays a couple of days and the kids in the house get used to having him around. He's huge, sensitive, absolutely great with them." Carl looked at his wife. "He seems to know *exactly* what you're feeling."

"Really weird." Jen drew the words out.

"We figure he's here to stay, but one day he takes off. No stopping him. Out the door and gone." Carl shot his hand into the air. "A couple of days later he comes back, adamant that we follow him. He stands at the front door raising a racket, refusing to come in, running up and down the sidewalk... so Jen hops into the van and I follow behind." Carl paused with a new thought for Jen. "Don't you think it's weird that *we* know exactly what *he's* thinking?" Carl squinted. "Anyway, he leads us across town to an alley where we find Kelly huddled behind a dumpster. A big man is holding onto her, and the dog runs up to them like he knows them.

"First we thought it was this man's dog, and then we figure its Kelly's... then the guy disappears before we can ask him anything."

"Weirder," Jen intervened, "is that Stewart just shows up at the apartment where Kelly was staying, just like that, out of the blue. And it's the dog that helps her to get out before the guy who beat her up comes back."

"You're saying a dog that showed up on your doorstep orchestrated this whole thing?" James asked.

Carl shrugged. "Pretty much."

"He sits and stares at the ceiling like he's hearing voices," Jen said. "He's not your normal dog. Nothing about this is normal. It's as if this dog was sent to be her guardian or something. Isn't that what it seems like, Carl?"

"Pretty much," he repeated.

The most natural thing was for Pat to lock eyes with her husband, discussing the conversation between themselves without words, a true test of manners to carry it off without alerting the bearers of such a story to any scepticism. Practice had made perfect. The entire exchange took one half of a second.

"How did you find out about Ellen?" James asked.

"I've never had a conviction so strong about contacting a parent," Jen told him. "The thought came to me the first time I sat down with Kelly... it was so urgent. Kelly had told us the date she'd left and her first name, and we got information from the constable at the police station. He gave us your message about Kelly's mom."

"A guardian dog," Pat mumbled. It didn't make the hair on her neck stand up, but it did arouse intense curiosity, and as uncomfortable as she was with the idea herself, it was at the very least an inroad to get James to consider the option of their help. "We'd love to come and meet your... dog, and see your group home."

"Of course," Carl offered. "You're more than welcome."

"We're a little overwhelmed that you're offering your home and your help for Kelly. When the time comes to make a decision, at least we know we have some options. I think we have to sit down together with her after Ellen is gone and discuss it again." James nodded in Pat's direction. "We're not prepared to make any decisions without Kelly, until we know how she feels about it."

"For sure," Carl agreed. "Absolutely."

"Should we look in on her?" Pat asked.

James checked his watch. "No. Let her sleep."

"She might be awake," Jen said. "If it's okay, I think I'll peek in the door, just to make sure."

◊

Kelly shifted, snuggled deeper into Ellen's side before her eyes blinked open. Tov was standing at the end of the bed, having been there since the sun put an appearance in the room. His mind was silent, his purpose clear. Kelly's face was puffy, little eyes buried deep in marshmallow flesh. When she fully awoke it was as if she'd never rested. She planted her face against Ellen's shoulder and sobbed.

Tov had mingled with her dreams as she slept, feeling her guilt and remorse as she could not take rest and leave of it. She needed forgiveness. Ellen was still here in a sense, but she could no longer offer absolution. The wisdom of heaven needed to impart itself, because he had dissected every angle of the situation and was left with the loose ends. The deep indigo space between heaven and the physical felt like this, a vacuum on his brain. Kelly was the key in releasing him, and something had to happen for Ellen to be released as well. The three of them were bound and he had no idea how to untangle the cords.

"I don't know what to do for you," he confessed. "For all of us, I don't know what to do."

Someone came to the curtain behind him and parted it. He turned to see Jen hesitating, not sure to approach. "Kelly…" she whispered. She heard sniffling. "It's me, Jen." She waited. "Do you need anything?"

Kelly sucked in through a stuffed nose and to Tov's surprise she answered. "No." Her head lifted and she looked to the end of the bed.

"Oh, no…" Jen muttered. "Just a minute…" She went to the bathroom and let the tap run cold to come back with a wet facecloth in hand, fighting for control as she approached the bed. It was her first look at Ellen, gaunt and lifeless, the shoulder of her nightgown drenched. She held the cloth to Kelly's forehead, dabbed her cheeks, spread the cool sensation over her eyes until Kelly groaned. Jen folded and unfolded, finding the coldest spots.

"Thank you," Kelly whispered. Jen nodded, smoothed her matted hair, pushing it away from her face, running her fingers through it like a comb. "This is my momma," Kelly told her. She turned her face back into Ellen's nightgown and closed her eyes.

"I knew she would be pretty," Jen said softly. Her hand stroked, massaged, cradled Kelly's head. "I took one look at you and knew your mom would be pretty."

"You did not."

Words were hushed, voices skimming over them almost, soothing to their ears. "Yup. I did too."

Tov heard the comfort in their speaking, the desiring of something originating from the mouth and not the heart.

"Her eyes the same colour as yours?"

Kelly nodded against Momma's chest.

"Even if you were not side by side, I would have figured you belonged together."

"Really?"

"Yup."

The room went silent.

"When I was little I used to snuggle up to Momma like this."

"You did?"

"She used to sing to me. I put my head on her chest and listened to the sound, deep, deep down... where the music comes from."

Drops overflowed Jen's eyes. She fought to keep them silent.

"I'm pretending."

"Pretending?"

"If I lie real still I can hear her singing."

It was work to gather her voice. Jen looked away, swallowing. "What did she used to sing?"

"Church songs mostly."

"Yeah? Which ones?" Jen looked up to empty her eyes. "Any favourites?"

Jen's hand kneaded compassion, beads of sweat cooling her own forehead as she sculpted and tucked stands of hair behind Kelly's ear.

"I think right now I would like them all."

Jen leaned down and put her cheek to Kelly's. "I'll get this cold again." She walked through the angel to the bathroom, using the cloth to dab at the mess on her face.

"Bless you," Tov said to her. "Bless you," he said louder. He could see into the bathroom. Jen fixed her hair, splashed water on her face, let the tap run in the sink while she regrouped. After a few minutes, a very composed Jen walked back through him to Kelly and began the ministrations again.

The angel felt lighter, one with the souls on the bed. He had been wrong. It was not three but four that needed to come together, the final pieces of a once-daunting puzzle swivelling and falling into their places. Cords were loosening, and Tov craved to hear his voice in such consecrated space. "Heaven bless you, Jennis Croft," he said. "From now until the end of time, heaven bless your mother heart."

◊

The room was quiet, Jen and Kelly caught up in the routine of Jen's hands.

"Do you think she knows?" Kelly asked.

"Yes. Yes, I do."

"I told her everything. Do you think she heard?"

"Yes."

Tov stirred, went to stand between them, connecting to Jen's spirit, reaching for Kelly's. A dam of empathy, pure and raw, broke inside of Jen. The colour of the room faded to a severe black and white, became the only thing she knew. She took hold of Ellen's daughter, hugging tight the knowledge that something between them could not be touched, that there was an exchange eminent that was not of this earth. It was the hallowed air, the lifeblood coursing through her lungs and veins.

"Do you know that she forgives you, Kelly?" Jen asked.

Kelly nodded. Her hands shook, her eyelids fluttered.

"She loves you so much."

Kelly turned to Jen, truth fitting into her heart.

"She knows how much you love her, Kelly." A pillar of peace solidified in Jen, a divine presence taking her body, giving her the sensation that she was too small for the room, and growing larger. "She knows."

Kelly sat up and looked at Ellen, the unchanging expression, the eyes closed in permanent sleep, their faces close, their noses almost touching, her words a wisp of hope to be captured. "Do you, Momma? Do you know?"

The words were audible only to the angel.

"Do you know how much I love you?" She took Ellen's nightgown, pulling her closer, clutching at the ribbon of life floating beyond her grasp.

Jen wrapped her arms around Kelly from behind, her chin on Kelly's shoulder, absorbing every movement of Kelly against her chest. "When you love someone that much, they know," Jen whispered.

They wept. Kelly leaned back against the arms. "I love you, Momma. Do you know I love you, Momma?"

"Yes." Jen answered each time. "Yes, she knows."

◊

The angel alone felt the full force of the moment, stronger than the power that had propelled him to earth, stronger than he. The source he knew intimately, and willingly he gave himself over to its purpose. Kelly was being filled. What he had been entrusted with he put there—every prayer, every ounce of love, the knowledge of being held, of being covered with divine hope that she was completely known and understood—he put there. He held her securely, his body rigid, until the storehouse of Kelly's emptiness and uncertainly was full. In the days to come, she would need this memory to continue healing.

The smug face of Grief flashed across his thoughts and he cringed, putting all his effort into wading against a current that threatened to sweep him from the two he held. He leaned into it, his lips on Kelly's ear.

"Doubt is coming," he told her. "When it does, you come back here, to this moment when you knew, when you believed…" Words faltered. He tried to anchor himself to Jen and Kelly, pummelled against the rushing force that worked to pull them apart. He leaned heavy into his warnings. "Come back to what you know. Come back to this time. Never forget that God loves you, that you are forgiven." The angel cried out, his voice penetrating eternity with reverberating clarity. "He loves you Kelly… He loves you…"

His grip was loosening. He grabbed for her, fought to speak words into Kelly's heart before the connection dissolved. "You will be with her one day… your momma will be waiting for you. She will wait for you…"

Kelly was quiet, listening. She opened her eyes and looked at Ellen, her thoughts given voice in the angel's head. "I know." She put her face on Ellen's cheek. "Don't worry anymore, Momma. I know."

A tornado of emotion blew through the angel, power and light pulling him away as it whipped him from their embrace and settled to the ground like a cloud of dust. Everything went absolutely still. It had happened. It had finally happened. He was in the moment, right now, that he had been sent for. And it was finished.

He was instantly released, bolting upwards, flying around the room in a streak of light. He cried in his laughing and laughed in his crying, a chorus of voices stringing along behind him. He could hear heaven celebrating as if he were actually there.

"Oh..." He slapped his knee, laughing the laugh of a crazy man along with the familiar voices of those who knew and had been here too, the older ones who had sent him off. Their presence, their kinship, their understanding of his elation and weariness kept him whipping around the room, following the walls as if he were bound by them. "How do we do this?" he shouted back, drained and full, satisfied and saddened. "What power is given to do all this?"

His mission was over. He had done what he was sent to do. The heavenly sounds faded. The room went still. Looking down, he saw Kelly in Jen's arms, locked together in the presence and power of the Spirit. This was how he would leave, heavy with endings, giddy with beginnings.

His mission was over.

The thread pulled.

Passing through the curtain and covers, he stood before Ellen. The room dropped away, and there was nothing left but them.

Chapter Twenty-Eight

Ellen watched Tov approach with a smile on her face, the one that gave him no choice but to return it. "I'm still here," she said.

Tov looked around. It had changed from when he had been here last. She wasn't in her garden anymore but in the middle of a sunset, rich with irrepressible oranges and shades of burnished rose, luminous colours that rolled and moved, parting slowly and wonderfully as the sunsets of earth. It was magnificent.

"Will it be much longer, do you think?" she asked.

"Tired of waiting?"

"It's peaceful, but I am anxious to be on my way." Ellen was studying him. "Who are you?" she asked quietly.

He hesitated, for dramatic effect. "I am Tov. I'm only an angel."

"Oh," she answered, before processing it. "Only an angel…" she repeated. "Are you the one I saw before?"

"Yes."

"You were faint then. You're much clearer now." Her head was tilted. "Have we met before that?"

"In your living room."

"Oh…" It was a gust of breath. "Really?"

"Yes, the day Kelly left."

"You were with me?" she asked quietly. "The presence I felt was you?"

Tov chuckled. This was marvellous. "It was."

"Did you see Kelly?"

"I found her, after I left you."

She asked politely for explanation.

"You led me to her."

Ellen's face softened. "With my prayers…"

"Yes."

"It's funny. I know all this as you tell me. It's like I've always known this…" She looked around. "So, is this…?" She paused, looked at the angel through the corner of her eye.

"Oh, no…" he replied quickly, "not yet."

"My goodness, it gets better?" She turned a circle. "I've had so many different pictures in my mind of what it would be like. This would be fine if it was heaven, you know. Just fine." She looked nervous for asking so many questions. "Where is this, then?"

"You are still in the physical realm, but you are changing. Kelly is with you." As he spoke, she understood.

"I can't see her?"

"Not right now."

"She is fine, though?"

"She is with you now. With your body, I mean."

A funny expression crossed her face. "You know, I don't feel sad when you talk about her. I cried and cried for days, but now I don't feel sad anymore."

"She will be joining us one day."

Ellen's countenance changed, steeling, and then softening. "Thank you…" she whispered, over and over. "Thank you…"

"I have also met Ben."

Her hands fell. "Ben? My Ben?"

"That's the one. The day he left, I was given the privilege of being his escort."

She was speechless. Her mouth closed then opened, another smile, an almost permanent one now. "This is so amazing. This is so absolutely *amazing!*"

"Oh, Ellen," Tov told her, "just you wait."

"How long? How long do I have to wait?"

"Not much. It seems we are more than on our way already."

"Do you know everything?" she asked.

A laugh spurted from the angel. "No, and after spending so much time on earth, I don't know if I want to." He saw he was confusing her. "I'm afraid you are as much of a mystery to me as I am to you. The more I learn of you humans, the more complicated things become." Stewart popped into his mind and his voice dropped. "The more wonderful things become…" His face lit up. "Tell me, what do know of dogs?"

"Dogs?"

"Have you ever had one?"

"When I was a girl." His enthusiasm was contagious. "Why?" she laughed.

"I met the most wonderful dog, Stewart, a very faithful and loyal friend."

"Mine was my best friend too. I told Ratchet everything."

"Ratchet?"

"My dad named him."

"Ah." He would have to give more thought about how one goes about naming dogs. "It was my first experience with one, and it was incredible. Do you know he could hear me?"

"The dog could hear you?"

Tov nodded.

"Well, that explains a lot." An idea hit her. "Will I see Ratchet?"

"Well…" His lips stuck out, then stretched tight.

"You don't know?"

"My duties are different than other angels. There might be some that escort animals, but I don't know about it myself. I do know that the Creator takes all things back to himself." He looked at her the same way she was looking at him. "We need to ask what that provision is." He was thinking and talking mostly to himself. "That would be wonderful. Something to look forward to." More than he could hope for.

Ellen couldn't hold back. She stepped into his thoughts. "Do you know how crazy this feels? I am standing here talking to an angel. What I have always believed is really happening."

"You have always believed," Tov told her. "It was your power."

"I know. But to finally be *living* it…"

It was hard to contain excitement. "I will be with you until it's time to leave."

"Do you know how long that will be?"

"No."

"Are we waiting for Kelly?"

"She is still with you. As long as she needs you, we will stay."

Her face was asking, her heart requesting. "I wish I could see her."

The angel remained silent, allowing the sediment of the final request that he had asked of heaven before his mission ended to settle in the sea of his growing faith in the way of things here. It all worked according to the will of the One who sent him. "Kelly loves you very much. Do you know that?"

Ellen looked the picture of pure joy, submerged in it, drenched. As the angel spoke, so she knew. "Yes," she said breathless, "I know."

◊

Ellen changed again as they moved in and around the clouds of colour. Tov held her hand, floating beside her. It wouldn't be long before he could let go and she would be able to follow on her own. They hadn't spoken for a while. There wasn't the need. The angel was in his element, enjoying the effortless wander through the spectacular foretaste of things to come. It was in front of him and all around him, but not a part of him as it would have been if he was home, and he was very aware of Ellen marvelling at her presence here. He loved this job so much.

There was no going back. He was attempting to tie up his emotions in a neat bundle so he could leave this place in peace, but as much as he thought he should let go of the bad, he realized he didn't want to. The jarring and painful experiences that initially upset him were embedded deep within. He needed a piece of Kelly, of Jen, Stewart, Reese, even the crazy old lady. He had changed, as Ellen had, and to be true to who he was now, he needed to carry it all in his heart. As they drifted in and out of yellows and crimsons and oranges enfolding them in tentacles of the promise of glory, he was coming to terms with that. The humans were a part of him now, however quirky and unpredictable they tended to be.

Ellen jerked at the end of his arm when Tov stopped. A tilt of her head asked him what he was thinking, entreating him to break their silence. Tov dropped her hand and realized she was floating on her own.

Ellen's curiosity won. "What?"

"Do you have any idea how much God loves you?" he asked.

She didn't reply immediately. "I have an idea." She watched his face to see if she answered right. "I thought I did, until all this." She spread her arms around her. "I think I am about to learn, though, right?"

There were no words left to describe to Ellen what awaited her. "That makes both of us," he said.

◊

Pat convinced Kelly to go to the cafeteria for a break, if for nothing but to get up and move her legs. Jen and Kelly, who seemed to be joined at the shoulder, had left only after Pat promised she would not leave Ellen alone. The face of her friend required an element of imagination to recognize it, the eeriness of it playing games with her.

"What's it like?" she asked the strange, skinny Ellen. "Are you in there?" She played with Ellen's flat hair, tried to fluff it with her fingers. "Are you in any pain?" Her friend's face was plastic. Pat turned her head so Ellen would look at her as she would have done had they been talking. The cheek absorbed the push of Pat's fingers. She waited for the chest to rise and fall, but it was a long time between.

"Oh, God..." Pat gasped, sitting through another agonizing interval before her stomach iced and tears ran. She stood abruptly, knocking the chair back, and rushed into the hall. James was in the lounge, his head on the back of his chair, eyes closed. She waved, frantic, running in slow motion it felt, startling him as she shook his arm.

"I think Ellen is going..."

"What?" James lifted his head.

"I think it's time," she said. The message delivered, her words hung in shock before striking deeper. James took her hand and pulled her back to the bedside, Pat voiceless behind him as he checked for pulse, timed the interminable interval between breaths.

"You're right," he said quietly.

"What do we do?"

"Get Kelly."

Pat's started to shake. "How long?"

"I have no idea. Minutes maybe. Minutes, at the most," he said. He took Ellen's hand. He was not going to let his friend think she was doing this alone.

Pat had been holding her breath. "I'll get Kelly."

The door closed, and in the quiet James could hear Ellen's slow intakes of air thick and laboured, making him feel sick. He was concentrating, absorbing them, making his own chest heavy. He pled silently with her to acknowledge him, to let him know somehow that she knew he was there. His body felt opposed to hers, blood and thought accelerating in him as hers was diminishing, winding down slower and slower. His voice was clear.

"It's okay Ellen," he said, praying to penetrate her stupor, to transcend the need for hearing, for the words to fall directly into her heart. "It's okay if you need to go."

Her chest rattled as her body shut down.

"You can leave now. You go home." As a doctor, he had an intense need to know what was happening inside of her, what it was like to be in the throes of death. As a friend, he had the need to shake her, to pull her back. But as a realist he spoke, knowing in his heart that they were the words that had given many in Ellen's place the peace and the permission needed. "Ben is waiting."

The elevator dinged like a timer. He imagined hurried footsteps before he heard them. "It's okay Ellen. You go now…" He leaned in, closed his eyes, and gave Ellen her last kiss. "You go…"

◊

Ellen's hand, the one Tov was holding, changed. Wonder painted her face as thick as the colourful clouds that ushered them. She was the one to let go, holding them both up to study them front and back. "It's time, isn't it?"

"I think so."

"Oh…" She inhaled deeply.

Tov grinned, eyes almost as wide as her mouth.

"What now?" she asked, preoccupied. "I feel so different," she breathed… "so *different*…" She looked to the angel. "But I'm still here."

"You have just received a new body," he informed her.

"Am I air?"

"There is no such thing as air anymore. You are spirit."

Ellen was inspecting herself, inch by amazing inch. "I have a body, but I don't."

"This one won't get in your way, I promise." He smiled. "Here, try something." He had her enraptured attention. "Look over there at that swirl of red." He pointed into the distance. "Think about being there."

Suddenly Ellen was looking at him from far away. He couldn't see the expression on her face, but heard her laugh echoing across space. It grew loud as she was instantly beside him again.

"This is going to be so much fun! No tears. No pain, right?"

"Never again," Tov promised.

"Fly with me," she urged, "right now!" She took off straight up, stopping a distance over his head.

"You have one last prayer to be answered," he told her.

"I can't imagine what that would be!" She was giggling. "I think this would just about cover any I had left."

"You wanted to see Kelly again."

Ellen went sober, was back at his side.

"I heard you pray it on the couch, that day in your living room."

"I did," she confirmed. "I can see her now if I want to?"

"Do you want to?"

"Yes, of course."

"You can see her, but she cannot see you."

Ellen contemplated the image of herself she could see in his eyes. "Well now, that will be different. But, so am I now." She looked around. "Where is she?"

"In your hospital room."

"We can go there?"

Tov nodded.

"This will be the last time?"

"For now."

She had her lip between her teeth.

"Are you okay?" he asked.

"Yes, I'm fine. I just want to clear my head of all this…" she motioned around her, "… so I can really *see* her. I don't want to miss a thing."

"Tell me when you're ready. There's no rush."

They turned in unison, moving slowly, close together, completely in sync. "You can come back anytime you want? To earth? To see people?" she asked.

"No, I have to be sent." He knew what her next question would be. "It is not the same for you. I was made to minister here to the souls of the saved. It is my existence. You are at the beginning of a new life. The old one is finished. Trust me, you will not regret leaving this one behind."

They walked on before Tov put a hand on her. "You will be surprised. It will not make you sad."

"I know. Somehow I know that." She was struggling. "It's just… so… different."

There was always one thing that sealed it for the new ones, the point of not wanting to look back, of never returning. "You will meet him, face to face, and you will know that you were always meant to be there, with him."

The lines on her face vanished. She blinked slowly. "Thank you. Thank you for being here."

"Ellen," he laughed, "believe me, the pleasure is mine!"

"I think I'm ready." She looked to him for the strength she need-ed to let it all go.

"Take my hand. We'll be there in an instant."

They connected and Ellen was aware of a ceiling, lights glaring above her. She was high up in a room. She gasped, causing the hand in hers to squeeze tighter. To her left a curtain was pulled half way around a circular rod. She could see herself on the bed, could hear crying. There were people in the room. "Look! There's James and Pat!" She saw two others she did not know.

"Ellen, meet Carl and Jennis Croft," Tov said. "They will be join-ing us one day as well. "

Ellen wasn't listening. Her eyes were fastened on the back of a head of long black hair spread out on the bed beside her body, the face buried in the blankets beside the pillow.

"Kelly..." Ellen whispered. She held out her hands, reaching, but did not move from the ceiling. "Kelly!" she cried out. Pat went to Kelly and pulled her up, a cry escaping Ellen's mouth as she beheld the face of her baby. "What happened?"

"She's all right," Tov assured her. "Believe me, she's fine."

"She's okay..." Ellen echoed. "She's all right..." she said over and over. She laughed through tears. "She's back. She's all right."

"Your prayers have been answered, Ellen. Every prayer that you prayed in faith is alive in her."

Ellen did not turn her head or move. She was not going to miss one fraction of one second of her Kelly. "You were with her the whole time?"

"Pretty much."

She was taking in as much of Kelly as she could. "She is beautiful, isn't she?"

"Yes, she is."

Her face beamed. "She's going to follow one day."

"Yes."

Ellen chewed her cheek, turned to the angel. "Then there is not one more thing I want or need. I would not change a thing."

"The prayer of a righteous person availeth much..." Tov said quietly.

"Does Kelly know that?"

"She'll learn, as you did."

They watched the end of Ellen's life play out, Kelly inconsolable, Pat, James, and the others encompassing her in sympathy.

"I feel so removed from it," Ellen said. "I should feel sad but I don't, like you said." She was watching, completely absorbed. "I have never felt so much love..." She paused in wonder. "Or so full."

"That is what you have given Kelly, the legacy you have left her," Tov answered. "Mission accomplished for both of us."

"Unbelievable," she said. "Now it will be the opposite for me. My faith is fact, and what I had always hoped for, I know."

"Quite a system, isn't it? And you haven't seen anything yet!" The angel made a move to go.

"Just one more minute?" Ellen's hands moved to her chest and covered where her heart used to beat. "I love you," she whispered to her baby. "I love you so very, very much." Suspended in space between time and eternity, she held the moment for exactly what it was. Her last. Eventually she took the angel's hand. "Okay."

The magnet pulled. Tov, too, looked on the room one last time, his heart tightening. "Don't give me reason to come down here again," he said quietly to Kelly, and chuckled. He had followed her enough to know better. Who was he kidding? If Kelly needed him and he was sent, he would be back on the next bolt of lightning.

"What?" Ellen asked.

"Nothing," he said softly. He took one last look, as Ellen was doing. "Are you ready?"

"Yes," she said.